Dedication

To my dear mother and father, my sources of inspiration and without who I wouldn't be where I am today.

Table of Contents

A Close Encounter

He withdrew the gun from his shoulder holster as he proceeded towards the elevator. As the elevator ascended en route to the observation deck, Charles Bronze wondered how this day started.

It was 5:00 a.m. when the alarm clock rang. Bronze was always an early riser, since his formative years. His day began as any day would; he sprang out of bed, headed to the kitchen and started making some scrambled eggs. Bronze then put the kettle to boil and started to make the usual cup of dark roast coffee and toasted some whole wheat bread. Once the eggs were cooked, he turned on his 50 inch HDTV and watched the BBC World News.

After gobbling down the eggs and toast, he took out some biscuits. It was about 5:45 now, and the sun was starting to rise. He proceeded to the balcony of his Miami Beach penthouse and gazed at the ocean for a good fifteen minutes. Then, he decided it was time to go for his two-mile long beach jog. Upon his return, Bronze took a steamy shower and let the hot water run through his sore muscles. Finally, he took a close shave with his straight razor and advanced to his closet.

Bronze's closet was full of designer clothes with famous names such as Ralph Lauren, Tommy Hilfiger, Tommy Bahama, Perry Ellis, Geoffrey Beene, and Lacoste. He put on his work attire. As Bronze looked in the mirror, he was amazed at his mahogany suntan from his recent Cancun getaway. He felt that because he was returning to the office for the first time since his vacation, he had to dress to impress. Charles Bronze decided to wear a yellow Alfani shirt and a blue J. Garcia tie, which had watercolor accents on it. He wore dark suit pants. He then put on his Rolex watch, Cartier cologne, and headed for the front door.

Bronze exited the elevator of the condo building he was living in and paced towards his white Lexus LS. As he entered the car, he started to think about what procedures he would have to perform today. Charles Bronze is an ophthalmologist, with an emphasis in eye surgery. He is part of a private practice with two other physicians, the owner of the practice, Dr. Henry Smith, and the beautiful Dr. Claire Scarlet. Dr. Smith and Bronze met at a medical convention many years ago shortly after Bronze graduated from medical school. Dr. Smith immediately took note of Bronze's aptitude and quick yet accurate answers to his questions.

When Dr. Smith found out that Bronze was going to specialize in ophthalmology, it was as if fate had brought these two together. Apparently, Dr. Smith was looking for two new ophthalmologists, because the other two who were with him before left due to family reasons. Dr. Smith, who was probably in his late 60s, Caucasian, short, stocky, clean-shaven with salt and pepper hair offered the newly titled Dr. Charles Bronze to work with him. When Bronze realized that the practice was located in Miami Beach, he was inclined to affirm. However, one of Bronze's gifts was his ability to profile people on first glance. He classified Dr. Smith as one of those people who it would take a long time to gain his trust, but once he did, they would become close co-workers. Considering that Bronze already lived in the Miami area, he agreed.

Dr. Claire Scarlet is a striking brunette, about 5'10", thin yet well endowed, with sharp features and blue eyes that would pierce any man's heart. Dr. Bronze and Dr. Scarlet were friends since their first year at Johns Hopkins School of Medicine and were always very close. Dr. Scarlet's primary reason for her deep affection for Charles Bronze was not because of his 6'4" lean yet fit body frame, nor his spice skin color, jet black hair, brown eyes nor his chiseled features. Dr. Scarlet loved Bronze because of his uprightness, honesty, and his humble demeanor despite all of his accomplishments. Most importantly though, Scarlet loved Bronze because of his respect towards women and his elders, which she thought was very difficult to find in a man especially when they reach fame and fortune.

Bronze reached the office at 7am, which was only a fifteen-minute drive from his house. He slipped on his white coat and entered the office. Bronze went through the waiting room to his office, whereby he saw Scarlet on the way. When she saw him, her eyes sparkled. "Charles!" she exclaimed, but not in a loud tone. She hugged him and Bronze could feel her soft lips touching his cheek. She squeezed him so hard that Bronze could feel the soft warmth emanating from her breasts on his chest, and he knew that they were real and not plastic like some of the patients he had to deal with during his rotations in medical school. She said, "It's so great to see you again! I've missed you very much!" Bronze said, "Yes Claire, I have missed you as well." Claire said, "We've known each other for so long and it feels strange not seeing you everyday." Bronze and Scarlet have known each other for over twenty years. During their second year in medical school, they did have a fling. However, they decided to call it quits, but since then, they have had a brother-sister relationship. Bronze then said, "It's only been two weeks!" Scarlet responded, "I know Charles, but it feels a lot longer to me."

As soon as Scarlet said this, he immediately thought of the Shakespearean quote, "Absence makes the heart grow fonder." This was one of many occasions where the validity of that very statement was proven. After their touching reunion, Bronze proceeded to his office where the administrative assistant had placed the patient roster for the day. He observed that he had to perform a cataract surgery, a glaucoma surgery, and a variety of pre-ops and post-ops. During his lunch break, however, his mobile phone rang.

His normal phone was a Blackberry for work purposes, but the phone that rang was his other phone, the Motorola. Bronze's Motorola doesn't ring often, probably only twice a week. However, he answered. "Detective Bronze, we need you to come in after work today," said a deep husky voice. Bronze said, "No problem Lieutenant, I should be finished by 5pm this afternoon, and I'll head on over right after." "Excellent, we'll see you then" said the Lieutenant.

Charles Bronze is an undercover detective for the Miami-Dade Police Department, which was a kept secret from Dr. Smith, his boss, and Dr. Scarlet. They knew he had a side job with the government, but only to that extent.

After seeing his final patient for the day, he told both Smith and Scarlet that he was leaving. "Leaving so soon?" asked Claire Scarlet. Bronze said, "Yes, unfortunately I have been called for my other job. However, I'll take anything I have to sign and some patient files home." Scarlet said in a stern yet pleasant tone, "Oh, you and that government job. One day you'll tell me more about it." "One day indeed," replied Bronze. After this, Bronze smiled and drove his Lexus to the police station. He took off his white coat, put on his shoulder holster with his Smith and Wesson .40 caliber compact handgun, threw on his jacket, put his badge on his belt, and proceeded inside. "Good evening Dr. Bronze", the receptionist said. "Lieutenant Baker is waiting for you in his office." Bronze thanked her and proceeded to the Lt. Baker's office.

"Good evening Detective Bronze," Lt. Baker said. "It's great to see you again. I'm sorry for bringing you out here, especially since you were on vacation and this is your first day back to work. However, this is of dire importance." Bronze replied, "Not a problem, Lieutenant, that's what I'm here for."

Lieutenant Baker was a male Caucasian of average height with chestnut hair and green eyes. His tailored made suit oozed sophistication, and gave the metro sexual Bronze some stiff competition.

Baker handed Bronze a file and said, "Victor Murray, the famous ruby smuggler, has stolen the Pigeon's-Blood-Red Burmese ruby, currently the most expensive ruby in the world. The ruby was at the Grand Egyptian Museum, which you are familiar with when you traveled to Egypt not so long ago." Bronze indeed remembered this and said, "Yes, but isn't that museum still under construction?" Baker responded, "You are correct, but they built a secret wing that can be accessed even though the museum is still under construction. When the Egyptian Government gained custody of the Pigeon's-Bloody-Red, they decided to hide it in the wing, thinking that no thief would be able to find it. However, we got the tip off from our friends in Cairo that Murray had a mole within the Egyptian government. Murray sent his most trusted companion in crime, the glamorous yet deadly Natalie Riviera to steal the ruby."

Bronze was tired after a long days work, but Lt. Baker brought some coffee that rejuvenated Bronze. After hearing all of this, Bronze asked, "How are we privy to this information? Is it a reliable source?" It was a frequent habit of Bronze to carefully analyze every detail of the situation before coming to a conclusion. He used this approach in both his undercover work and in medicine. Lt. Baker responded, "When the American government got the tip off, they sent CIA Agent Khaliq Ahmed to do some reconnaissance in Egypt. He reported back to the CIA, which then reported to us, NYPD and LAPD." Bronze agreed with himself that this was indeed authentic. He had worked with Ahmed about eight years ago on a case in the Middle East. Because of Bronze's fluency in Arabic, he was often assigned to cases with a Middle Eastern connection.

"This is a picture of Natalie Riviera. Ahmed caught a picture of her in the alleys in Cairo about a week ago. You do agree that she is quite beautiful, right?" asked Lt. Baker. "Indeed," said Bronze. He studied her image carefully. She was Hispanic and had the body of a model. She had large breasts, firm buttocks, a straight abdomen, cinnamon-colored skin, and soft features. Bronze looked at her facial features, and even though she could pass for a model, she did have a kleptomaniac quality about her. He noticed that her eyes were very shifty, even though it was only a picture and profiled her immediately to be the seductive type. Lieutenant Baker then said, "She is indeed the seductive type that we've seen before (just like Bronze predicted), but she does have a distinct quality. Riviera is very intelligent and acts on instinct. I believe that this is the primary reason she is Murray's right-hand woman." Bronze said, "I will definitely keep that in mind as I approach this case. However Lieutenant, its 6pm on a Monday evening. Where do I come in?" Lieutenant Baker grinned and said, "I thought you'd never ask."

Lt. Baker said, "Murray has gained possession of the ruby. We have reason to believe he is going to sell it to a wealthy Chinese industrialist named Ho Yi. Tonight at 9:30pm, in the SkyCity restaurant in Seattle's Space Needle, Murray is having a black-tie banquet. You are going to the banquet as Henry Coomes, a wealthy businessman who wants to match Mr. Yi's price for the ruby." Bronze thought for a moment and said respectfully, "With due respect Lieutenant, it's a little after 6pm. How am I going to get to the banquet on time? Also, wouldn't it be more sensible to send someone from LAPD where it's a lot closer?" Lt. Baker said, "I understand where you're coming from Detective Bronze, it is a long trip. However, we have a jet that travels five times faster than a normal jet and will get you there in two and a half hours. In addition, because Seattle is three hours behind us, you'll have plenty of time. Ahmed has requested that you, Detective Charles Bronze, to go and capture him. I guess you made a more lasting impression on Ahmed than you thought." Bronze looked a bit perplexed, but agreed. He said, "Very well then. So when does the jet leave?" Lt. Baker replied, "About fifteen minutes. We have tailored a black tuxedo for you, and since I know of your fashionable taste, courtesy of Giorgio Armani himself." Bronze smiled with the folder in hand and proceeded to the jet hanger.

Victor Murray was drinking a martini on a Sunday night as he nervously awaited her arrival. He was going to have his banquet in Seattle the following day, but at this moment, he was dressed in casual clothes in a corporate suite. Pacing back and forth, Murray's palms started sweating. He glanced at his watch every few minutes wondering if she would show up. It was 7:28pm, meaning that she should be arriving in two minutes. As soon as his watch struck 7:30pm, there was a knock on his door. "I never thought you were going to show up Natalie," said Murray. Natalie Riviera was standing at the threshold wearing shades and a black trench coat. She carried a briefcase with her. "Do please come in," said Murray. "So do you have the ruby?" Natalie replied, "Indeed I do darling." She opened the briefcase, took out a large stone wrapped in felt cloth and unwrapped the cloth. Murray had never seen anything like it. It glowed like the full moon on a clear night. "Excellent work as always Natalie. This is exactly why you are my one and only." She replied, "That's very sweet of you honey, but may I have my share please?" Murray replied, "Before I give you the money, let's have some champagne first to celebrate. Is that ok?" Riviera smiled and said, "Why not."

Natalie Riviera had worked for Victor Murray for the past thirteen years. He met her in Crete, where she was smuggling diamonds. The two became instantly attracted to each other, but not to the point of having an intimate relationship. Murray knew she was smart, for he had heard of her through a contact in London. Murray asked Riviera out to dinner, and they enjoyed some fine Greek dining. Afterwards, they went to a gazebo where they looked out at the ocean. Murray started caressing Riviera's back. He looked her in the eyes and said, "You're one of the most beautiful women I've ever seen." Riviera smiled and said, "Sorry dear, that's not going to work with me. I know exactly who you are. You use women for your pursuits and don't think a statement like that is going to turn me on." Shocked with the aggressiveness of her statement, Murray was in awe. He had met one or two intelligent girls during his seasoned career of smuggling, but never one that caught onto him so quickly. "Alright," said Murray, "You got me. However, I think we would be excellent working together as partners." Riviera thought for a moment and replied, "Victor, I just met you this morning. What makes you think I wouldn't trick you and walk away?" Murray said, "You're not that type. You think that because you're smart you can use your abilities to try and outsmart me, like you have with men in the past. However, it's not going to work with me." Riviera reluctantly said, "OK, you've made a good point, but you're going to have to prove yourself to me before I join you." Murray then took Riviera to a special room full of scintillating emeralds and sapphires. Upon seeing this, Riviera hesitantly agreed. Riviera still wasn't sure if she could trust him.

As Murray and Riviera were drinking champagne, he said, "Do you remember when we first met?" Natalie replied, "Yes, I do. I remember how reluctant I was to join you, especially because I was doing fine on my own. However, over the years I grew to trust you, and now I trust you with my life." Victor Murray then said, "Do you also remember that one night?" Riviera would never forget. One night they were drinking and made love. It happened very naturally, but they woke up very confused. Natalie said, "Whatever I can remember that is. We were so drunk we didn't know what we were doing. Tell me something Victor, why are you bringing this up?" He said, "Just thoughts running through my mind as we sit here so high up in the air on this lovely evening."

It was high indeed, for they were drinking champagne in a corporate suite on the 140th floor of the Burj Khalifa in Dubai. Murray chose this location because many business dealings went down here, and he didn't want to be conspicuous, especially since this was a large payoff. Natalie Riviera then said, "Alright Victor let's stop reminiscing and get down to business. I want my money now." Victor then sat back and said, "I have one more request. Let's go out to the balcony and view the city. Have you ever seen Dubai from 140 stories in the air Natalie? It is quite breathtaking." Natalie smiled and said, "You know me too well Vic. You know I never refuse a view of the city." He took her arm and they went to the balcony where they gazed at the city. Natalie said, "This reminds me of when we first met in Crete and we were looking out at the ocean." Victor laughed and said, "Yes, it does." A few moments later, Victor said, "I'm sorry Natalie." Confused, Natalie responded, "For what?" Victor replied coldly, "I've poisoned your champagne to kill you."

Tears started to fill in Natalie's eyes. She started to sway from side to side, as if she were about to collapse. Natalie asked, stuttering, "But why?" Victor responded, "The Pigeon's-Blood-Red Burmese Ruby is the most valuable ruby in the world. It does indeed hurt me on the outside that I have to do this to you, especially since we've known each other for so long. However, I will not pay you off for the work that you have done. You stole the ruby because I asked you to. Natalie, you claimed when we met you knew who I was, but you still barely know me. If you think that I was going to let you leave here alive, you are sadly mistaken. I knew damn well that you were going to kill me and take the ruby for yourself." Natalie looked surprised, fell to the floor and said, "He's coming for you."

Bronze was going over the file handed to him by Lieutenant Baker a while ago. It had a dossier of Victor Murray and his conviction. Bronze did notice, however, that there were some holes in his file yet to be filled. He was still a little confused that Ahmed would recommend him, Dr. Charles Bronze, of all detectives to catch this man. A bartender came and asked, "Can I get something for you Dr. Bronze?" He said, "Yes, I'll just have a ginger ale on the rocks please." Charles Bronze did not consume alcohol. He admired the portrayed refinement of drinking an alcoholic beverage, especially since he was a socialite, but as a physician, he of all people knew the intoxicating effects.

The jet was about to land, and he was surprised that the Lieutenant kept his word. The flight was exactly two hours and thirty minutes. Right before he landed, he noticed a piece of paper in the file that was somewhat hidden. It said, "Do not take a taxi to the Space Needle. It's a waste of time. We have a helicopter waiting for you that will take you there faster." The note had Lt. Baker's signature, but Bronze still checked it to make sure it was authentic. Bronze was always on his p's and q's, and even though it seemed unlikely, someone could have slipped that into the file, someone dangerous.

Bronze got off the jet, and the helicopter was waiting for him just as the note said. "Welcome Detective Bronze. Its nice to see you again after so many years." The man was Agent Ahmed, who Bronze didn't even recognize. All of Ahmed's black hair that he had turned grey. Ahmed told him, "You haven't aged a bit Charles, compared to me." Both of them laughed. The helicopter reached the Space Needle fairly quickly, and Bronze observed a Chinese man had just exited a helicopter a few hundred feet away from theirs. Ahmed said to Bronze, "That's Ho Yi. I assume Lt. Baker has told you about him." Bronze replied in the affirmative and the two gentlemen proceeded to the elevator, which took them 500 feet in the Space Needle to the SkyCity restaurant.

Bronze looked from side to side, thoroughly examining his surroundings and looking for an escape route. This was a frequent habit for his, especially when in a foreign place. In Bronze's line of work, there always had to be a Plan B, especially where the risk is so high. For this case, the risk is even higher because he will be meeting Victor Murray face to face, not just lurking in the shadows and remaining undercover. The elevator opened, and Bronze had to show his passport for security purposes. He gave it to the security guard in front. He noticed that there were armed men in suits walking around. The security guard said, "Welcome Mr. Coomes. We hope you have a great time tonight." Bronze thanked him and treaded carefully.

He decided to go to a table where there were some fine looking women and introduce himself. "Good evening Ladies. Do you mind if I join you?" "Sure" they all said. Bronze said, "My name is Henry Coomes, the owner of Coomes Enterprises." They all introduced themselves, but he was so engrossed in their good looks that he didn't pay attention to their names, or what they were saying. Bronze did his normal profiling and came to the conclusion that they were just fillers, women that Murray probably hired in order to entertain the guests. "Do you all know where I can find Victor Murray?" They looked a little concerned and one of the tall redheads said, "Oh Mr. Murray? He's over there."

There was a reserved table very close to the stage where the senior gentleman was sitting. Bronze thanked the ladies for their time and company, and proceeded to the bar. He ordered a cold Coca-Cola. As Bronze was enjoying a refreshed Coke, he noticed that the famous Sonny Rollins and his jazz band were performing for the evening. Bronze has been a jazz buff for a long time, and preferred the 1940s-1970s jazz. Out of all the famous artists of the time, Sonny Rollins is one of the only few that is still alive. He was taken by Murray's exquisite taste.

Bronze smiled and walked around. He was stopped abruptly by one of the armed men. "Are you looking for someone?" he asked. Bronze said very calmly, "Yes, my name is Henry Coomes and I'm looking for Mr. Victor Murray." The man said, "Mr. Murray's expecting you. Please join him at the table." Bronze sat down at the table, and Mr. Murray glanced at him, but was paying attention to the performance. Bronze sat right next to Ho Yi, who was grinning. The armed man who stopped Bronze whispered to Murray that it's Henry Coomes. Murray nodded and dismissed the armed man.

The performance had finished and Murray formally introduced himself to Bronze. Bronze noticed that Murray was very cool and calm, as if Murray was expecting Bronze to seem the way he did. Murray ordered the starter, some Russian Beluga caviar and biscuits, whereby they all ate. Ho Yi and Murray were discussing the status quo of the Chinese economy, and Bronze gave in his normal intellectual input. Bronze relied on various news sources for his information, and Murray seemed somewhat impressed with Bronze considering Coomes Enterprises was operated solely in America and didn't have any foreign ties.

Victor Murray then said, "Mr. Yi, I have invited Mr. Coomes here tonight because he has great interest in something you want to buy." Ho Yi looked a little shocked and said, "Victor, I thought no one knew about the ruby." Murray said, "Mr. Coomes here has friends in high places and found out about the ruby." Ho Yi said, "That is very impressive for an American." Bronze took the comment nonchalantly and asked Murray, "Are you sure you have the ruby?" Murray replied, "Of course, what makes you say that?" Bronze replied, "Well, you never thought that one of those beautiful ladies over there would love to have a big ruby like the Pigeon-Blood-Red for their collection?"

Bronze was setting up a trap for Murray, and Murray was taking the bait. Murray started to look worried and asked one of the guards to search all the women. Upon that, Murray said, "OK gentlemen, its time. Mr. Yi, you are going to come with me to the observation deck. As for you Mr. Coomes, I have someone who wants to meet you first." Bronze knew exactly what Murray was up to, but went with Murray's game. "OK," Bronze said. "I'll wait here then." Yi and Murray proceeded to the other elevator that specifically went up to the observation deck.

One of Murray's armed men escorted Bronze to the kitchen. Bronze was ready. He knew what was coming. Three of the armed men were there, accounting for four in total. One of them struck Bronze in that back in said, "OK Mr. Coomes, let's talk. Victor wants to know how you found out about the ruby and why you want it so badly." Bronze screamed in pain and said, "OK, I'll tell you, just let me stand up." In a swift stroke, Bronze knocked the main armed man, struck him unconscious, and used the man's body to shield him when the other three were firing away. Bronze then took the poor multiple-shot fellow's gun and shot the three men.

One of the guests heard the gunfire in the kitchen, saw Bronze with the gun after the three men had been killed, and headed for the kitchen door. "Call the police at once!" the man was about to say, but Bronze knocked him out and dragged him to a closet. He couldn't let anyone know yet and most importantly, Bronze didn't want to make a scene.

Because the fellow's gun was a machine gun, Bronze washed his face in the sink, combed his hair to a left side part, and headed out of the kitchen. He was back in the main restaurant and swiftly headed towards the elevator that goes to the observation deck. He withdrew his Smith and Wesson from his holster as the elevator proceeded towards the observation deck.

The elevator opened, and there was an armed man. Bronze shot him in cold blood and strolled along his path, focused. He was heading towards the observation deck, whereby he felt a cold muzzle towards his head. One of Murray's guards was pointing the gun to his head and said, "Mr. Murray's expecting you." Charles Bronze proceeded, greatly worried as to how he was going to handle the situation. Bronze had a tendency to panic internally, but had a fantastic ability to seem cool and calm on the outside.

Ho Yi and Victor Murray were drinking champagne, where Murray said, "Ah, there's our guest. Have a seat Mr. Coomes." Bronze said, "It's ok, I think I'll stand." "Very well then," said Murray. Murray nodded to another guard who was standing in a corner and shot Ho Yi directly at his forehead. Murray said, "We won't need Mr. Yi at this time. You see, Mr. Yi has officially given me the keys to his organization." Bronze, again, kept very cool headed and said, "I'm not surprised at all." Murray then said, "Of course you're not, Henry Coomes. Or should I say Dr. Charles Bronze of the Miami Dade Police Department?"

Bronze was a little taken. "So Victor, how did you know?" "Well Detective Charles Bronze, its quite simple. Bring him in.," said Murray. The same guard who shot Ho Yi brought in Agent Ahmed. Murray said, "Agent Ahmed here has been working for me the whole time." Ahmed said, "Sorry Charles, but Victor's offer was better." Murray said, "Indeed it is."

With that Murray winked at the same guard who brought in Ahmed and the guard shot Ahmed in the heart. Two corpses on the ground, Bronze thought, "How the hell am I going to explain this one to Lt. Baker?" Murray said, "You see Charles, I'm one step ahead of everyone. I fooled you, Mr. Yi there, Agent Ahmed, and of course my favorite deception of all, the American government." Bronze then looked to the left, even though he still felt that cold muzzle against his head. He saw a briefcase. Murray noticed this and said, "Ah, Bronze, you're wondering what's in the briefcase. Most importantly, you are wondering how you can escape this observation deck. Don't think I didn't see you looking around when you were brought in here. I'm sorry to inform you my friend, but the only way out of here is through that same elevator you came in." Murray then went for the briefcase and said, "So, this is what you want to buy isn't it?" He took out the ruby and it had a glow like the sun. Bronze replied, "Indeed. And I'm still willing to make you an offer. I am willing to offer $400 million for the ruby." Murray replied, "C'mon Bronze, the government won't give you that kind of money, even for a situation like this." Bronze said, "You are right, but need I remind you I am also a physician and let's say I've earned a lot over the years." Murray looked a little surprised and said, "O yeah, I almost forgot. How is it that someone who went a world renowned medical school allow himself to be in this situation?" As Murray said this, Charles Bronze was starting to get worried. He was trying to analyze the details, two armed men, two corpses, no escape route, and not to mention Murray himself. Bronze also wondered whatever happened to Natalie. As far as he knew, she was still alive, and if she was Murray's right hand person, why wasn't she present this evening? Detective Bronze's mind wandered a little and he agreed with himself that it would be very difficult to escape this situation. Out of all the cases none were so close to the chest. In all of Bronze's previous cases, when the enemy thought he outsmarted Bronze, Charles Bronze always had a comeback. Give the current situation; it is hard to wonder how exactly he would get away this time. However, Bronze did predict the worse case scenario, so he was prepared to deal with the present circumstance.

Charles Bronze chuckled and said, "Murray, you may think you know who I am, but you have no idea." Murray laughed sinisterly and said, "Bronze, you can stop bluffing." Bronze yelled, "Now!" With that, the pressure of the muzzle was released from Bronze's forehead. The guard aimed directly at Murray and planted three bullets in Murray. Right before the bullets hit Murray, he then realized before his death what Natalie meant before her untimely death. She knew of Detective Bronze, and that fate would eventually cause the two to meet. "Good work gentlemen," said Bronze to the two guards. He waited for the police to arrive. He then told them that he was working for MDPD, but it seems the Seattle

Police had a detective of their own present at the banquet. The Seattle detective saw Bronze hastily proceeding towards the elevator leading to the observation deck and assumed that Bronze would take care of the situation. Bronze asked the chief Seattle police officer present to ensure that the Pigeon-Blood-Red ruby be delivered back to the secret wing in the Grand Egyptian Museum and left.

Charles Bronze was now very tired. His body was aching and his head was pounding as he left the Space Needle to go back to the Learjet. He almost fell asleep on the jet back to Miami when the phone rang. It was Lieutenant Baker. "Excellent work, Detective Bronze. I knew you would help us get rid of this smuggler. Turns out that Natalie knew of who you were and warned Murray before Murray killed her. However, I guess he didn't realize what hit him." Bronze replied, "Thank you sir. If you're going to send me on another mission as tiring as this one though, please let me do it on the weekend when I'm not in the office." Lieutenant Baker laughed and said, "I'm sorry Bronze. Sometimes I forget that you're a thriving ophthalmologist. We will try our best to acknowledge your request. Have a good night and congrats again."

It was now 2:00am on Tuesday when Bronze got back to his penthouse in Miami Beach. He was so tired, but still brought himself to brush his teeth, floss, and change into his pajamas. As he was about to go to bed, he realized how close the enemy got this time, probably the closest he's ever encountered. He also learned that careful profiling does help make informed hypotheses, but to never assume too much about a person or situation. With that, he set the clock at 5:00am, realizing how hard it would be to get up (but did it anyway) and fell asleep immediately.

The Scent of the Culprit

"Intruder Alert! Intruder Alert!" said the alarm. Bronze could hear the alarm ringing constantly in his ears as he was trying for find an escape route from the warehouse. He started to hear gunfire. Bronze ran as fast as he could, sprinting towards a helicopter that was conveniently located right outside.

Dr. Charles Bronze woke up at 5:00 a.m. as usual, and proceeded on with his normal morning routine. He ate his breakfast, drank a cup of dark roast coffee, and went for his normal beach run. Bronze really wanted to take a dip into the ocean, but was very hesitant. He knew that the salt water would cause fatigue, but his muscles were so sore that he decided to do so. In addition, it really didn't matter seeing as it was a Saturday morning and all he had to do was sign a few patient files and fill out some prescriptions.

Charles Bronze was really glad he opted for a sea bath. Upon his return to his Miami Beach penthouse, he took a shower to wash the salt off of himself and took a nap. He woke up for the second time at around 8:00 a.m. Bronze was so accustomed to being a morning person that even if he was tired from activities from the previous night, he would wake up no later than 9:00 a.m.

After doing his normal weekend paperwork for his patients, he picked up Ian Fleming's *Goldfinger* and continued reading from where he left off. When Bronze was ten years old, his parents took him to see his first James Bond film, and instantly fell in love. He decided to buy all the movies as a young teenager and watch them. After watching all the movies, he bought all the books and felt closer to the true gritty character of James Bond. He reflected on how his life as an undercover detective was analogous to 007 in many ways, but it did indeed have its differences.

After reading a few chapters of *Goldfinger*, Bronze reflected and smiled about the previous night. It was the holiday season of 2010, and every year around Christmas-time, his beloved friend Dr. Claire Scarlet threw a holiday party. There was always a lot of food, dancing, and good company. It wasn't black tie, per se, but it did require formal dress code. All the ladies were dressed up in cocktail dresses, and the gentlemen in suits. Bronze remembered each part of it detail for detail, dissecting each moment, and relishing the moment.

It was a busy day at work. Fridays were never too busy, but since it was the holiday season and people were traveling, many patients had to get their eyes checked before going on vacation. Since Miami Beach had a relatively large geriatric population, this was probably one of the busiest back-to-back patient influxes for the whole year. For the day, Bronze had two cataract surgeries, one refractive surgery, and one vitreo-retinal surgery to perform in one day. However, he didn't have any clinical duties for the day since so many surgeries were scheduled. After his long day at work, he drove his Lexus LS back to the penthouse and started to get ready for the real festivities.

Since this was once a year, Charles Bronze felt he had to dress for the part. In addition, Dr. Henry Smith and other senior ophthalmologists from the Miami Beach area would be there, so he really had to look outstanding. Bronze wore a navy blue Calvin Klein suit with a white Geoffrey Beene dress shirt, a bright red tie with stripes, and a puffed white silk pocket square. He didn't want to dress too flamboyant, but had to be fashionable yet conservative. He took a close shave with his straight razor for this special occasion and combed his hair accordingly. Bronze put on his normal Cartier cologne, and donned his platinum Rolex he wears for special occasions.

While Dr. Claire Scarlet did have a formidable beach bungalow in Miami, she always rented out a rather large beachfront house to host the party. Scarlet had exquisite taste when it came to interior decorating, so she normally took it upon herself to decorate the whole place on her own. She has been doing each part of the house bit by bit over a week prior to tonight. The food was always well catered as well, and Bronze was really glad especially since his stomach started to growl.

Because there was valet parking, Bronze saw it fit to use his other car for this auspicious occasion. He opened his drawer, took out the car keys and proceeded to the underground garage. Bronze then drove his black Audi R8 out, ready for a night on the town. As he was driving, he was wondering what Claire would be wearing. Since she is the host, he thought, she would have to wear something appropriate yet sexy. Instead of Bronze doing his normal predictions and proving himself right, he decided that for this one time he was going to wait and see.

When Bronze arrived, there were already a good amount of people. He saw a few physicians he knew from a variety of ophthalmologic conferences, and talked to them for a while. However, even though they were talking to him, Bronze wasn't really paying attention. He was waiting for Claire. He excused himself from the conversation. After a tedious day at work, Bronze was in no form to discuss patient cases. Besides, the weekend had already begun. With that, Bronze proceeded to the bar and ordered a virgin strawberry margarita. Still no sign of Claire.

Bronze saw one of Claire's close lady friends that Claire met while in Miami. Even though Claire Scarlet was single, that doesn't mean that she wasn't looking for a suitable companion. She reached a point in her life where she was really ready to settle down and get married, but after all these years, there was still no man to that could fit all of her needs. Bronze talked with Claire's lady friend for a while. Scarlet's lady friend knew that her and Bronze were really close friends. She actually alluded if they were seeing each other, even though Bronze knew very well that Claire's lady friend already knew the answer. "Sorry," he said, "We called that quits a long time ago." Claire's lady friend chuckled and left.

Now he was sort of roaming around, and finally caught a glimpse of her. Claire was talking to some of the ophthalmologists that Bronze was speaking with earlier. Once again, Claire never ceased to amaze him. She was dressed in a sequined red dress. The dress covered her breasts modestly, and had two straps that flung over her shoulders. Her buttocks were well pronounced, but firm and tight. Bronze enjoyed the dress length the most, as it extended to her ankle, emphasizing her lean 5'10" stature. She wore white flat shoes, and Bronze always smiled upon a red and white color combination.

Scarlet finally made eye contact with Bronze. He grinned from ear to ear, while Claire excused herself from the conversation with some of the most prominent ophthalmologists in Miami. They approached each other and embraced each other in the normal fashion. "You look outstanding, Claire," Bronze said. Claire blushed a little and said playfully, "You look very handsome yourself Dr. Bronze." She continued, "And what's even better is that my dress and your tie match." Bronze always loved Claire Scarlet for just that. She was one of the very few of Bronze's lady friends to notice the little things, very much like him. They talked for a while, during which Bronze complimented Scarlet on the color combination of her dress, shoes, and the contrast of her skin color. Also, Bronze commended Scarlet on the decorating of the place.

As they were talking, some tango music started playing. Bronze asked her to tango, whereby she agreed. Claire always knew that Bronze was a terrific dancer, for Bronze was on the ballroom dancing team during his undergraduate years at the University of Miami. Claire Scarlet and Charles Bronze took center stage where other elderly folks were dancing, including the great Dr. Henry Smith, and really displayed an outstanding performance. Bronze could feel the warmth of her body against his as they were dancing. Once the music ended, Dr. Henry Smith started laughing and initiated an overwhelming round of applause.

Bronze then continued to mingle with some other folks after he and Scarlet were the center of attention for their encore. Then, he felt a vibration in his pocket. It was the black Motorola. Bronze went into the house, found a private corner and answered the phone. "Detective Bronze, you are needed at once," said the brash voice of Lieutenant Baker. "Alright sir, I'll be there in about an hour." Lt. Baker said, "Make that thirty minutes Bronze, we need you asap." Bronze started to get a little angry especially because he was having such a good time. Lt. Baker didn't hear a response and asked, "Hello, are you still there?" Bronze reluctantly said, "Ok boss, thirty minutes." Bronze hung up the phone, somewhat frustrated.

Claire then came in and saw Bronze was a little annoyed and softly said, "Charles, are you ok?" The breathlessness of her voice immediately calmed Bronze down and he said, "Yes, but unfortunately I have to leave." Claire then said, "It's that government job again, isn't it?" Bronze said, "Yes indeed." Claire then smiled and said, "One day." "One day indeed," Bronze said. Charles Bronze then kissed Claire Scarlet on her rosy cheek and left.

Driving his Audi R8, Bronze hid his frustration from Scarlet, but he was still very annoyed. He then put on some Miles Davis jazz, which calmed him down. Bronze went inside the police station. Since it was so late at night, no one was there. However, a light emanated from Lt. Baker's office and he went inside. Baker was sitting there, rummaging through papers and for a second didn't even notice that Bronze had entered. "Good evening Detective Bronze," Lt. Baker said. "I'm sorry we had to take you away from Claire's party, but this is important." Bronze had introduced Claire Scarlet to Lt. Baker a long time ago as his boss, but he was still a little confused. Lt. Baker noticed this and said, "We had a man at the party to make sure you were ok."

Bronze somewhat peeved said, "Good God Lt. Baker, is that really necessary? Although I didn't have my gun on me, need I remind you that I'm a black belt in Tae Kwon Do?" Lt. Baker replied, "I know Detective Bronze, but we had to be sure that you were safe." Bronze's mind wandered a little, wondering how exactly the police force works. Given Bronze's great aptitude and ability to figure things out, this was one issue that was too complex to resolve. Bronze had calmed down and said, "Ok Lieutenant. Let's get down to business. It's obvious that you wouldn't call me out here on a Christmas Eve unless you had something important. You're not spending time with your family, and you were rummaging through papers when I came in, not even noticing that I had entered. What's going on?" Lt. Baker then responded, "Ok Bronze, let's begin."

Lt. Baker said, "Tell me what you know of a man named Daniel Greene." Bronze thought for a moment and replied, "Daniel Greene, wanted for arson, smuggling, blackmail, the whole nine yards. Our friends in Madrid nearly caught him, but Greene narrowly escaped. No photograph available." Lt. Baker said, "You are right about everything Bronze, except we did get a photograph when he was escaping in Madrid. We just didn't feel right showing neither you nor anyone else. It is something that remained strictly confidential between the Captains and Lieutenants of the police force." Bronze glanced at the photo, studied Greene's features carefully, and did his normal profiling. Bronze then said, "From the looks of it, Greene is very cunning and will do whatever means necessary to get what he wants. He also looks like a cold-blooded murderer, which would explain why he's wanted for so many things." Baker said, "Excellent Bronze, now let's proceed."

Lt. Baker went to his filing cabinet and took out a thin file, not filled with much information. He gave it to Bronze, not saying anything. Bronze then said, "But sir, why are you giving me a file on Len Steinberg, a German blackmailer, after asking about

Daniel Greene?" Before Lt. Baker could answer, Bronze exclaimed, "Unless…Steinberg works for Greene!" Lt. Baker said, "Almost there, Bronze. It's the opposite, Greene works for Steinberg." Then Bronze said, "But Lieutenant, that doesn't make sense. If Greene works for Steinberg, then shouldn't Steinberg's file be much larger with more information?" Baker said, "Yes, Bronze it should be. But it's not. Also, the information that's in the file about Greene is fake. Greene had an inside person working with the American government, the same inside person who's set up the President of the United States." Lt. Baker then further explained, "It seems that Greene wants to blackmail President Obama for some secret information that he has obtained through his contact I just mentioned. However, Bronze, you know very well that a blackmail of such large proportion couldn't be simply done by Greene. No, it had to be someone higher. We think that Len Steinberg is the man behind the curtain. Greene has gotten away with a lot, but it wasn't due to his personal intellect. It's because Steinberg has been the puppet master the whole time. So here's what we want you to do. Greene has a warehouse in Bermuda. I want you to travel there and do some recon. We need to find some factual information about Greene, and we still don't know to what extent this blackmail is. You will report here, and the file with all the information you need will be at the front desk. Pick it up, and your flight leaves at 11 a.m. Best of luck Detective Bronze."

Bronze then drove home in his R8 and started to think about what a fun weekend this was going to turn out to be. Yes, he was disappointed that he had to leave Claire Scarlet's party so abruptly, but a weekend walking in pink sand in exotic Bermuda.

What could go wrong?

As Bronze continued thinking about last night, dancing with Claire, getting a mission from Baker, traveling to Bermuda in a few hours, he had his second cup of coffee for the day. He then packed his clothes, wore dark Perry Ellis suit pants, a Tommy Bahama island shirt and straw hat. Bronze drove to the police station, picked up the file per Lt. Baker's instruction and hopped on the Learjet to Bermuda. He arrived, drove by the beaches, checked himself into the Presidential Suite, and started to think about his plan of attack.

Bronze was a savant in his own right; he firmly believed that in his business of undercover work, it was vital to think three times before acting. He decided that the evening of his arrival, he was going to dress in all black and sneak into the warehouse. He put on his shoulder holster with the Smith and Wesson .40 handgun, and drove his Toyota Camry to the warehouse. Even though he wanted to rent a Lexus or Mercedes, he had to keep a low profile despite his rakish clothing.

He drove up to the warehouse, but parked in a side corner of the warehouse by some crates. He proceeded quietly. Bronze circled around the warehouse undetected to make sure that there were no guards. There were only two. He put the silencer on his Smith and Wesson and shot both of them. Then, he dragged their bodies to the crates where he parked his car and made his way inside. Although there were guards, for some reason, the warehouse didn't have a lock. He snuck in, looking for any traps. He then saw a random haystack that covered about ten feet of ground. Bronze thought for a moment and knew something was there. He felt the floor feeling through the haystack for any handle. Bronze was spot on. He found a handle, like a door, on the ground.

Detective Bronze turned the handle and saw a safe. However, there was no key lock, fingerprint pad, nor combination. He examined it thoroughly for a few minutes and saw a pinhole. He took a paperclip, which he had and tried to press into the pinhole. The pinhole was smaller than usual, so one needed to have a steady hand in order to press down. Luckily, Charles Bronze has extensive experience in performing eye surgery, or he would have never been able to stick the paperclip into the narrow pinhole. He pressed as hard as he could, and the safe popped open. He opened it and saw a bunch of papers. Bronze heard some dogs outside. "Damn, they must have smelled the dead bodies," Bronze said to himself. He crawled up to one window and saw that there were two Dobermans and two guards snooping around. Bronze saw that they noticed the Camry randomly parked there. They shot all four tires. He saw them mumbling, but couldn't hear what they were saying. The two guards were looking for a number plate, but there was none. Charles Bronze was very wise and predicted that this may happen, so he removed the number plate from his car before driving to the warehouse. Bronze saw a helicopter landing through another window. It was Daniel Greene.

Daniel Greene came out of the helicopter, with the pilot. They landed about 100 feet from the warehouse and he saw them proceeding towards the warehouse. He got down and without thinking, grabbed all of the papers that were in the safe. As soon as he grabbed them, red lights started blinking. "Intruder alert! Intruder alert!" exclaimed the alarm. He climbed up to the window where he had seen

Greene, and Greene called for backup as the alarm was screaming like a crying child. Bronze started hearing gunfire. He examined the helicopter carefully (the ophthalmologist himself has 20/20 vision, even at night) from the window and noticed that Greene and the pilot, guns in hand, were coming around to the front of the warehouse. Bronze jumped out the window and landed on his feet. He then sprinted 100 feet towards the helicopter. Greene and the pilot entered the warehouse, noticing immediately that the safe was uncovered and the window had been broken. They went around the warehouse and saw a man running towards the helicopter. The pilot started running, shooting at Bronze.

Bronze could hear the gunshots, but channeled his hearing to hear from which angle they were coming from. He ran as fast as he could and started the helicopter. Before the pilot could see who it was, Bronze was now in the air. The pilot shot at the helicopter, but to no avail. Charles Bronze had narrowly escaped.

Bronze went back to his hotel room after nearly getting caught and packed his things quickly. It was only a matter of time before they tracked the VIN number of the Toyota Camry. Luckily, he always gave a pseudonym, even when he didn't have to, in order to protect his identity. He headed straight for the Learjet and flew to Miami.

During the flight, Bronze analyzed the papers carefully. He was wearing black gloves when he stole them, and changed to surgical gloves so his fingerprints won't contaminate the documents. They were stamped "Top Secret" and he saw a copy of a letter to President Obama of the United States, Prime Minister Cameron of England, and King Abdullah of Saudi Arabia. In these letters, Daniel Greene told them that he had obtained secret information about each government and that for $500 billion-$1 trillion, Greene would keep silent about it. Then, he saw another paper that was an agreement signed by Len Steinberg and Daniel Greene where Steinberg agreed to give Greene 25% of his share since Greene was working under him. At the bottom were both of their signatures. Lastly, he saw a card with a red "L" marked on it.

It was now early Sunday morning when Bronze arrived back in Miami. He called Lt. Baker on his cell phone and told him he had vital information. Baker then agreed to meet Bronze later that morning, about 7:00 a.m., in Baker's office at the Miami-Dade Police Department headquarters. After their conversation, Bronze fell asleep for a few hours.

They met at the appointed time in Baker's office. Baker ordered the documents to be sent to forensics for a fingerprint analysis. It was confirmed that Greene and Steinberg's fingerprints were on the documents. Once Baker saw all the information, he told Bronze to keep his Motorola on him at all times. Bronze then reminded him that he has to work during the week, and Baker told Bronze to come back to the police station the Friday night coming.

Charles Bronze, M.D., had another busy week at work. It was the beginning of 2011 and there was still a steady flow of patients for the New Year. On Friday night, he went to Lt. Baker's office in the police station. Baker then said, "Detective Bronze, we've gained a lot of information since our last meeting this past Sunday. It seems that the documents you retrieved in Bermuda are in fact very true. The FBI has warned President Obama, so he's currently on his p's and q's. Also, our friends in the British and Saudi Arabian embassies have warned

Prime Minister Cameron and King Abdullah respectively. We have been in contact with a variety of countries around the world, because this blackmail is an international threat. We're giving Steinberg the benefit of the doubt that he's not joking due to his notorious record of blackmailing. However, this is his biggest blackmail yet." Bronze listened carefully to what Lt. Baker said and asked, "What about the card with the red "L"? Any leads?" Lt. Baker replied, "I'm afraid not Bronze. Its probably a publicity stunt by Steinberg since his first name is Len." Bronze then said in a casual manner, "Yes, of course." However, Charles Bronze knew very well that that card had a more significant meaning. Now it's just a matter of finding it to prove Bronze's theory.

Bronze asked, "Alright Lieutenant, what's going to be our plan of action on this one?" Lt. Baker replied, "Our contacts in Australia have told us that Len Steinberg is having a meeting with Daniel Greene in the Sydney Opera House during a concert tomorrow night. You're going to take our special jet that is five times faster than a normal one and attend the concert. However, we want Steinberg alive. Although he is a deep-seated criminal, he will be of more use to us alive." Bronze agreed. Before leaving, Lt. Baker whispered something in Bronze's ear. Bronze nodded and left to the Learjet that was now going to Australia.

On the jet, Bronze opened up his laptop and searched for a floor plan of the Opera House. He then thought to himself, where is a nice enclosed soundproof place where Greene and Steinberg can discuss their business? He called Lt. Baker on the phone and asked him for a more detailed government version of the floor plan for the Sydney Opera House. Bronze always wanted to travel to Australia, but never had the chance to. Money wasn't the problem; he just never got the time. However, this was his chance, especially since it was on the government's dime. Despite the excitement, Bronze was very nervous because he wasn't familiar with the configuration of the Opera House to plan his escape route in case anything went wrong.

Bronze landed in Australia, checked himself into another Presidential Suite, and got a massage by the rapturous and sexy masseuse. He studied her body shape very carefully before having the massage. Bronze was very respectful and asked the masseuse about her life in Australia and where were some good places to eat. Before she left, he gave her a tip and kissed her hard on the lips. She giggled and then left.

He dressed in an Alfani tuxedo and was chauffeured in a Rolls Royce to the concert. Bronze was somewhat in awe. Even though he memorized the floor plan of the Sydney Opera House, seeing it in real was completely different. Since he distinctly remembered Greene from Bermuda, he looked carefully for him without being conspicuous. Bronze was very outgoing; he introduced himself to a few people and chatted with some native Aussies. Because Bronze was an outstanding cook, he talked to them about the origin of various Australian dishes and they were very impressed. During the concert, he saw Greene talking to an older man wearing a suit and a fedora in the VIP section. He assumed that it was Len Steinberg. Immediately after the concert ended, there was a reception in the Northern Broadwalk. Bronze ignored the rushing crowd and kept his eyes affixed on Steinberg. There were so many people, that neither Steinberg nor Greene would have ever noticed a tall, stately gentleman in an Alfani tuxedo looking at them.

Bronze saw that they were heading to the kitchen. He went to the kitchen, took a towel and started rolling a fruit cart, pretending to be a waiter while keeping an eye on Greene and Steinberg. He saw they were heading to the Utzon Room. Bronze followed them, still rolling the fruit cart. He realized that going to the Utzon Room would be in the opposite direction of the Northern Broadwalk. Detective Bronze observed that Greene looked like he was in a hurry to talk to Steinberg, and therefore, Bronze implied that they would be talking for a while. On his way to the Northern Broadwalk, Bronze stopped a waiter whom he saw. He told the waiter he wasn't feeling well and asked the waiter if he could take the fruit cart instead. The waiter was very sanguine and agreed, giving Bronze a chance to head to the Utzon Room.

Daniel Greene told Len Steinberg nervously, "Some whack job stole the documents from the safe in Bermuda. He had the audacity to run towards my helicopter and get away." Steinberg's face turned red and said in a thick German accent, "Damn you Greene! Those documents were very sensitive. They had some of the details for our plan! Most importantly, they had our agreement of your share." Len Steinberg was a tall, blond hair blue-eyed German who was medium built. Daniel Greene, on the other hand, was a short, brown-haired Irishman with a slight accent. Steinberg asked Greene if he caught a glimpse of the man responsible for this. When Greene replied in the negative, Steinberg slapped Greene across his face. Steinberg then said, "After all I've done to guide you and protect you, you do this to me! I could have had you caught in Madrid but I chose not to out of my mercy. Get out of my sight! Come back in an hour and we will discuss what we'll do next."

Greene left the room a little disheartened. Daniel Greene was Len Steinberg's right-hand-man, and Greene felt that after all the years of loyalty, Steinberg shouldn't have slapped him in the face. Bronze was heading towards the Utzon Room. He could smell trouble. Daniel Greene was too nervous. He took out his Smith and Wesson and strolled cautiously. Bronze saw Greene as Greene was making the corner. Bronze swiftly placed himself into another corner. Luckily, Greene didn't see Bronze. Greene did hear a "whoosh" sound and said "Hello," but no response. Greene then headed to the men's bathroom and Bronze followed him.

Bronze went inside the bathroom as Greene was defecating. He could see Greene's brown shoes. Bronze noticed that Greene was the only one in the bathroom. Since this bathroom was close to the Utzon Room, no one was around. Bronze had his Smith and Wesson in one hand and turned on the bathroom faucet with another hand, pretending to wash his hands. Then he put his hand under the power dryer and left the bathroom. Bronze positioned himself by the doorsill of the men's bathroom. When Greene opened the door, he looked down the barrel of a gun. Bronze said calmly, "Take me to Steinberg now." Greene was more surprised than scared. Greene told Bronze he had good timing as he was just going to see Steinberg. Greene led Bronze to the Utzon Room, but no one was there. Bronze still had his Smith and Wesson against Greene's head, as Greene opened a secret passageway behind some artwork. He led Bronze to a room where Steinberg was sitting behind the desk. Greene told Steinberg, "I brought us some company Len," and started laughing.

Steinberg asked, "Who the hell are you?" Bronze said, "My name's Charles Bronze of the Miami-Dade Police Department." Steinberg said, "Miami? Why the hell would the police department send someone all the way from Miami to here?" Bronze replied, "You don't need to know that right now." Steinberg then said, "It's ok Mr. Bronze, you can shoot Mr. Greene if you'd like." Greene was in shock and Steinberg said, "After all, he did tell me an hour ago that some buffoon stole our agreement." Greene was about to gasp when Bronze said, "Yeah, I believe I was that buffoon." Steinberg was in shock, and took out a 9mm and pointed it at Bronze. He asked Bronze, "What do you want? Why are you here? You're just a policeman. You don't even know who I am. You may have stolen the documents, but you have no idea."

Bronze then said, "I wouldn't say that Steinberg. We know bloody well that you're a very accomplished blackmailer and have used Mr. Greene here, your puppet to do all your dirty work. We know about the $500 billion-$1 trillion payoff that you want from President Obama, Prime Minister Cameron, and King Abdullah." Steinberg said, "Well Bronze, you make a good point, but you are in no position to do anything. Yes, you may have a gun pointed at my right hand man, but I have a gun pointing at you. So can we sit down and talk like gentlemen?" Bronze replied calmly, "Here's the deal Steinberg. You are going to put that gun down." Steinberg laughed and said; "Now why would I do that?" Bronze replied, "We have some very classified information about your partner here. Either you put your gun down and turn yourself into the police, or we will let out the secrets about Daniel Greene." Steinberg looked a little surprised and said, "Prove it." Bronze then said, "Wir sind zusammen, wir sind eins." Steinberg was traumatized and put his gun down. Bronze decided to savor the moment for a little bit. The German phrase he had just mentioned, "We are together, we are one," was kept confidential between Greene and Steinberg. No one knew about the phrase and that one phrase was an indication to Steinberg that Bronze and his colleagues knew much more.

Charles Bronze told Greene to call the police and turn himself and Steinberg in, which Greene did while at the mercy of Bronze's Smith and Wesson. Steinberg had a sense of guilt mixed with revenge in his eyes. Bronze saw this, and he knew that Steinberg wanted to pick up that gun and shoot Greene, but didn't do it because Bronze was too intelligent. The authorities eventually arrived, keeping Steinberg and Greene at gunpoint. The police threw both of them in jail temporarily until the court hearing. After doing this, Bronze asked Steinberg what the card with the red "L" meant. Steinberg told him, "Mr. Bronze, if I had known you were so stupid, I would have shot Mr. Greene here. In another life perhaps. The "L" obviously stands for my name." Bronze was annoyed with Steinberg's smart remark, but replied, "Wow, Steinberg, I didn't realize you were that arrogant." Bronze then laughed and left the police station.

Dr. Bronze was now on the plane back to Miami. He didn't receive the normal call from Lt. Baker this time. Instead, he landed and Lt. Baker was waiting. "I'm proud of you Detective Bronze. I never thought you would have been able to understand what I whispered to you. However, I had a feeling you would have used your reasoning skills and brilliant mind to figure it out. Congrats my friend."

Even though the case was closed, Detective Charles Bronze still wondered deeply about what that red "L" meant. It was obvious from Steinberg's jaw clenches when he spoke to Bronze from the jail cell that he was lying. It dwelled on his mind for a few days, and he decided to do some investigative work. However, nothing turned up, so Bronze ignored it.

Dr. Charles Bronze returned home about 1:00 a.m. Monday morning. He thought about the whole 2010 holiday season and how far he traveled in the past two weekends from Bermuda to Australia. Even though he went to bed so late, he still woke up at 5:00 a.m. as always and continued his normal morning routine. However, right before he left the house phone rang. It was President Obama who said, "Detective Charles Bronze, I want to thank you personally on behalf of my family and I for being an integral part to our safety. It is people like you who make America a safer place and you deserve to be commended." Bronze replied, trying to sound awake, "Thank you Mr. President, it is an honor sir." President Obama then hung up the phone. Charles Bronze took his patient files that he brought home for the weekend and headed for the front door, smiling.

The Unraveled Sign

It was April 2011, and the weather had warmed up to about the high 70s-low 80s. Bronze conducted his typical morning ritual, a run the beach, and took his perfunctory hot shower. He then picked up a copy of Ian Fleming's *On Her Majesty's Secret Service* and continued reading from where he left off. As he read the novel, he started to remember how exactly he ended up working for the Miami Dade Police Department in the first place.

On June 9th, 1995, Charles Bronze began his day of residency like any fourth year resident would. He woke up early, got ready, and headed to the Bascom Palmer Eye Institute. Bronze was chief resident, so he had to do rounds with the younger residents for the day. After rounds, he had a patient named Thomas Brown, who was a 50-year-old Englishman who previously worked for the law enforcement there. When Brown moved to the United States, he requalified in police work and was now one of the chief sheriffs in Miami. Mr. Brown needed radial keratotomy, a refractive surgical procedure to correct nearsightedness.

Bronze did his normal routine of gathering patient history and reading Brown's patient file in order to ensure that radial keratotomy would be the correct procedure to perform. Although he specialized in ophthalmology, Bronze had sound knowledge in general internal medicine. He was no internist, but he always kept himself updated. Bronze believed that even though he was specializing, he still had to be an all-rounder when it came to medicine. Thomas Brown was not a doctor by any means, but his uncle who he grew up with was an internist, so he was familiar with some medical terms.

Brown asked Dr. Bronze why would he even bother looking into the physician that referred him. When Bronze explained his idea of how every doctor should have a comprehensive knowledge of general internal medicine, Brown was very impressed. Brown took mental note of this, and started chatting with Bronze. Since childhood, Dr. Charles Bronze was always gregarious so Bronze talked to him as well. Bronze himself was very glad that Brown was a talker, because it made the patient interaction a lot easier. When Bronze told Brown that he's a Hopkins medical school alumnus, Brown was very impressed. However, Brown was more intrigued at where Charles Bronze obtained his undergraduate degree.

Bronze obtained a degree in Chemistry from the University of Miami. He loved his time in Miami. Bronze's parents were from Highland Beach, an affluent community only an hour from Miami, so his mom was especially glad that Bronze would be staying close to home. Brown asked Bronze what sort of course work he did as a Chemistry major and asked Bronze details about his experience at the University of Miami. After telling Brown that he was on the ballroom dance team, an emergency response team, and did research in Chemistry, Brown understood why Bronze got into Hopkins. Brown really admired Charles Bronze's humility in telling him all of his accomplishments. Bronze said, "You are one of my first patients throughout my whole residency who's so interested in my time at the University of Miami. Almost all my patients question me about the experience at Johns Hopkins Medical

School, not realizing what a terrific school Miami is."

Thomas Brown then said something that Charles Bronze would never forget. Brown said, "Well, since you were a Chemistry major, I think you would be a fantastic crime scene investigator. CSI is a lot of chemistry, and I can tell that you are a very brilliant young man with the reasoning skills that apt CSIs need. I feel you would be a great asset to the police force." Bronze was a little taken with such a bold and profound statement, especially after speaking with this patient for only twenty minutes. However, Bronze said very respectfully, "Thank you Sheriff, it's an honor to hear that from someone of such high rank. I will definitely take it into consideration."

As Bronze finished up his final year in residency and commenced his one-year fellowship at Bascom Palmer, Brown's statement kept going on in his head like a broken record. Charles Bronze couldn't believe that he was taking this quote so seriously. After watching so many James Bond movies, reading all the novels, and being a fan of *Sherlock Holmes* and *Dick Tracy*, Charles Bronze started to think he would make an excellent secret agent. Bronze did bring himself back to reality though, realizing that not all cases will be so glamorous as portrayed in fantasy books. Nevertheless, the idea grew on Bronze.

After working a few years, when Bronze was thirty-five years old, he decided to enroll into the police academy, and pursue it as something part time. He got a 100% on the admissions test, and when the evaluators saw his academic credentials, they sent him to the CSI department. After talking with the Lieutenant of the Miami Dade CSI and telling the Lieutenant the kind of investigative work he would enjoy doing, the Lieutenant suggested that the go back to the police department and wait for a while. The CSI Lieutenant told him that once they observe him for a few months, he would be appointed to the detective position.

Just like the Lieutenant predicted, the police department noticed Bronze had a gift when it came to problem solving. He could take the most random details of a case and put them together to create one magnificent picture. Also, they noticed that Bronze was a great predictor, for he could read people very well and predict the moves they made, of which most of the time Bronze was correct. In addition, the person who was evaluating Bronze noticed he was very diplomatic, which was perfect for international cases. After nine months of working weekends for the police force, he was appointed to be a detective.

Because of Bronze's fluency in Arabic, he was assigned to a lot of international missions, with a concentration in the Middle East. Lt. Baker was in charge of the international aspect of the police force, and was the liaison between the major police departments in the U.S., the CIA, the DEA, and the FBI. Bronze always showed the utmost respect to Baker, and as a result Lt. Baker helped Bronze, especially when it came to not having his missions during the week because of Bronze's work in ophthalmology. As a result of Baker, Bronze was able to travel to many locales in the world at such a young age. Also, since Bronze was working for the government, the government paid off all of his medical school loans. While other doctors were struggling to survive at the age of 35, Charles Bronze was enjoying life, working as a doctor at Bascom Palmer during the week, and traveling to some of the hottest destinations in the world on the government's dime.

Charles Bronze was in his patio finishing up the last chapter of *On Her Majesty's Secret Service*. Afterwards, he decided to call Claire Scarlet to see how her weekend was going so far. Bronze felt like a brother to Claire, and since she didn't have any partner or spouse yet, he called her at least once on the weekend to make sure everything was ok. They chatted for about thirty minutes. At first, they were talking about work related affairs and wondering if Dr. Henry Smith would eventually hand over the practice to Scarlet or Bronze after deciding to retire. Then, they reminisced a little bit about medical school and their residency and how funny it was that they ended up in the same place as residents, especially considering how random "The Match" process is.

After his lovely chat with Claire Scarlet, the black Motorola that was on the little side table was ringing. Bronze smiled, waiting for the moment when his weekend would really get exciting. He had finished all of his paperwork for the weekend, as he was excellent at time management. Charles answered the phone, and as always, it was Lieutenant Baker. The husky voice said, "Bronze, get over here at once. We've got something for you." "Right away Lt. Baker," Bronze replied. With that, Bronze put on a Tommy Bahama flower shirt and white Calvin Klein pants and headed to the police station in his Lexus LS.

Bronze entered Lt. Baker's office and said, "Good afternoon Lt. Baker. What have you got for me?" As soon as Bronze asked that question, he chuckled slightly, for he remembered always saying that when patients would be coming into the ER during his residency. Lt. Baker replied, "Pay attention to this one Bronze, it's a very interesting case and we can't send one of our normal international detectives for this job. It requires someone who has great intelligence. That's why we chose you." Bronze said, "Thank you sir, I'm honored. Now shall we get on with the briefing?"

Lt. Baker showed a portrait and said, "Amadi Omotoso. Nigerian environmental engineer. Born into a poor family, Omotoso was an astute child who was fortunate to receive full scholarship to study at Oxford University. While at Oxford, he built a network of high politicians in Africa and African kingpins who were part of wealthy families. After graduating from Oxford, he did a one year fellowship at Harvard." Baker paused, knowing what was going to come out of Bronze's mouth. Bronze said, "Alright so we have someone who apparently went from rags to riches. You are talking about this gentleman because he's done something of international threat. Judging from his curriculum vitae, he used the contacts he made in Africa in order to get what he wants. Since he's an environmental engineer as you said, he somehow manipulates the environment to fulfill his greedy desire. Also, if Omotoso looks like that portrait in real, then he must have a lot of money. He wants more though. I find with all the cases you have given me over the years, all these guys and sometime gals want in the end is money."

Lt. Baker then smiled and said, "Top marks, Detective Bronze. Except for one thing. He is not interested in money. No, all Omotoso wants is power. The only reason we know so much about him is because of his inflated ego. So the question that must be in your head Bronze is "How is he going to gain all this power?" Before you even speak, let me say this. Omotoso ultimately wants to make all of Africa his empire. We are still not too sure how he is going to do it. Our sources tell us that he is in Sudan, and is gathering some of his disciples by the East-West Sudan border, the Nile River. You are going to go to Sudan and do some investigative work. I don't want you coming back right away like what you did when you were in Bermuda. It is important that this time you lie low for a few days and obtain as much information as you can. Then, go to the U.S. embassy in Khartoum, Sudan and call me. Do not, I repeat, do not call me from anywhere else. Since Omotoso has so many high political contacts, including the current President Omar-al-Bashir, nowhere is safe to call from. It looks like you're going to have to take this next week off from work." Bronze then replied, "I understand Lt. Baker. I'll take a vacation week per your suggestion. I have one question though. You said that nowhere is safe to call from because of Omotoso's affiliation with Omar-al-Bashir. If that is the case, what is stopping al-Bashir from tapping into the embassy? Also, do you want me to kill Omotoso?" Lt. Baker replied, "Although you make a good point, the embassy works with the U.S. and other major superpowers. We ensure their safety. Therefore, phone tapping shouldn't be an issue. However, I've known you for eleven years now and even though this is the case, I know you'll be on your guard. As for Omotoso, although he would be a great asset alive, he would be able to even make contacts in whatever jail we put him in so yes, kill him, but only if necessary. Good luck Detective Bronze." Bronze said, "Thank you sir." Right before Bronze opened Lt. Baker's office door to leave, Baker said, "Bronze! Be careful. There's a lot of turmoil going on in Sudan. Lie low, make your own cover and be safe." Bronze smiled and headed for the government's Learjet to fly to Sudan.

Before taking the Learjet, Bronze took a detour to his house, seeking Baker's permission. Since this was going to be in Sudan, Bronze had to get out the appropriate clothing. He packed some long gowns, skullcaps, and pieces of cloth to wrap as a turban. Bronze decided that he had to become one of the Sudanese in order to find out information. Bronze came to the conclusion that this time, he was not going to wear his normal designer clothes. Sudan is not the place where Bronze's fashionable taste was necessary. Fortunately, since Bronze had to make frequent trips to the Middle East, he had many Arab clothes in his closet.

He decided to be Abdullah Muhammad, an Egyptian who studied medicine in America. Bronze was going to Sudan as a volunteer to help those poor women and children who are suffering from eye problems. The eye problems stem from the smoke of the kerosene lamps used at night to learn. Charles Bronze settled in a village located on the Upper Nile in Sudan. He helped the women and children during the day and did some investigating at night.

Even though Bronze was doing undercover work in the evening, he felt very proud of the work he was doing during the day. Bronze wanted to become a doctor for humanitarian reasons, not income purposes. By helping the less fortunate women and children, he felt he was achieving this goal. As Bronze was asking the locals around, some of them started to talk about Bronze. They would whisper to each other in Arabic how this tall stately gentlemen dressed like us just randomly came and is now asking all these questions. Bronze noticed they were whispering, and approached the people who were talking about him. He introduced himself as Abdullah Muhammad, and told them he was greatly honored to finally come over to the Upper Nile to assist the women and children. The men smiled at Bronze, showing their golden teeth. Bronze then left them alone to talk, not asking them any questions.

It was now day two of Bronze's stay in the Upper Nile. Bronze continued asking around, to no avail. However, one person did tell him that if he wanted to find out more about Amadi Omotoso to travel to Khartoum and go to a man named Kareem Sayid. Sayid would tell Bronze about Omotoso. After helping out more women and children in the Upper Nile, Bronze called for a Land Cruiser and took his briefcase with him. He bid goodbye to everyone, and the men who were talking secretly about him hugged Bronze, thanking him for his service to the village. Bronze then thought of how he would approach Sayid.

From the man's description of Sayid, he was a sophisticated gentleman. Therefore, Bronze wore western clothing, but nothing designer, just normal clothes. Bronze went to the U.S. embassy and called Baker, informing him of his progress. Baker commended him. He also asked Lt. Baker to do a cross-reference of Kareem Sayid and where Bronze would be able to contact Sayid. After receiving the information from Baker, Bronze told Sayid that he was a friend of Omotoso and to meet him at a local café in Khartoum.

Charles Bronze was waiting patiently for Kareem Sayid in the café where they agreed to meet. He saw that Sayid was five minutes late and became a little annoyed. Charles Bronze's pet peeve was tardiness. He couldn't stand it. However, Bronze swallowed his annoyance and thought out how he was going to pick information from Sayid and not volunteer any info.

Kareem Sayid finally arrived fifteen minutes late. Bronze heard what Sayid had to say. Bronze noticed that Sayid had an excellent command of the Arabic language. Sayid was speaking in an almost poetic fashion. Sayid seemed like a really kind man, but Bronze profiled him from the start and knew he would be a gentleman that would be difficult for Bronze to probe for information based on his mannerisms. Sayid briefly told Bronze about Omotoso, and Bronze was getting the impression that Sayid was praising Omotoso in a divine way. Bronze realized he wasn't getting anywhere with Sayid. Sayid then excused himself to use the restroom.

Bronze followed him into the bathroom and saw that he was in a stall. Bronze washed his hands and face when he heard a gun clicking. Sayid then told him in English now to turn around slowly. Bronze complied, wiping his face on his shirtsleeve. Sayid asked, "Now Mr. Abdullah Muhammad, what do you really want? I know you're after Omotoso. The fact of the matter is, he is an inspiration to all of Africa and when he claims Africa to be his empire, he will make a change for the better!" Bronze replied, "Kareem, you really don't need the gun. I'm not armed. Look." Bronze lifted up his pants cuff and Sayid yelled, "Stop! Hands up where I can see them." Bronze then tackled Sayid to the midsection against a stall, while using his left hand to try and crack Sayid's right wrist that was holding the gun. Bronze was successful, as Sayid released the gun. Sayid punched him in the gut, and Bronze mustered as much energy as he could and dived to grab the gun. Then he pointed it at Sayid. "Hands up and on your knees!" Bronze exclaimed. Sayid complied. Bronze asked, "Now, let's talk. First, where is Omotoso?" Sayid asked, "Why would I tell a policeman like you?" Bronze turned red and said, "Because if you don't, I'll plant a bullet through your foot, and then your head." Sayid said, "Alright, alright he is in Morocco." Bronze said, "Why is he there, and how is he going to claim Africa to be his empire?" Sayid said, "He's in Morocco on business. As for how he's going to claim Africa, I can't exactly tell you. He gave me an amber envelope and told me not to open it until tomorrow. It has his plan in it. However, it's in my house." Bronze then asked him, "What makes you think I can trust you?" Sayid said, "The same way I know I can trust you. Your name is obviously not Abdullah Muhammad." Bronze thought for a moment. He realized that he needed some bait to make Sayid talk. Bronze said, "Where's your mobile phone? Dial your American business partner, Jake Weston." Sayid was in shock, taking the bait, and said, "How do you know Mr. Weston is here on business?" Bronze said, "You don't need to know that now. Just tell me where the envelope is and we'll let bygone be bygone." Sayid said, "Ok ok don't shoot! It's in my car." Bronze said, "Shall we?" Sayid took Bronze to the car while Bronze still had him at gunpoint and took out the amber envelope. Then, Bronze and Sayid went back to the bathroom. He ordered Sayid to open it and read it to him. Sayid read a two-page document that was in the envelope. He read, "Attention Mr. Sayid: In two days, we will strike. I will use my political contacts in Africa and dump nuclear waste into the Nile River. The pollution will disperse throughout the Nile and it will kill many innocent people. Then, they will bow down to me. As for you, I have a big reward planned for you. Sincerely, Amadi Omotoso." Bronze ordered Sayid, who was still at gunpoint, to hand him the document. He then told Sayid, "Kareem Sayid, it is a pity that you will never have the privilege to receive that big reward that Mr. Omotoso so ably described." Bronze then shot Sayid in the head and put the gun in Sayid's right hand. Bronze took out a bottle of solution from his pocket in order to remove his own fingerprints, making it look like suicide. He put the document back into the amber envelope and left the café.

Bronze was starting to get tired, but still remained focused. He ordered room service, vegetables and rice with Sudanese coffee. He examined the document with all of the information very carefully. He then looked into the envelope to see if anything else was present. Bronze saw a little white piece of paper. He took it out and it wasn't a piece of paper, it was a card. It had a red "L" on it. Bronze's mouth opened wide open in shock, not making a sound.

One day while Omotoso was doing a fellowship in Harvard, he received a letter in the mail asking him to meet a gentleman in Harvard Yard. The gentleman told Omotoso what clothes he will be wearing. Omotoso arrived at the Yard in the prescribed time and asked the man why he wanted to meet Omotoso. The man replied, "You'll see." The man put a piece of cloth of Omotoso's mouth, knocking him out.

Omotoso woke up in a restrained chair in a dark room. He couldn't even tell if he was in Harvard anymore. A man of average height wearing a cloth across his face introduced himself as "L". L said, "If you ever utter one more syllable, I'll have your throat slit." Mr. Omotoso yelled, "Who are you? Why do you want me?" L replied, "Calm down, I want to tell you something. It was because of me that you were offered that fellowship in Harvard. I've noticed what a brilliant man you are after doing some inquiries with my friends in Oxford. I'm here to offer you a job. You want the African empire, and I'm going to give you the tools to achieve that goal." Omotoso said calmly, "And what do you want in return?" L replied, "I want your trust, and you are going to work under my supervision. However, you have a lust for power, and I am going to grant you that freedom. Despite this, if you do not agree to my wishes, I'll have you executed. Also, whenever you tell someone about my grand plan, you must give them my card." L then showed Omotoso the white card with a red "L" on it. L then said, "You'll be hearing from me soon." Then, the man who knocked him out the first time was present again. He put a cloth over Omotoso's mouth, knocking him out for the second time. Omotoso woke up in Harvard Yard, with no trail of the man.

Charles Bronze was still in shock. He knew the whole time that the card wasn't just linked to Len Steinberg, a master blackmailer who he busted a few months ago. Bronze then realized that it's a whole network of criminals who want international attention. Questions started to flood in Bronze's mind, "Who are these people? What is the motive behind this marking of a red "L"? Is there a man in charge?" For a good thirty minutes, Bronze pondered and pondered. He used every reasoning skill he had, but it still didn't lead up to anything. Bronze then focused back onto the case at hand.

Detective Bronze observed that the return address of the envelope was in Morocco. "Omotoso must be there," he thought. He headed to the U.S. Embassy and called Lt. Baker. "Lt. Baker, I've got something big." Baker replied, "Go ahead Detective, but make it quick." Bronze said, "After questioning Sayid, I have reason to believe that Omotoso is in

Morocco. Is there any link or anything we have about Omotoso being in Morocco before?" Lt. Baker responded, "Hold on let me check. Yes, we've got something. It seems that Omotoso has contacts there as well in the government. However, he always books the penthouse suite at the Le Royal Mansour Meridien in Casablanca. There is a good chance he is still there, and he will probably execute the plan you sent me via email from that suite. Be careful Bronze and good luck. I don't want to cut you short but I have to go." Lt. Baker hung up. Bronze then took the Learjet to Casablanca.

As Charles Bronze was flying to Casablanca, he continued wondering what the white card with the red "L" meant. He recognized that it was the same one from his mission in Sydney, but still couldn't come up with a link. Bronze was surprised at himself and a bit disappointed. He was beginning to accept that there are some things that he couldn't solve. However, he ignored these temptations and tried to stay focused. He calmed himself down with some herbal tea that was on board, and told himself, "Come Bronze. Focus on the case. Take care of Omotoso first, and the facts regarding the card will fall in line. Focus."

Bronze finally arrived. It would be too obvious booking himself in the same hotel as Omotoso, but he did it anyway, especially because Le Royal Mansour Meridien was the most prestigious hotel in Casablanca, and he couldn't refuse such a grandiose offer. As the porter escorted Bronze up the elevator, he noticed that the penthouse had keyed access. He was staying on the fifth floor.

Charles Bronze was starting to get nervous. It was around midnight and he was wearing a Perry Ellis suit. He was sipping some ginger ale at the bar when a tall, thin Moroccan belly dancer came up to him and sat next to him. She was heavenly. Bronze analyzed how tight fitting the top part of her costume was. Dr. Charles Bronze also scrutinized how toned her abdomen was and how it glistened in the moonlight. He bought her a drink, and started asking about some great places to sightsee in Morocco. Bronze started telling himself, "It's about time I finally saw a beautiful woman. All this traveling and no females to keep me company." Bronze spoke to the woman, named Nadia, in a very respectful manner and asked her a few questions, especially about the man in the penthouse. Nadia told him that his name was Amadi and she was invited twice to perform for him. She said he had a very harsh tone, but he was strangely very kind towards her. After speaking with Nadia for a while, she kissed Bronze on the cheek and bade him goodnight.

1:00 a.m. came around fairly quickly, when Bronze decided it was time to pay Mr. Omotoso a visit. He saw one of the porters and told him that he had some luggage in the elevator. When the porter went inside with Bronze, Bronze closed the door, withdrew his Smith and Wesson from his shoulder holster, and told the porter to take him to Mr. Omotoso's room. The porter agreed, having no say in the matter. Bronze could feel a lump in his throat, and he was getting really nervous.

The porter took Bronze to the penthouse floor. He told the porter, "I'm going to need your word you never brought me up here tonight. If not, well let's just say it won't be pretty." The porter, who was actually very jolly but scared, agreed. He went back down and Bronze tiptoed to Omotoso's room.

Bronze opened the door slowly and saw it was pitch black. He started to wonder if Omotoso was actually sleeping. Bronze reached for the light and turned it on. When he did, three men were pointing guns at him, asking him to drop the Smith and Wesson. He agreed, and they took him to Omotoso.

Omotoso was sitting in a maple chair, lined with a red cushion. He collected Bronze's gun from one of the armed guards and said, "Smith and Wesson .40 handgun. Standard issue for those bloody Americans. So why is an American agent sitting here in my penthouse suite in Casablanca, Morocco?" Bronze replied, "Let me ask you Mr. Omotoso. Why are you here? The sweat trickling down your forehead indicates you are nervous about something. Also, since you had the guards strategically placed, you knew I, Abdullah Muhammad, would be here tonight. Of course, judging from who you contacts are, you probably know my name is Charles Bronze and I work for the Miami Dade Police Department." Mr. Omotoso grinned and said, "Very good Mr. Bronze. Continue." Bronze said, "Well, you want Africa as your empire and are going to use nuclear waste to dump it into the Nile River. My question I want to pose to you tonight Mr. Omotoso is "Why?" Why would you do such a thing and kill so many innocent people?" Omotoso replied, "Well Mr. Bronze, I mean, Detective Bronze, you are as intelligent as your file says you are. The reason is very simple. As you are doubtlessly aware, I was born into a very poor family. And now I have access to a lot of money, money that I wished I had when I was younger. However, I don't want money. Money is something that goes away after a while. I want all of Africa to call me King Omotoso and bow down to me."

Bronze listened very carefully to what

Omotoso had to say. He then asked, "Mr. Omotoso, I want to ask you something personal. However, I think that you should dismiss your guards. We don't need them here. Let us talk like gentlemen, the way civilized people talked. You have my Smith and Wesson, which is the only arm I carry around with me. You don't have any guns on you, for I sized you up when your goons brought me inside. So let's talk." Omotoso laughed so loud that one could hear the echo throughout the whole floor. Omotoso said, "I know how dangerous you are Bronze. You're looking at everything I have in this room and thinking what you can use to kill me. Am I right?" Bronze laughed voraciously himself and said, "What you say may be true, but I give you my word I won't harm you. However, I still don't understand why you want to deprive people of their livelihood by adulterating the Nile. Don't you remember where you came from? Whether you like it or not Omotoso, you were once a poor boy as well who just got very lucky because you were smart." Mr. Omotoso face went like a prune and dismissed his guards. He said, "You are too straightforward to just kill me with anything you can find. No, you want more, you want information so tell me." Bronze thought about the white card with the red "L" very deeply. He knew that Omotoso could sense this, but he buried that feeling. However, it just couldn't escape Bronze. He started sweating, while Omotoso was starting to cool down compared to when Bronze first arrived.

Bronze asked, "What is the white card with the red "L" on it?" Omotoso replied, "Ah, I was wondering when you were going to ask. It's something I like to keep with me at all times, and I am in no position to discuss it. What I will tell you is my plan will work. They will bow down to me." Bronze then said, "Sorry but its not going to happen. It seems what you said will come to past Omotoso. You will be dead before I leave this room." Bronze tried to muster whatever confidence he had. Bronze reasoned out the situation and realized that only one of them would leave the penthouse suite alive. Omotoso said, "Well since you're so positive, let me show you this briefcase. It has the control to dump the nuclear waste. All I have to do is press this button." Omotoso pointed to it but didn't push the button, even though he was about to. Omotoso and Bronze heard gunfire from outside the penthouse. Bronze had a feeling that Lt. Baker had sent some help through the U.S. Embassy in Morocco. A man entered, handing Bronze a gun. Bronze pointed the gun at Omotoso and told him to put his hands up. Omotoso agreed, and Bronze shot the briefcase. Omotoso was disheartened and turned red. Then, Bronze pointed the gun at Omotoso. Omotoso asked, "Are you going to kill me Detective Charles Bronze?" Bronze dropped the gun and said, "No, you are more worth to us alive." Omotoso then laughed and took out a knife from his back pocket and slit his own throat. "No!" Bronze yelled. Then he rushed to Omotoso as he was dying asking, "What is the white card? What does it mean?" Omotoso replied, "You'll never find out! To hell with you!" and dropped to the ground.

The Moroccan police took care of the situation in Omotoso's suite, thanking Bronze for his assistance. Bronze was presently on the Learjet heading back to Miami. The phone rang, and Bronze knew it was Lt. Baker with his usual call. Baker said, "Good work Detective Bronze. I must admit I was worried, especially having you out there for such a long time, but I'm glad you stayed in one piece. And good work taking care of Omotoso. I know you didn't exactly kill him, but you warped his mind so much that he felt better if he killed himself. For that, you deserve great credit. Get some rest now and we'll be in touch." Bronze replied, "Thank you sir." Charles Bronze sipped a cup of tea on the Learjet as he kept thinking about that white card. He knew that it was a whole network of people who want power and money. Bronze was going from anger to depression, as he couldn't figure out the link. As he was pondering, the phone rang. Bronze said to himself, "What the hell does Baker want now? I need some rest." However, it wasn't Baker who was on the phone.

Claire Scarlet said, "Charles! Where have you been? Are you ok?" There's just something about Claire Scarlet's voice that always uplifts Charles Bronze. He became bright and alert saying, "Yes I'm fine thank you darling. I had to take a week off because I had some business to take care of in the Middle East, but it's all done. I'm on my way back." Claire responded, "Ok, I was worried because I saw you hadn't come into work and you didn't even tell me you were going away. Does it have to do with that government job of yours again?" Bronze laughed and told Scarlet, "One day." Claire Scarlet chuckled and said, "One day babe." Scarlet hung up the phone and Bronze immediately dozed off.

4

Venus

Indeed today was a very special day. Charles Bronze woke up and got out of bed and began his normal morning routine. However, he had a joyous feeling when he woke up. Bronze was always very optimistic and was an inspiration to others. Nevertheless, he felt something special today, as if there was warmth emanating from his heart. Bronze found it profound, for he never had such a feeling before. He thought something significant would happen today. Be that as it may, Bronze still could not pinpoint exactly what would make the day special.

Dr. Charles Bronze drove in his Lexus LS to work as always, and sat down in his office pondering about this special feeling. Bronze knew himself pretty well, especially seeing as he was 46 years old. He had gone through many experiences in his life, some which he sanguinely reminisces and others which he regrets, but never had this feeling. Bronze decided to ignore it for the time being. After all, he did have a full list of patients for the day.

It was now 5:00 p.m., and Bronze had seen his last patient for the day. It was a patient who had cataract surgery last week and it was a simple post-op. After seeing the patient, Bronze returned to his office whereby he had a stack of patient files to do some paperwork for. He always went through his patients for the day to make sure everything was correctly documented, because in medicine that is key. Dr. Henry Smith also had his fair share of patients, but left early in order to be with his wife. Charles Bronze and Claire Scarlet always admired how diligent a husband Dr. Henry Smith was, especially because neither of them were married.

At this point, it was around 6:00 p.m. when all of the administration for the office left. Therefore, it was only Charles Bronze and Claire Scarlet left in the office. She came on over to his office and asked him how his day of patients went. He told her that it wasn't anything special, but he had some interesting conversations with some of his patients. Charles Bronze was very charismatic, and loved talking to patients. It also made them feel a lot more comfortable and contributed to his renowned bedside manner. Claire noticed that Bronze was smiling for the day and even though he always did, this was different. She asked him, "Charles, you seem a little happier than you usually are. Is everything ok?" Bronze replied, "Yes indeed Claire, its just I had this unusual feeling of joy this more that I've never had before. I have been trying to figure it out, but still to no avail." Claire replied, "Well Charles maybe you should stop looking for a reason, and let the reason find you." Bronze said, "Very wise of you Claire, but then again you have always been an amazing person." Claire blushed a little and smiled.

It was about half an hour later now and she had just left his office to go back to her office. Then, the black Motorola rang. "Bronze, we need you," said Lieutenant Baker. Bronze replied, "Right away sir. I'm in the office now and I'll be there in 20 minutes." Bronze stopped by Claire's office and told her that he was leaving. Claire Scarlet replied, "It seems I have perfect timing then. Don't worry Charles; I'll lock up the office. See you on Monday. Have a good night!" Bronze replied, "Thanks Claire, you too. Take care and have a fantastic weekend!" Bronze left the office, hopped into his Lexus LS and drove to the police station.

Bronze arrived right on time. He entered the police station and was greeted by the receptionist as always. The receptionist always loved Bronze's courtesy towards her and the way he conducted himself around people. Charles Bronze then entered Lt. Baker's office. Baker was on the phone with someone and looked a little confused. Bronze read into the situation and realized that it must have been his wife wondering when he would be home. After Lt. Baker hung up the phone, he said, "Sorry, Detective Bronze. That was my wife. She was wondering when I would be coming home. After all it is 7:00 p.m. on a Friday night." Bronze smiled. Baker said, "Let's begin with the briefing, shall we?"

Lt. Baker said, "Subject, Larry Rucker. You know of Rucker, correct?" Bronze said, "Of course. You know that I am a technology enthusiast. He is the CEO of LaRu, the famous computer company. I was reading the 2010 Nielsen Report just yesterday, and it said that LaRu is now the Number 2 hardware computer company in the world after Apple Computers. It seems that at the rate they're going, they may even surpass Apple." Baker replied, "You are exactly right Bronze. I tell you, you would make a very convincing economist. Are you sure you're a doctor?" Bronze laughed and said, "Lieutenant, you never cease to amaze me. Let's continue."

Baker said, "Rucker formed a small investment company on the side in 1992, which has been very successful since. Not many people know about it, because he wants to keep his top ten clients a closely guarded secret. However, you know how the American government works. Rucker has a sidekick who is running the investment company with him." Charles Bronze then started to think of what Rucker looked like from the website he was reading yesterday. He was Caucasian, short, thin, and had gray hair. He always wore expensive clothing and looked like a millionaire. Baker showed Bronze a picture of Rucker's sidekick. He was an African-American gentlemen, a good six feet in height and muscular. It seemed to Bronze that this gentleman worked out everyday, for he had bulging muscles, especially in the picture Lt. Baker was showing him. Lt. Baker then said, "His name is Tyrese Jones. Rucker and Jones have been partners since 1990, and when Rucker formed the investment company, he let Jones run the company. However, Rucker still makes the major business decisions. They agreed to split all of the profits 50/50." Baker then continued, "Now here's where you come in."

Baker said, "Jones has kidnapped a Swedish woman by the name of Annalina Kristensen. Unfortunately, we don't have a picture of her on file. She is the CEO of Kris Cosmetics, a beauty supply company. The company is not very well known in America, but has gained a lot of revenue from Europe and the Far East. We still don't understand exactly why Jones would kidnap her." Bronze then replied, "How many people know that Kristensen has been kidnapped?" Lt. Baker replied, "Not many. Only the top officials in the police force. In fact, you are one of the first people below my rank to know about it." Bronze said, "Well Lieutenant, Jones looks like a thug. Although I do complement him for wearing sophisticated clothing, I still don't understand why Rucker would choose him. However, even though Jones gives that vibe of a blunt instrument, he does seem very intelligent. To be able to kidnap someone and not let anyone know requires great intelligence. As for why, it's pretty simple. Kristensen has found out information about either LaRu computers or Rucker's investment company that Rucker doesn't want others knowing. The question is: "What?" and also "How did she know about it?" Allow me to infer, Lieutenant, you want me to free Kristensen and bring her back here. Then we will question her as to what she knows about the company." Lt. Baker smiled and said, "My dear friend, this is exactly why I suggested to the chief of the MDPD that you be the first one to know about this case besides the big bosses. I can't believe that we were so dumb in figuring out why they would capture her. The answer is so obvious." Bronze then replied, "Don't worry Lieutenant, I can tell you from experience that we all make foolish mistakes."

Bronze asked Baker, "Where are they keeping her hostage?" Baker said, "On the rooftop of the Ritz-Carlton resort in South Beach." Bronze thought for a moment and said, "With due respect Lt. Baker, don't you think that it is too conspicuous of a spot to hold someone hostage?" Baker replied, "You make a good point, but our sources have lead us to that spot. One of the MDPD helicopters was flying around the area this morning and saw that she was there sitting in a chair, wrists tied." Bronze replied, "Very well then. Do you mind if I take one of the undercover police cars?" Baker said, "Not a problem Detective. Before you leave, another important thing. Your hunch about Jones is correct, he seems like a thug just working as Rucker's sidekick. We still don't understand why Rucker would trust someone like Jones so much. However, it's very important that you bring Ms. Kristensen here. Do whatever means necessary. If Jones is preventing you from Kristensen and he doesn't give you any information, kill him." Bronze replied, "Of course sir."

As Bronze was driving to the Ritz-Carlton, he was thinking about his plan of attack. He reached the Ritz-Carlton in the MDPD Dodge Charger. He went to the elevator to the top floor. Then, he noticed a stairwell to go on the roof. He withdrew his Smith and Wesson .40 handgun from his shoulder holster and proceeded cautiously. He opened the door ever so slightly and saw two guards. However, he didn't see the chair with Kristensen like Lt. Baker described. Another guard was coming up the stairs, but Bronze was so focused on how to eliminate the two he didn't notice. Det. Bronze felt something poking him behind his back. "Hands up," a voice said. The armed guard who was going up the stairs took his gun and told him to open the door and walk slowly. Bronze was starting to sweat and complied. The two guards pointed their guns towards Bronze. The third one, the one who initially found Bronze, took out a walkie-talkie and called someone and said, "Mr. Jones, we found an intruder." A deep voice said, "Kill him." The third guard said, "Very well then." Bronze was getting really nervous now. He said, "Hold on! Before you shoot me, I want to talk to your boss. Maybe we can come to some arrangement." The guard who was holding the walkie-talkie asked, "What makes you think Mr. Jones wants to hear from a fox like you?" Charles Bronze bluffed and said, "I have some information that will be of great use to him." The guard told this same statement to Jones, and Jones said, "Put him on." Bronze took the walkie-talkie from the gentlemen. Then, Charles Bronze threw the walkie back to the guard and told him to catch. As soon as the third guard let his gun down to catch it, he ran toward the rear of the third guard. He then pointed the gun to the other two guards and shot them. He punched the one who caught the walkie and kicked him hard. Bronze took the guard's gun and pointed it towards him. Bronze said, "Where is the girl that was here?" The guard replied, "Does it matter? They're probably torturing her at this point." Charles Bronze repeated the question and said, "If you don't answer me, you will have the same demise as your friends there." The guard said, "Ok ok, don't kill me! They have her at a warehouse on US1 and NW 79th Street." Bronze said, "Thank you my friend." Det. Bronze shot the third guard and took back his Smith and Wesson from the man's jacket pocket. Bronze then said, "I believe this belong to me," and headed back to the police station.

He entered the police station, but only two people were there. One of them was the captain. Bronze asked the captain whether or not Lt. Baker had gone home. The captain replied in the affirmative and Bronze headed back home in his Lexus LS. When he returned to his Miami Beach penthouse, he checked his messages and got a message from Baker. He said, "Good evening Bronze, this is Lt. Baker. Call me when you get this message on my Motorola cell phone and update me on your progress." Bronze called Baker from his own Motorola phone. Lt. Baker picked up immediately and said, "What's the update Bronze?" Bronze replied, "Sir, I'm sorry, but Rucker is one step ahead of us. He knew that the police helicopter was snooping around so he moved Kristensen to a different location." Baker said, "Good God, did anyone tell you where she is?" Bronze said, "Luckily, there were only three guards, one of which knew. She's being kept at a warehouse on US1 and NW 79th Street." Baker replied, "Alright, meet me in my office tomorrow morning at 8:00 a.m. and we'll talk about it."

Detective Charles Bronze went to Lt. Baker's office the following morning just as planned. Baker said, "Bronze, I'm really sorry. I should have trusted your judgment. Clearly, Rucker was only using that location as a decoy. We investigated into that warehouse, and it's actually a shack. However, we have our satellites giving us live feedback, and there are armed men guarding the shack so it seems your guard friend from the Ritz-Carlton was correct. Go there later, and proceed with extreme caution. Our contacts have told us that there is a good possibility Jones is there questioning her. Good luck." Bronze headed out and proceeded towards the shack.

When he reached the area, he parked a good distance away. He didn't want to be too discernible. Bronze did an analysis of the perimeter, noticing if there was anything else besides guards. There were two guarding the door and one behind the shack. Bronze crept up behind the one at the rear of the shack and put his hand over his mouth. Then, Bronze snapped his neck, laying him on the ground quietly. Bronze took out his Smith and Wesson and put on the silencer. He boldly went to the front door. One of the guards asked, "Who are you?" and Bronze shot both guards coldly. He then continued looking around and opened the door.

Kristensen was sitting in a chair. Her face was bruised but the rest of her body seemed to be intact. Her wrists were tied, just as Baker described. She had been knocked out. However, when she heard the door open, she woke up. It was at that point when Charles Bronze laid his eyes upon the most beautiful woman he had ever seen. She was tall, thin, had very plump and erect breasts, what looked like rock hard abs, and a firm bum. Her skin was a golden white color, probably from tanning in Miami. Bronze felt a lump in his throat, and tried his best to focus on the mission. Bronze put his finger on his lips, telling her to keep quiet, and circled the inside of the shack. He told her to stay quiet, took out a pocketknife and starting cutting the rope.

Tyrese Jones was heading to the warehouse by himself. He came alone to check up on the girl. Kristensen gasped and whispered to Bronze that he was coming. Bronze took out his Smith and Wesson, which still had the silencer, stood up in front of Kristensen, and pointed his gun directly towards the door. Jones noticed that the two guards in front of the door had been shot. He took out a 9mm handgun and proceeded towards the front door. He opened the door, seeing Bronze pointing the gun towards him. Bronze said, "Put the gun down slowly." Jones replied, "I will as soon as you do." Bronze didn't budge. He said, "Mr. Jones, I said put down the gun." Jones said, "Well, it seems you know who I am. The question is how much do you know?" Bronze replied, "I know enough. Now put the gun down." Jones replied, "No." Bronze then said, "Ms. Kristensen, please close your eyes." She closed her eyes, and Jones then asked, "Don't you want to know who did that to her?" Bronze replied, "Obviously, it was you." Jones said, "Well, maybe you're right, maybe you're not." Bronze said, "Are you going to put the gun down or not?" Jones said, "No." Jones aimed at Bronze's head and shot, but Bronze ducked in time. Then, Bronze shot Jones in the chest, followed by the head.

Kristensen screamed slightly and asked, "Did you kill him?" Bronze replied, "Yes." Kristensen said, "Good, you don't want to know how badly I wanted to, especially for beating my face." Bronze said softly, "Well, it's all over now. Come with me." Bronze took her hand and they dashed towards his car. As Bronze was driving, Kristensen asked, "Who are you?" He replied, "My name is Charles Bronze, and I'm a detective for the Miami-Dade Police Department." He drove for a mile or so when he saw that the bruise on her face had scathes, which started bleeding. Bronze pulled aside. He reached for the back seat and grabbed the first aid kit. Bronze brought it because he didn't know what condition Kristensen would be in. He put some peroxide on her bruise, followed by Neosporin. Bronze said, "This may hurt a bit, but it will make your bruise better." Kristensen let out a small cry and after Bronze taped gauze on her face said, "Thank you Detective Bronze."

As he was driving on, he said, "So your name is Annalina, correct?" She said, "Yes, but everyone calls me Anna." Anna asked, "So what else does the Police Deparment know about me?" He replied, "I'm afraid that's all, except that you're the CEO of Kris Cosmetics and that you operate primarily in Europe and the Far East." She chuckled and said, "Well you do know more about me than I know about you. Do you think my bruise will be ok? Jones hit me pretty hard." Bronze said, "Yes, it will be fine. It doesn't seem to be infected which is good and you have to ensure that you do not rest on it. Otherwise, it will delay the recuperation process." Anna said, "You sound like a doctor." Bronze smiled and said, "Actually, I am. I'm an ophthalmologist." Anna said, "But I thought you said you were a detective." Bronze told her, "Yes, I am. However, I do the detective work on the side for special cases." Anna replied, "I'm glad you consider me a special case then." Bronze laughed and a few minutes later, they were at the police station.

Bronze entered the police station with the 5'9" golden blonde hair, blue-eyed Annalina Kristensen. She was wearing a corporate suit, with a skirt bottom. Bronze told Anna to wait in the lobby and he will be back soon. Det. Bronze entered Baker's office. Baker said, "Well?" Bronze replied, "She's waiting in the lobby downstairs. Where do you want me to take her?" Baker replied, "Take her to one of the rooms. We will both talk to her since she knows who you are." Bronze said, "Very well then."

Bronze took Anna to an interrogation room with the cameras. Baker asked her a lot of questions, while Charles Bronze was standing on the side listening carefully. Bronze was a multitasker, so although he was listening, he also took a considerable amount of time to analyze Anna. "Wow, this woman really is beautiful," he thought. Anna had a slight Swedish accent, but nothing heavy at all. In fact, Bronze found it very attractive. He started to feel that inexplicable warmth from his heart that he felt the previous morning. Bronze then realized that he had fallen in love.

Baker didn't ask her the most important question, which was, "What information do you know that others don't?" Lt. Baker was much smarter than that. He knew that Bronze should be the one to ask her, especially because Anna liked him, calling him her hero once or twice during her discourse with Lt. Baker. Baker then said, "Ok Charles, is there anything you want to ask Anna here? She is a very sweet person." Bronze asked the big question. Anna thought for a while and smiled. Then she explained, "About two years ago, Larry Rucker called me while I was on business here in Miami. He told me who he was, the CEO of the world-famous LaRu computers. Rucker said that he had a small investment company and that I was one of a few selected people to be his key members in the company. I detected a menacing tone from Rucker and knew immediately I couldn't trust him. He told me that his wingman, Tyrese Jones, the creep who bruised my face, is the Vice President of the investment company and to talk to him. I respectfully told Rucker that I wasn't interested. He seemed indifferent and hung up the phone. A few months after our conversation, one of my best friends, who was the CEO of the world-famous Proactiv Solution, told me that she made an investment five years ago and saw a substantial increase in her revenue within the first year. When I say substantial, I'm talking about $10 million. My friend, Laura, then told me that as the years passed, she made more and more money. I started to have a great interest in who she invested in. When she told me that it was Larry Rucker, I was a little shocked. I told myself that if my best friend could put so much faith into this man, maybe I should give it a shot. However, I'm the kind of person that has to think about the details of the situation before I make a big decision." Bronze smiled upon hearing all of this, especially the last sentence. He analyzed her pouting lips carefully as she continued.

Anna continued, "Therefore, I started to do some investigative work behind the scenes through some business contacts about what exactly this on-the-side investment company of Larry Rucker is. They all started seeing large profits as well. I continued to do further investigative work, and Rucker's company seemed to be legitimate. I thought about approaching Laura, but she had so much faith in Rucker that she would have a bias for him. After a year of investigating, I got a call from Laura saying that after acquiring billions of dollars, she started seeing a few billion diminish from her investment fund bit by bit. I told her not to worry and I would call her back in a few days. I thought deeply about what happened and then it hit me like a baseball. I realized that Rucker was swindling one of my best friends. I called her phone immediately and told her the scenario. She didn't believe me, and it caused a great rift between us. A few days later, I got a call from Jones, not Rucker, telling me that I had a package at my front door. When I opened it, they kidnapped me and took me to the shack. Rucker told me Laura spilled the beans to him and that they had to kidnap me because my inference was correct and that I knew too much. They kept me there for about a week, feeding me and giving me water while my hands were tied. Jones then told me that they were going to execute me three days from today."

Charles Bronze and Lt. Baker analyzed what Anna said very carefully. Charles Bronze analyzed the facts, this woman was captured because she knew too much and two officers were sitting right in front of her. There was no way that this woman just lied to them. Bronze profiled and looked at Anna from head to toe when they met, and he could see in her eyes that she had an innocent heart and wasn't like those corrupt CEOs that are present today. They told Anna to wait in the interrogation room while Baker and Bronze went outside to talk. Baker asked, "Well Detective, what do you think of Anna's story?" Bronze said, "I think it's legitimate. She is in no position to lie to us. I profiled her and she is a woman of honesty." Baker asked, "How do you know we can trust her so quickly?" Bronze replied, "Trust me." Baker said, "Well, you've never let me down before Bronze so I believe you."

Bronze and Baker went back into the

interrogation room. Bronze asked Anna, "Anna, is there anything else you can tell us? Do you know where Rucker currently is?" Anna replied, "Yesterday, I heard Jones on the phone with Rucker talking about what they were going to do with me. Rucker said that he was still in Miami, and won't be leaving until after I was executed. I guess he wanted to make sure I was dead before he left this area. However, I don't know exactly where." Baker said, "Ok, let me see what I can do. Detective Bronze, do you mind if you take Anna to your penthouse for the night? She can't be on her own until we catch Rucker. Keep an eye on her and protect her at all costs." Bronze was a little shocked. In his eleven years of working in the police force, Baker never asked Bronze to take a victim with him to his house. I guess Baker thought that Kristensen was very intelligent, too intelligent for her own good to be on her own. Bronze said, "Alright sir, we'll see you at 8:00 a.m. tomorrow."

Bronze and Anna really didn't talk much on the way home. She asked him what his interests were, and sensed that she started liking him. Fortunately for him, the feeling was quite mutual. Once they arrived home, Bronze put the kettle to boil for a cup of tea. Anna complemented him on how lovely the place was, and walked out to the patio where she could see the ocean. Even though it was nighttime, and the ocean was pitch black, she still told him that she loved the sound of the ocean and the smell of the salt air. Bronze and Anna talked for a while. Bronze asked her, "So Anna, did you always live in Sweden?" Anna replied, "Hmm, well I was born in Sweden to Swedish parents. However, they moved here to Miami when I was four years old. Since then, I've only been back to Sweden once when I was about twenty years old." Bronze listened to her carefully. He loved the breathlessness of her voice. She was like a Venus, and Bronze started to care deeply about her.

Anna asked, "What about you? Where are you from? How did you get to have such a nice place like this?" Bronze replied, "Well, I was born here in South Florida. My mom is from Barbados and my dad is from Grand Cayman. Both islands are located in the Caribbean. I grew up here in Florida as well and as for this house, I bought it a few years ago. I always dreamed of owning a penthouse right on the beach so I saved my money from the very beginning." Anna asked, "But I thought medical students have really large debts to pay off? At least isn't that how it is here in the U.S.?" Charles Bronze was a bit taken and replied, "I received full scholarships from the University of Miami where I did my undergraduate studies. When I went to Johns Hopkins Medical School, I did take many loans. However, the government helped me pay those off as soon as I joined the MDPD." Anna smiled and said, "Wow, Hopkins? No wonder why you were recruited as a detective." Bronze laughed and replied, "No my dear. That was long after medical school."

Bronze and Anna talked for a while about a variety of subjects: politics, economics, medicine, business, and the overall status quo of America after the economic downturn in the early 2000s. Bronze was very impressed with Anna's knowledge of so many topics. He got the impression that Anna felt the same way, for when he started talking about the benefits of the free market system, Anna shook her head surprisingly in accordance. Anna then asked him, "Tell me something Charles, do you like me?" Charles Bronze was pleasantly shocked with her daring question. He then said, "Why do you say that?" Anna replied, "I see the way you look at me. You seem to be quite infatuated. You see, I have a gift in reading people for who they are. I know for sure you are an honest man who has worked hard from his humble beginnings. I've also noticed that you speak in a very respectful tone, which is one of my favorite qualities about you. In addition, I have observed that you don't drink and it is because you are a doctor. Am I correct?" Again, Charles Bronze was astonished. It was as if a female version of himself was talking to him. Bronze replied, "Yes, you are quite right. I must say, I'm amazed at how our abilities are parallel. I also detect that you are very honest. That's why I urged Baker to believe your story about Rucker. Also, even though you are gorgeous, you carry yourself very modestly." They smiled at each other. Bronze looked at the time and it was 1:00 a.m. Bronze said, "Wow, I didn't realize we were talking so long. It's getting late and I think I'm going to go to bed now. Feel free to take any food if you want. You can sleep in the guest room over there." Anna stood up and sat next to Bronze. Bronze was starting to feel that warmth emanate from his heart again. He was slightly blushing. Anna said, "Thank you so much for taking care of me Charles." She kissed Bronze on the lips hard, to the point where Bronze was starting to run out of breath. Anna then rose from her seat and went to the guest room, whereby Bronze went to his room.

The next morning, Bronze and Anna went to the police station. It was Sunday at 8:00 a.m. when Baker was expecting them in his office. Baker asked to speak to Bronze privately. Therefore, Anna waited outside Baker's office. Baker asked, "Slept well?" Bronze laughed and said, "Yes, now what's the scoop?" Baker replied, "We've found Rucker. He's going to be having lunch at the Crandon Park Marina and then go for a ride on his yacht. Sneak aboard the yacht before he finishes lunch. Detective Steele will lead him to where you will be on the yacht. Then, the police will sneak up on him from behind. I am sending you Bronze as the main man because you know the most about the case." Bronze agreed.

Charles Bronze did as planned; he went aboard the yacht before Rucker finished his lunch. Bronze was waiting for him, Smith and Wesson in hand. Bronze told himself, "This is going to be an easy catch." He started to get a little nervous when he saw that Rucker was fifteen minutes later than when Steele was supposed to escort Rucker to the yacht. Bronze started asking himself, "What is going on? I hope Steele didn't mess up the operation." A few minutes later, Detective Steele entered instead with a gun pointed at Bronze. He told Bronze to drop the gun and kick it towards him. Bronze did as told, and Rucker entered. "Good work, Detective Steele," Rucker said. "Now Mr. Bronze, you have been caught. Get on your knees and put your hands behind your head," Rucker said. Bronze did as told. Rucker then took the gun from Steele and pointed it at Bronze. Bronze said, "Perhaps." Bronze then wolf whistled whereby a stampede of police officers came in. Bronze got up and told some of the officers to take Rucker away. Then, he went to Steele, looked him in the eye and said, "I should have known. I wonder what Baker's going to say." Then he asked the remaining officers to take Steele away as well.

The officers tied Rucker to a chair, and now he was in an interrogation room. Baker and Bronze entered the interrogation room. Bronze had a lie detector, and attached it to Rucker. Baker then said, "It was very wise of you to recruit Detective Steele to do your dirty work. Very smart indeed. I didn't even see that one coming. After all, Steele's been on the force for fifteen years. Now let's talk. Tell us about the swindling." Rucker calmly responded, "Well Lieutenant, all I know is that Jones and I used the investment company to create one large Ponzi scheme. However, that's all I know. It seems that you, Lieutenant, in your great stupidity, killed the person through your puppet Detective Bronze here, who was the head honcho. That's right; Tyrese Jones was the man in charge the whole time. I joined him long afterward. However, we wanted to fool everyone so we pretended that I was the man in charge and he was my right hand man." When Bronze and Baker looked at the lie detector, he was telling the truth. Baker knew from Rucker's dossier that Rucker wasn't trained to surpass a lie detector, so he must have been telling the truth. Baker left angrily, and Bronze followed.

Lt. Baker was now in his office with Bronze, and Baker was enraged. "How the hell could I have allowed that to happen?!" Baker exclaimed. Bronze replied, "Calm down sir, it seems that Rucker is a lot smarter than we think. However, he is telling the truth. We will have to be more careful next time." Baker yelled at Bronze, "Charles! That's easy for you to say! The Captain is going to have my skin for this! It's your fault! You shouldn't have killed Jones, even though I ordered you to! Get the hell out of my office!" Bronze was shocked. He never saw Baker act like this before. Bronze said calmly, "Very well then," and left to head back home.

Charles Bronze's workweek had begun full swing. It was two days after Baker yelled at him, which Bronze was still trying to figure out. He was also wondering about Anna. Anna stopped Bronze after Baker yelled at him and gave him a card with her phone number. She said to call her anytime, and she would love to go out with him. Bronze agreed, and was very glad that he wasn't doing all the work to take the relationship to the next level, as he had done in his past two relationships. Bronze decided not to call Anna for another week until things were better at the police department. He wanted to tackle each problem one at a time. Claire noticed that Bronze was under stress, and asked him if everything was ok. He told her very calmly that everything was all right, just a little stressful right now.

Baker called on the black Motorola phone. Although Bronze didn't want to answer it, out of his compassion he decided to anyway. Lt. Baker and Bronze talked for a good thirty minutes. First, Baker apologized to him for his behavior. He told Bronze that at the debriefing, he took full responsibility because he was the one that told Bronze to kill Jones if necessary. Then, he updated Bronze on where the government stands with Rucker and Steele. Since Jones is dead, the charges are off him, but Rucker has been giving life in prison for fraud. He swindled over $200 billion in total alone. Steele was given 50 years behind bars for assistance to fraud. Baker apologized again to Bronze and he agreed not to act like that ever again. Bronze was very forgiving, and pardoned Baker.

Bronze then cooked himself some dinner. He started to think about how all this began with that warm feeling in his heart that one morning last week. He cooked some curry shrimp with rice, one Caribbean dish among many that he learned from his mother. He realized that sometimes you couldn't always follow orders. Bronze also grasped that he will have to use his own one-of-a-kind reasoning before hastily deciding to consent to Baker's demands. Bronze then thought about calling Anna, but decided not to until tomorrow. As he fell asleep, he envisioned her radiant face and body.

A Poignant Conundrum

He moved stealthily up the stairs, step by step with his gun in hand. It was a large mansion, but Bronze had to be careful not to make a sound because it would echo. He finally made his way up to the main room. Bronze was like a fox waiting to pounce on its prey. As he opened the door, he couldn't believe what he saw.

It was around noon when Bronze went outside with a cold orange juice in hand. He could feel the Miami sun toasting his skin, as it was the summer of 2011. Bronze went to his beachfront patio, and joined Anna who was tanning. He laid down on the beach chair that was adjacent to hers. She then got up, sat on Bronze's lap and planted a hard kiss on his lips. "Love you babe," she said. Bronze replied, "Love you too sweetheart."

Bronze and Anna had been dating for about three months now as Bronze had met her on one of his missions earlier in the year. They became instantly attracted to each other, and fell in love. Of course, Charles Bronze had to face the responsibility of telling Claire Scarlet a few weeks after dating Anna that he had a girlfriend. Much to the surprise of Bronze, Claire took it in good stride. Bronze was a little worried because even though Claire and Bronze hadn't dated for over twenty years, he knew that their friendship wasn't strictly platonic. It was then when it occurred to Dr. Charles Bronze that Dr. Claire Scarlet had moved on, which he was very glad about.

Anna and Bronze were talking for a while

about business and medicine. They were also talking about the new healthcare plan passed by President Obama that was going to take effect in 2014. Bronze found it very interesting, especially because they both had exceptionally different, but valid viewpoints. On one hand, you had Charles Bronze's analysis of the new plan from a medical perspective and on the other hand, you had Annalina Kristensen's perspective from a corporate standpoint.

Anna didn't only have intelligence, but she proved it through her actions. For the most part, she made wise decisions, especially in her field of cosmetic work, which Bronze really admired. He loved her the same way she loved him. They both had mutual respect not only for each other, but for others as well regardless of race, belief, or socioeconomic circumstances. During their conversation, the black Motorola phone rang. Anna knew what this meant, for Bronze had been called out quite a few times during their relationship. After all, the two of them met on one of Bronze's cases. When they heard the phone rang, Anna said, "Go ahead Charles. I'll go inside."

Lt. Baker said, "Detective Bronze, we need you. We have an interesting case that requires your exceptional talent." Bronze replied, "Of course, Lieutenant, right away." He entered into his penthouse, put on some clothes, kissed Anna goodbye, and headed towards the police station. Anna was very accepting that Bronze was an undercover detective, and never got in the way when he was solving a case.

Bronze entered Baker's office and greeted him in the normal fashion. Lt. Baker asked Bronze, "Why is there a strong odor of suntan?" Bronze laughed and said, "My apologies, Lieutenant. I was sunbathing on my patio when you called." Baker said, "No worries Bronze. Let's proceed with the briefing."

Baker started the briefing in an unusual fashion. Instead of going into the suspect directly, Baker made a stern warning. He said, "Now, Bronze, I want to alert you that this case may seem a bit personal to you. However, you are the only man on the force with the analysis and rationalization to capture the felon." Bronze was a little surprised and said, "It seems a bit strange that you would make such a forewarning Lieutenant. However, I will keep my emotions in tune." Baker said, "Very well then. Let's begin."

Baker said, "The subject is a French madam named Claudine Fournier. She is a global human sex trafficker. Madam Fournier brings in women from Eastern Europe, Asia, and South America. She offers them the incentive of an American job with American currency that can be earned immediately. Fournier lures them by telling them that they can send their money back to their respective home countries. This woman is cruel. She makes these women work under forced labor, and puts some of them out on the streets as prostitutes." Baker handed a picture to Bronze. Baker said, "One of our agents caught this picture before he was killed. Despite the demoralizing nature of Fournier's business, she is well educated, which is why we put you on the case. She attended Cambridge University and received her Bachelor's and Master's degree there. Then she obtained a PhD in Psychology from the University of Geneva in Switzerland. Fournier makes occasional visits to America, for both business and pleasure. At the moment, she is in New York, but the MDPD doesn't know exactly where."

Charles Bronze scrutinized the snapshot

carefully. The madam had very chiseled features, and a mean face. She had black hair, brown eyes, pale white skin, and looked quite crazy. However, Bronze read deeper into the picture and realized that behind all the madness was a brilliant woman. He then told Baker, "Ok so here we have a very well educated woman who is participating in currently the fastest growing criminal industry in the world. Judging from her global base of women, she simply cannot correspond with the ones she is trafficking directly. No, she probably has intermediaries from each country of some sort that she works through. The question is Lieutenant, "How do we capture her?" Baker smiled and continued.

Baker said, "Your intuition serves you well Detective Bronze. She is fluent in French, Taiwanese, Tagalog, Russian, Spanish and English. Therefore, she can easily communicate across borders. Because this woman is very well educated, she will be difficult to capture. As a result, I want you to be fully prepared before you make the arrest. You need to use your charm, skill and wit in order to capture her. She is very smart and always has a plan B. I'm going to give you three months to travel abroad to various destinations at different times, and acquire as much information as you can. I understand that you are a man of great reasoning and can get out of any situation. Also, I realize that you have made some of our most difficult cases seem easy. However, I feel that you are going to need a lot more time on this one. In addition, be very careful with your emotions. Always remember the mind controls the body. I know you have great love and respect for women, and this case will be sensitive to your heart. Nevertheless, let this be a lesson that when you are on the job, you must bury your emotions. Bear in mind that we want Fournier alive. Let's go outside for a moment, shall we?"

Bronze was taken with Baker's suggestion. They never went outside together before. Bronze thought to himself, "Wait a minute, Baker would never take me outside to talk to me. He probably wants to tell me something outside the police station, for the stations is wired and has cameras all over. Now I know for sure that this case is a very delicate one." Baker told Bronze, "I'm sorry I lied to you." Bronze said surprisingly, "Lied to me sir?" Baker said, "Yes. Inside my office, I told you that we don't know where exactly Madam Fournier is in New York. However, that statement is not entirely true." Bronze said, "What do you mean sir?" Baker smiled and said, "Bronze, you are probably aware that I have never brought you outside to talk to you in all the years you have been working for me. However, you have proven to me based on your performance on your missions that I can really trust you. In my line of work, that is very hard to come by. I have a European contact. His name is The Sleeper. He works for the American government. Whether it is FBI, CIA, or DEA, I have no idea. He has always given me the tip off for the most sensitive information. Luckily for you, he is currently in New York."

Detective Bronze was puzzled beyond explanation. He asked, "Why did you bring me outside to tell me this? Also, if you don't even know which agency he works for, how do you know we can trust him?" Charles Bronze only trusted people once in a blue moon. Although he had a network of contacts, that was only in the medical world, not in the life as a detective. He was always a lone wolf, and finding out this was perplexing. Baker replied, "I met him while in the police academy, whereby he had an alias name. I tried looking up his name in the files, but couldn't find it because I never obtained his real name. Five years after I graduated the police academy, I received a phone call from him. I knew it was he because he has a signature accent that I will never forget. He told me from now on call him The Sleeper. Since then, he has given me vital information about a plethora of cases. I know what he looks like, but he told me he had plastic surgery to guard his identity. I brought you outside because he is my closest contact, and no one, not even the Captain, knows that I know The Sleeper. The Sleeper told me he has very important information about Madam Fournier. However, he said that it is so delicate that he can't say it over the phone." Bronze's head was spinning at this point. He was still doubtful as to whether or not he could trust this Sleeper. Lt. Baker wrote some information on a piece of paper and showed it to Bronze. Baker said, "I want you to memorize this and repeat it to me." Bronze was a master absorber. After all, he was a doctor and had to memorize so many different topics and details. Following Bronze's memorization and repetition to Baker, Baker took out a lighter and burnt the paper.

Baker told him, "For this weekend, just worry about getting the information from The Sleeper. Also, do some investigative work in New York. When you return, resume your normal ophthalmologic work during the week and every Friday night, travel abroad. You pick the destination. You have reached the point in your undercover career where you can figure out things on your own. Use your own mental ability to reason where to go next. Every Sunday night, report back to me. Good luck. Exactly three months from now come back to my office and tell me what's the plan of action to capture Madam Fourier.

Good luck."

Bronze then hopped onto the Learjet and went to New York. While he was on the plane, he made his plan of action for New York. First, he will talk to The Sleeper and obtain the "delicate" information that he claims he has. Next, he will see where that leads him and try and figure out why exactly Madam Fourier is trafficking when she is a psychologist. Finally, Bronze will decipher where to go next. "Sounds like a plan," Bronze said to himself. Charles Bronze decided to call the house phone to see if Anna is still there. Anna answered, "Charles! Where are you?" He replied, "I'm sorry Anna but I'm working on a case. This is a big one. I'm on my way to New York. I'll call you tomorrow night when I return." There was a moment of silence. Bronze knew that Anna didn't like the sound of that. Anna said nonchalantly, "Its ok Charles. I understand. After all, not every woman gets to date a physician and an undercover detective. I look forward to hearing from you Sunday evening. All the best." She hung up. There was a part of Bronze that felt sorry for leaving Anna like that so suddenly. However, Bronze came back to his senses and thought about what Baker said about burying emotions.

Bronze landed at JFK airport and was always impressed with the hustling airport traffic, no matter the time of day. He was happy to be in New York again, as it was many years since he had been there last. Bronze took a taxi to the St. Regis Hotel. He proceeded to the check-in counter with his luggage and told the lady at the front desk, "Charles Bronze." The lady replied, "Ah, yes, Mr. Bronze. We have the Presidential Suite ready for you just as requested." Bronze smiled at the lady and thanked her.

It was about one hour before meeting with

The Sleeper. Bronze didn't know what to expect. He was supposed to meet him in an alley in downtown Manhattan. "Very sketchy indeed," Bronze thought. He wore all black clothes. Bronze always thought that pure black meant a funeral. However, fashion wasn't the key element in his attire this evening. It was inconspicuousness. Bronze then put on his shoulder holster with the Smith and Wesson in it. Bronze still didn't trust The Sleeper, and he didn't know what to expect, but he was prepared. Charles Bronze drove his Lexus to the agreed meeting place and was five minutes early. He waited patiently.

The dark alley was pitch black. The only light in the alley was a bright street lamp that shone on a two-foot radius. Bronze was a little nervous. Although he was always prepared for any situation, he was so confused about The Sleeper that his head started hurting. However, Bronze came to his senses. It was now 9:00 p.m. He stepped out the car and started walking. Bronze quickly turned around as he heard a voice. It said, "The nightingale sings in the dark of night." Bronze detected the thick signature European accent. Lt. Baker wasn't kidding. It was unique in its own right. Bronze then said, "But the rooster shrieks at the break of dawn." The Sleeper approached Bronze and said warmly, "Ah, Detective Bronze. You are just like what your dossier says about you." They shook hands. Bronze watched The Sleeper carefully. He couldn't see his face, for it was too dark. All Bronze could see is an average height skinny man with a black fedora and a long black trench coat. The Sleeper said, "So, you want to find Madam Fourier ah?" Bronze said, "Yes indeed. That's why I'm here." The Sleeper said, "No one knows where Madam Fourier is." Once The Sleeper said this, Bronze said to himself, "Why the hell would this man keep it so secretive if this is what he is going to tell me?" However, The Sleeper continued, "What I can tell you is that her French correspondent, who is her closest intermediary out of all of them, Ms. Rousseau, is staying at Room 1110 in the Le Méredian hotel in the heart of New York City. Tread carefully, for she is very dangerous and highly intelligent. No one knows she is there, because she is checked in as a pseudonym." Bronze thought for a moment. Then The Sleeper gave him a cylindrical case and a small picture. He said, "Take these. You are going to need them. The case has a special liquid inside a glass tube that when drank, causes forgetfulness for the next 24 hours upon consumption." Bronze then thanked The Sleeper, but before he could say it, The Sleeper was gone.

As Bronze was driving back to the St. Regis, he still didn't know if he could trust The Sleeper. When he reached his room, Bronze ordered Kona coffee and biscuits. It was now 10:30 p.m. Det. Bronze was going to be staying up until about 3:00 a.m. so he ingested the coffee hoping it would help him stay up. He took out a briefcase and then a box. Bronze opened the box, and it was rectangular with a piece of glass on the top. He then turned on his laptop, plugged in the device, took a drop of the chemical that The Sleeper gave him, and used some old software from his undergraduate years as a Chemistry major at the University of Miami to analyze the composition of the chemical. It was a benzodiazepine, or also known as "benzo". Bronze then realized that The Sleeper was telling the truth. This psychoactive drug has been known to cause amnesiac effects.

Bronze got dressed in pure black. It was around 1:00 a.m. He obtained a blueprint of the Le

Méredian hotel from the NYPD database via the MDPD. Bronze started analyzing various air vents, seeing which one would lead to Room 1110. He couldn't go through the front door, because it would be too obvious. Also, he took out his night vision goggles, because he knew that Ms. Rousseau would be sleeping. Bronze found a vent that would put him directly over the bed, yet would also give him a peripheral view of entire room. Bronze knew his plan of action.

As he was driving to the Le Méredian, he still had the internal conflict as whether to trust The Sleeper or not. The Sleeper has been earning Bronze's trust bit by bit, but Bronze still wasn't convinced. Charles Bronze thought to himself, "What if The Sleeper is a double agent working for Madam Fournier?" Nevertheless, Bronze realized that Lt. Baker would trust The Sleeper with his life. Since Lt. Baker trusted The Sleeper, Bronze decided to as well. He circle round the back of the Le Méredian. Bronze entered stealthily through a door. It was the pantry of the kitchen, just as the blueprint had indicated to him. He peeped through the pantry door. There were only two chefs, because after all, it was 1:00 in the morning. Bronze went through the air vent, remembering to place back the air vent in its original position. After he spoke with Ms. Rousseau, he was going to leave through her front door.

He went through the labyrinth of the air vent. Finally, he was in the vent that he predicted. It had 1110 engraved on it, so Bronze knew he was in the right place. He put on the night vision goggles. He looked all over her room from the air vent, and saw that no guards were around her bed. There was no one else in the room except Rousseau, who was sleeping comfortably in her bed. Bronze checked around the room again and saw no one. It seems The Sleeper was right. Since Rousseau was in the room under a pseudonym, no one would know that she was there. Rousseau was sleeping on her side, but when she turned, Bronze could see her face. It was the same face that was on the picture The Sleeper gave Bronze, so he knew this was the right woman. Bronze opened the vent as quietly as possible. He used his steady surgical hands not to make a sound. He took out his Smith and Wesson and put the silencer on.

Bronze held the glass tube in the other hand. When Rousseau's mouth opened and faced towards the vent, he poured the chemical The Sleeper gave him, which directly landed in her mouth. Rousseau woke up immediately whereby Bronze plopped on the bed. As soon as Bronze landed, he covered her mouth, pointed the gun to her temple, and told her to keep quiet. Then, he asked her to turn on the light, which she did. There was no one in the room. Bronze then told her that he was going to uncover her mouth and if he heard a peep, he would shoot her. He let go and she didn't make a sound. Bronze saw her hand reaching towards a pillow. He said, "Hands behind your head." Bronze cocked the safety, ready to fire and said, "Now." Rousseau agreed. Bronze then said, "Nod if you are Ms. Rousseau." She nodded. Bronze said, "Take off the pillows and throw them on the ground." She took them off, and her one hand from before was reaching towards a gun. Bronze told her to throw the gun on the ground, which she did. He then asked, "Where is Madam Fournier?" Rousseau then told him, "Why should I tell you? And what was that liquid you poured in my mouth?" Bronze replied, "You won't remember me. It eliminates your memory for the next 24 hours.

Therefore, you won't even recall this lovely conversation we're having. I'm not going to ask again. Where is Madam Fournier? If you don't tell me, I will shoot you in the head. Simple as that." Rousseau noticed the seriousness in Bronze's eyes. She thought, "Maybe if I made love to him, I won't have to tell him anything and I'll leave." Rousseau then was about to make a move on Bronze, but Bronze knew where she was coming from and got off the bed. He said, "This is your last chance." Bronze pointed directly at her forehead. Rousseau realized this man meant business and said, "Ok ok I'll tell you. The truth is, I don't know." Bronze was turning red and said, "You have three seconds. Three, two..." Rousseau interrupted and said, "Alright alright! Don't shoot me." Bronze said, "Now talk." Rousseau said, "It is as I told you. She booked me in this room, gave me my assignment. Although she trusts me the most, which is why you are here this evening sir, Madam Fournier never tells me where she will be."

Bronze said, "Listen, you are her most trusted person as you just said. You have a gifted mind, now please use it. She may have not told you where she is going to be, but I'm sure you can infer." Rousseau thought for a moment and said, "Considering her typical travel patterns, when she sends me to New York, that means she is going to be in Switzerland three months from today." Bronze thought, but didn't see how that made sense. He said, "How do I know what you say is true?" Rousseau said, "You don't. What I will tell you though is that I am currently at gunpoint and am in no position to lie. You don't believe that that is where she will be next because you don't see the connection. However, that is the point. Madam Fournier purposely makes her travel routes farfetched, so that way no one will ever catch her." Bronze then got back on the bed, with the gun pointed at her. He felt her hair and said, "You know you really are very beautiful." Bronze struck her in the neck and knocked her out cold. He rearranged everything, tucked Rousseau in bed, and left through her front door. Bronze saw a porter and asked him to show him the kitchen, for he wanted to see the fine work the chefs were doing. The porter took him there and he tasted one of the seafood dishes that were prepared for guests. The chef said, "You can't have that!" Bronze replied, "It tastes bland. Ease up the salt and add some pepper. That's what the boss said." The chef looked surprised, smiled, and said, "Of course sir." Then Bronze left through the back door and drove back to the St. Regis.

Madam Fournier received an invitation in the mail. It was for a ball being held in Geneva, Switzerland. "How convenient," she thought, seeing as she had one residence in Switzerland. Madam Fournier had her "business" for about five years now, which she started after obtaining her PhD from the University of Geneva. It didn't have a return address, or whom it was from. However, there was a red "L" at the bottom, like an insignia. Fournier decided to ignore it for the time being.

She wore a sexy, well-fitted red cocktail dress, with silver earrings and a silver necklace. Madam Fournier also wore glittered silver shoes. Fournier went to the grand hall where the ball was being held. She entered swiftly and with ease, taking note of her surroundings. Fournier noticed there were a few dignitaries from the Swiss Parliament. She also noticed that there were some other law enforcement officers. Fournier hadn't gained a reputation in crime yet, but she still got a little apprehensive. She decided to have a few martinis to wash away her anxiety. Madam Fournier felt the alcohol soothe her nerves and bones. A man of average height came up to her and asked her to dance, whereby she agreed.

As she was dancing, Fournier tried to discern whom this man was. However, she was getting drunk, and the man could smell the alcohol on her breath. She danced frivolously wondering that nothing could go wrong. After all, why couldn't Fournier enjoy herself a little if she wanted to? The man then told her to come with him. Fournier followed him. However, she came back to her senses, even though she was drunk. She took out a small handgun from a thigh holster and pointed it to the man. "Where are we?" she asked as her hand with the gun was shaking. The man replied, "Calm down my dear. We are going to my office. I just want to sit down and talk. We can either do this the easy way or the hard way." Fournier said, "Well I'm drunk at the moment so I'll take the easy way. Let's go."

As Fournier entered the office, she saw some intricate artwork. Fournier saw a portrait of Mona Lisa on one side, and other abstract art in the office. The man told her to sit in the chair. She complied. Then, he knocked her out.

Madam Fournier woke up a little groggy a few hours later. She was restrained and there were two guards. One of them picked up a walkie-talkie and said, "She's awake sir." A deep voice said, "Ok. I'll be there right away." The same man who danced with Fournier and brought her to the office entered. He slapped her on the face. "Wake up," he said. Madam Fournier said in a thick French accent, "Alright, alright I'm awake. Who are you?" The man said, "They call me "L". If you call me anything else, I will have you executed." At that moment, Madam

Fournier remembered the invitation with the red "L" on it. She then said, "You! You are the one that sent me the invitation." L said, "You are very right my dear. I brought you here because I want to offer you a job." Fournier asked, "What job? I already have a job. I traffic in this area and it brings in the money." L then said, "You see Madam Fournier, I think that women are an insult to the human race. I can't believe that they have so many rights. They are clearly second class citizens." Fournier said, "I agree with you L. We are here to serve you. But I am clearly a man in a woman's body." L then said, "I like your style. You are so ashamed of being a woman; you think you are a man. My job offer is that I will give you all the financial support to traffic internationally. I know exactly who you are. Yes, I know your whole background story. I know that when you were studying in England, you moved around royalty circles so you can establish a network. However, you didn't get anywhere. I will highlight a plan for you that is foolproof. If you follow it step by step, you will succeed. You have my word on that."

Madam Fourier thought for a moment. She was trapped with no way of escaping unless she agreed to this man's request. Fourier then agreed with him that they think very alike in their misogynistic ways. She said, "Ok I accept. And what do you want in return?" L replied, "You are going to work under me. Anytime you do something I ask, you leave my trademark. It is a white card with a red "L" on it. I will leave you free for the most part and connect you with the right people. I like the way you work, and I don't want to change that. Also, 30% of the profits go to me. Do we have a deal?" After thinking for a few minutes, Fourier asked, "30% is a bit low. Why such a low percentage?" L replied, "Because I want your trust. Your trust is more valuable than money." Fourier said, "Ok you have my word. It's a done deal." One of the guards knocked her out, and she woke up in her red dress back in her room.

It was now Sunday night and Bronze was on the Learjet back to Miami. He called Anna. Charles Bronze said, "Hello Anna, its Charles." She sounded a little depressed and said, "Hi dear! How was your trip?" He told her that it went pretty well. Then Bronze said, "Anna, it seems that this mission that I'm currently on will have me traveling abroad on the weekends for the next three months." Anna replied, "Oh, so what's going to happen to us?" Bronze replied, "Don't fret, I'll stop by your place some weeknights and we can talk." Anna sounded a bit more cheerful and said, "Alright, I'll see you then!" Anna hung up the phone.

As soon as Bronze finished speaking with Anna, he called Claire Scarlet. Claire answered the phone, and sounded a bit surprised. "Charles, how are you doing?" Bronze responded, "I'm doing pretty well thanks. I had to travel this past weekend, and I'm a little tired but doing well. Also, I'll be travelling on the weekends for the next three months. However, if you need anything, feel free to contact me." Claire said, "Aww Charles thanks!" Afterwards, her tone became more serious. She asked, "Is it for that government job again Charles? When are you going to tell me about it?" Bronze responded, "Soon, Claire, very soon. See you tomorrow." Bronze then hung up the phone.

Bronze had now landed back in Miami and took a taxi to his penthouse. He was thinking about what he'll do next. He recognized some Brazilian artwork in Rousseau's room when he was there that seemed like it was going to be packed away.

Therefore, Bronze decided that the following weekend he would travel to Brazil and see if he could find out more information about Madam Fournier. He did some research in the police database, and it indicated that one of her operations was in a factory in Rio de Janeiro. Bronze thought that if he could talk to the person in charge of the factory, which could in fact be one of Fournier's intermediaries, then he may be able to find out more information as to where to find Madam Fournier.

During the course of the week, Charles Bronze was all over the office like a busy bee. He had patients from 9am-5pm and had administrative work to get done. Also, Dr. Henry Smith needed help with a few things, so Bronze and Scarlet ran errands for him. Dr. Charles Bronze and Dr. Claire Scarlet took shifts, one day Bronze would run errands, and the other day Scarlet would take care of running errands. At night, Charles Bronze would go and visit Anna to see how her business Kris Cosmetics was going. It seemed very profitable, and Anna had to also travel some weekends as well on business.

Anna was very curious about this particular case. Bronze got that impression from the pointed questions she was asking him, with the slight allusions to the case. Bronze told her, "Anna, you know I love you dearly. However, the information about the case right now is very sensitive and I can't share it with anyone. Not even you." Anna looked disappointed and said, "Please Charles. I might be able to help you. I know when you are on the case you don't trust anyone, but can you make the exception this one time?" Charles answered in the negative. Anna was very upset now, and Charles Bronze knew it. He offered consolation, but she refused. He asked, "Ok, let's say I make an exception. What information would you be able to tell me?"

Anna responded, "Well, I know a little bit about the white card with the red "L" on it." Bronze was in shock and speechless for a moment. He then moved closer to her and asked, "Listen Anna, if you can tell me everything, and I mean everything you know about that card, I would really appreciate it." Anna smiled and said, "Now will you let me help you?" Bronze asked, "Well it depends if you're bluffing or not. I do indeed love you, but let's say that the nature of my undercover work involves not trusting anyone." Anna said, "I understand. You remember Larry Rucker, the villain who you caught on the case whereby you met me right?" Bronze replied, "Of course, I would never forget that case because that's where I met you." Anna smiled and continued, "Well, my friend Laura who was one of his subjects of swindling told me that Rucker had a white card with a red "L" the first time they met. Laura asked Rucker what the card was, and he said that he couldn't tell her. However, Laura gained Rucker's trust, but all Rucker could say is that it is a person of average height that goes by L. That's all unfortunately. However, from the way Laura had said it, I presumed that L probably has a whole network of people that he works with." Bronze then said, "Thank you very much darling. Even though it isn't much information about L, it definitely is a start. Do you know anything about Madam Fournier?" Anna replied, "Although I have friends in high places in Europe, I'm afraid not. Other then that she's a trafficker. However, I must warn you. Do not be surprised if L has recruited her. She seems to be the type of person he would want working under him." Bronze thanked her. Then, he left her place and continued his workweek.

Three months had passed, and Bronze gained a good amount of information. However, the most salient particulars were from Rio. While he was there, he went to the factory that the police database had referred him to. He was able to find out that Madam Fournier was indeed going to be in Switzerland, and that she was going to be hosting a black-tie party at her mansion in Bern. In addition, it seemed that Anna was right. He found a corpse, which was one of Madam Fournier's workers. The corpse had many scars and bruises from the beatings it received prior to its death. What struck Bronze the most was that a red "L", the same one on the white card, was branded on her forehead.

Bronze was now on his way to the police station to brief Baker about all the information he obtained and what his plan of action was. While Bronze was driving, he started to think three months ago when Baker had told him to be careful with this one because it may play with his emotions. Baker was indeed correct. Bronze had a feeling of emptiness within his soul. His face became thinner, and it was easier to see his cheekbones as a result of the depression. He felt so sorry for all the poor women that had been abused. Bronze had a deep-seated reverence for women, and always believed that they were special, and to see all these women being tortured and put on the streets sank his heart. He had parked up the car before he went inside the police station. Bronze needed a few minutes to put his thoughts in order and bury his emotions. Although Bronze's face was still gaunt, he forced a smile on his face and briefed Baker about the status quo of the case.

After the briefing, Bronze flew on the Learjet

to Bern. He was going to land just in time for the event that Fournier was hosting. Therefore, he was already wearing his black Armani tuxedo. He made his plan of action. Bronze wanted to enjoy himself and blend in very well without being too conspicuous. Det. Bronze knew that Madam Fourier would try and succeed in finding out who he is, so he didn't even bother giving the normal alias he usually did. He was going in as Charles Bronze.

After the Learjet landed 100 yards from the mansion, Bronze walked towards and entered Fournier's mansion. He saw some very elaborate paintings and a prominent sculpture in the middle of the main hall. The place was swarming with people. The ladies were dressed accordingly, the gentlemen were dressed in their tuxedos, and there was enough champagne to give away. Nevertheless, since Bronze didn't consume alcohol, he went to the bar and ordered some ginger ale. Bronze looked around for a while and finally saw Madam Fournier. Many people surrounded her when she appeared, yet there were two security guards standing by her side. Bronze approached the crowd around her, not paying attention to how many people there were. He squeezed in between and caught a glimpse of her. Since Bronze was so tall, he could always see over crowds without any difficulty. Bronze was now in viewing distance of Fournier. Madam Fournier extended her hand, which was covered in white gloves up to her elbow and approached Bronze. She said with her thick French accent, "Bonjour monsieur. I don't believe we have met. I am Madam Fournier." Bronze replied, "My name is Charles Bronze." Bronze pretended to be ignorant because he wanted to speak with Madam Fournier privately. He then asked, "So how exactly were you invited to the party?"

Everyone around him, including Madam Fournier, laughed at him. She said, "I am the host of the party." Bronze then said, "Wow, I didn't realize the host would be so beautiful. May I have this dance?" She took his arm and they went onto the dance floor.

Madam Fournier and Charles Bronze were now slow dancing in the middle of the dance floor. Bronze was no stranger to the dance floor and now was the perfect time to show his charm. Fournier then told him, "I know very well Mr. Bronze that you knew who I was. You just wanted to speak to me in private. So speak." Bronze was quite impressed, but not surprised. From Baker's description and given the length of this mission, it was a known fact that Fournier was very intelligent. Bronze then said, "You are quite right Madam Fournier. My main question is, you have a PhD in Psychology, yet you run a business in sex trafficking. Why?" Fournier looked a bit surprised at Bronze's straightforwardness in describing the nature of her business. However, there was no time for Bronze to beat around the bush. She replied, "Two reasons. One, I have a flare for traveling, and two, there is a lot of unlimited money in trafficking." Madam Fournier smiled at Bronze. As they were dancing, Bronze had lifted her leg to make a dance move. Then he took out a small handgun from her thigh holster and placed the gun on the ground. Fournier then said, "Very good, Mr. Bronze I'm impressed. However, our little meeting is over." She whistled, and the two guards who were guarding her before grabbed Bronze, one of them, which took his Smith and Wesson and put it in his pocket. Madam Fournier then said, "You know too much Mr. Bronze. Take him to the storage room. I have some business to take care of first, and then I will deal with him later."

The two guards took Bronze to a back room so to speak. He analyzed the two carefully. One was pointing his machine gun at Bronze, and the other was scrutinizing Bronze's Smith and Wesson. The one who was looking at Bronze's gun said, "This is a very nice gun you have here Mr. Bronze. What kind of gun is it?" Bronze replied that it was a Smith and Wesson .40 caliber. Charles Bronze then tackled the other guard that was pointing the gun towards him, aimed the gun at the guard with the Smith and Wesson, and shot him in the head. Then, Bronze cracked the other guard's wrist so he would let go of the machine gun and Bronze took the same gun and killed the other guard. Charles Bronze wanted to be inconspicuous since there was still a party going on, so he grabbed the Smith and Wesson only.

He knew that since Madam Fournier had business to do, she wouldn't be on the main floor. Bronze went through a roped area up the stairs. He took out his Smith and Wesson handgun and checked the magazine to make sure he had a full round. He stealthily climbed up the stairs. Bronze knew where Madam Fournier was by the scent of her perfume. It led him to a main room on the second floor. Bronze heard a woman screaming from outside. He didn't know what to expect. Bronze kicked open the door.

There were two guards who aimed at him, but he had the advantage on them. He killed them quietly and then pointed his gun to Madam Fournier. She had a whip in her hand, and was beating one of her female intermediaries, whom he recognized from Rio. He was shocked. Bronze closed the door with his left foot and locked the door, eyes fixated on Fournier. He told her to drop the whip, whereby she complied. Bronze then saw that the intermediary had some marks on her back. Bronze told her to go to the bathroom and wash up, while he and Fournier will talk privately. The intermediary complied, and went quietly out the room, locking the door. Now it was only Bronze and Fournier left in the room.

Bronze analyzed the surroundings while telling Fournier to kneel on the ground, hands behind her head. She agreed, as now Bronze was pointing at her heart. Fournier said, "You are not going to kill me Charles Bronze, undercover detective for the Miami Police Department. I know too much." Bronze smiled and said, "Madam Fournier, you have such a vast network that I'm not surprised you know who I am. You also know how much I know about you." She replied, "Yes I do Mr. Bronze, and you made a very convincing act of how ignorant you were in front of all those people." Bronze said, "You are a very knowledgeable woman indeed, but you have used your knowledge for the wrong reasons. I still don't understand how you can torture these women and allow them to be sexually abused when you are a woman yourself. It just doesn't make sense." Fournier replied, "Well Detective, let's just say I'm a man in a woman's body. I've always been a man since birth." Bronze knew very well that this woman was officially crazy. He cocked the safety of the gun, ready to shoot and told her, "I have one question. Who is L?" Fournier replied, "I don't know what you're talking about." Bronze took out one of L's cards and said, "Oh, I think you do. Now tell me who L is or I will be forced to shoot you." Fournier said, "I can't tell you. I have pledged my allegiance to him." Bronze took out another gun with his left hand. It was a tranquilizer gun. Bronze shot a dart into her, and she fell unconscious. Then, he took out his cell phone and dialed the Swiss police.

The Swiss police took custody of Madam Fournier. Bronze then decided to call Baker, telling him that she had been caught. Baker had a contact in the Swiss police department and had called him to find out if Fournier was talking. Baker's contact told him that they were torturing Fournier, and she talked about her whole international business of trafficking, but still didn't utter a peep of who L was. Bit by bit, Baker started finding out from different sources that her intermediaries had been caught in Taiwan, Russia, Latin America, and the Philippines and tried in the courts.

Before Bronze left the mansion, he looked for the Brazilian intermediary that Fournier was torturing when Bronze walked in. He found her in one of the ladies restrooms and she was crying. She told him that the marks hurt a lot and they were burning. Bronze hugged her, and told her that it would be ok and that it's over now. He called for a medical unit, which came to help her. She then bade him goodbye, kissing him on the cheek and thanking him.

Bronze was now on the Learjet heading back home. He thought about how long this mission took compared to his previous ones, and how vital it was to bury emotions. This case was very trying and depressing at times, but victory was his. After speaking with Anna on the phone telling her that he finally solved this one and thanking her for her help, his face became plump again. Bronze fell into a deep sleep and woke up when the jet landed in Miami. As he stepped out of the plane, he felt the Miami sunrays on his face, wondering what adventure he would be embarking on next.

A Catch in Paradise

Charles Bronze was sitting in first class aboard Caribbean Airlines when he heard that the plane was about to land in Miami. His palms started to sweat as he gripped the armrests firmly when the plane was descending. Bronze always got a little nervous during landings, so this was normal for him. The plane finally landed. As he was walking from the plane towards the Miami International Airport terminal, he started to reflect on his entire vacation, but kept in mind that this trip to Barbados was more important than ever.

It was August of 2011 and Charles Bronze decided to go to Barbados for some relaxation. Bronze's mother's family lives there, and even though he could have gone to visit family, he wanted to spend some time with close friends. When he landed in Barbados, it felt very strange being there because he hadn't been there in such a long time. However, he still had his network of contacts there that he would be meeting for lunch at the Crane Resort in St. Phillip.

Bronze was clad in a Tommy Bahama shirt, straw hat, khaki pants, and brown dress shoes. Bronze rented a Toyota Yaris because he wanted to maintain a low profile. As he drove the Yaris to the resort, he was starting to think about how much Barbados has changed since the last time he went. Dr. Bronze was not meeting his associates until the following day, so he decided to spend some time enjoying the island that he called for so many years his second home. He drove through the West Coast, and visited an old friend who had a catamaran. His friend was amazed to see how grown up Bronze was, and he offered to take Bronze on the catamaran for a few hours.

Bronze started telling his old friend about America, life as an ophthalmologist, and how being back in Barbados felt very strange. His old friend told him, "Well Charles, that's what happens when you leave Paradise." Bronze grinned at his friend calling Barbados "Paradise" and said, "I've been so busy that I really haven't had time to come back in a long time." Charles Bronze still maintained contact with his family, but couldn't travel much, especially since he was always travelling when he was solving cases for the Miami-Dade Police Department.

His old friend took out some Mount Gay Rum and offered Bronze a drink. However, Bronze refused, telling him that he doesn't drink but to "have one for him." Bronze's friend was starting to get a little tipsy from the excessive alcohol consumption, and Bronze started to frown. "This is the exact reason why I don't drink", Bronze said to himself. He asked his friend for an excuse, and went to change into a shirt and board shorts. After all, Bronze would have to take over sailing the boat, for Bronze wasn't going to let a drunken friend sail.

When Bronze was a teenager, his uncle taught him how to sail. Therefore, Bronze had quite a bit of experience sailing, even though he hadn't done it for a while. His friend was starting to have slurred speech, and it was at that moment when Bronze knew that it was time to go back. Bronze sailed the catamaran back to the port, changed back into his more formal attire, and was trying to tell his friend goodbye. However, Bronze could smell the alcohol from his friend, and he really didn't know whether or not his friend comprehended that Bronze was leaving. Nevertheless, Bronze left anyway laughing and said to himself, "That man will never change."

Charles Bronze continued on his drive up the coast, went to the Northern point, relaxed there for a while, and coasted through the eastern part of Barbados. This was the more hilly, rocky and rough area of Barbados. Even though there were a lot of new places, many of the old places were still there, so Bronze knew how to navigate accordingly. He went to a restaurant that his friend owned on Bathsheba, and dined there. His friend, just like his friend with the catamaran, was surprised to see how much Bronze grew. They caught up for a few hours and Bronze drove back to the South coast to his hotel room.

It was the following day, and Bronze was about to leave to The Crane Resort to have lunch with his colleagues. He wore a different Tommy Bahama shirt, Ray Ban sunglasses, and his normal Rolex watch, Cartier cologne, and straw hat. While he was showering, one of his associates called asking if Bronze had arrived on the island fine and if the service was outstanding. Bronze returned the call and told his associate that everything was excellent. Then, he proceeded to his Yaris and drove off to Sandy Lane.

It had been a good ten years since Bronze was in Barbados, and he was really surprised to see how much Sandy Lane had been renovated. He saw pictures of it online and in a travel magazine that was in his office, but seeing it in person was completely different. Bronze went to the lunch area that overlooked Sandy Lane Beach and some of his associates were already there. Mr. Stevens, Bronze's old friend who was in charge of importing and exporting all goods to and from Barbados, greeted him and told him that it was so great to see him again. Bronze told him cheerfully, "I hope I didn't get too old since the last time you saw me." Mr. Stevens chuckled and replied, "No, Dr. Bronze, not at all. In fact, you look the same, just a little darker." Bronze replied, "Yes, I was on a boat yesterday. Please though Stevens you're a good friend of mine. Call me Charles."

Bronze started to feel warmth of joy inside of him. It felt so wonderful being with some of his most exclusive friends on the island, all of which are members of the highest echelon of Barbados. Just as they were about to enter into the main restaurant from the balcony, Bronze's old friend Mr. Lawrence Thomas came in.

Thomas was a tall, thin African-American gentleman, clean-shaven and well polished. He was surprised to see Bronze and exclaimed, "Charles!" and shook his hand very firmly. "It's very great to see you again!" Dr. Bronze replied, "Lawrence my good man how have you been?" Bronze and Thomas sat next to each other for lunch.

They started talking while the rest of Bronze's associates were talking and Thomas was telling Bronze about his beautiful wife and kids and how Bronze must come one day while on holiday to meet all of them. Bronze replied in the affirmative, and told Thomas about the office in Miami Beach, life as an ophthalmologist, and Anna, Bronze's girlfriend. Thomas was very impressed with how Bronze was able to become so thriving in such a small period of time. Thomas said, "Well Charles, it seems you've beat me on the road to prosperity. The last time I had seen you, you were finishing up your ophthalmology residency, and I though you were going to be in debt from medical school forever." Thomas told Bronze, "We have to mingle with the rest of our friends. However, let's have lunch here again. My treat." Bronze noticed Thomas had a very serious face and agreed quickly. He loved Sandy Lane for it oozed elegance, which Bronze yearned constantly.

Bronze spent the next day touring around the island again. He could have called some of his family and tell them he was in Barbados, but decided not to. He relaxed at the suite he was staying in, and thought about what Thomas would tell him. Thomas did have a very serious face, and Bronze got the feeling that Thomas had something very important to tell him. However, he put it in the back of his mind and went to the beach to watch some tourists.

While he was on the beach, he saw some fine women. He didn't approach any of them, but many did see him relaxing on the beach. One of the locals came up to him offering him some weed, as Bronze could smell this guy from a mile away. The local said, "You look like a handsome young man, you want some?" However, Bronze talked in a Caribbean accent and said, "What's wrong with you man, I from here. Go long nah, and let me enjoy the beach." The local looked a little shocked that Bronze was a fellow local, and fled like a fox. Bronze shook his head and soaked up some rays.

It was the following day now, and Bronze was getting ready to go to Sandy Lane to meet his old friend Lawrence Thomas. The two had been in touch constantly for a while, but lost contact about three years ago. Lawrence Thomas is the managing director of all of Barbados' offshore bank operations. Bronze trusted Thomas with the most confidential material, for in the nature of Thomas's work, confidentiality was crucial. Many thoughts were flowing through Bronze's mind, and perhaps Thomas would need help with something regarding the bank, explaining Thomas' serious face. However, Bronze decided to go to Sandy Lane with an open mind, and hear what Mr. Thomas had to say.

Bronze entered though the gates of Sandy Lane and walked calmly to the lunch area. He wore another Tommy Bahama shirt, for Bronze brought many from home since he was in Barbados. He wore dark suit pants and black dress shoes this time. Bronze waited patiently for Lawrence Thomas, and Thomas arrived right on time. "Good afternoon Charles. Shall we?" Thomas said. Bronze replied, "Indeed we shall my old friend."

Thomas ordered some steak, while Bronze ordered salmon. Thomas ordered a Banks beer, while Bronze ordered a Bentley, a non-alcoholic drink indigenous to the Caribbean. Thomas laughed and told Bronze, "You still don't drink my friend? When will you just try a bit of beer or vodka?" Bronze smiled and replied, "For my 50th Birthday." The two men laughed together.

Thomas then said, "You are probably wondering why I called you out here today, aren't you?" Bronze said, "Yes, but from the seriousness of your face when you proposed this meeting, I knew it was something of the utmost importance." Thomas laughed and said, "I see you are still a master predictor. That is correct. I have a question. Do you still work for the Miami-Dade Police Department?" Bronze was a little taken by Thomas's brashness, but took it in bona fide. Bronze had told Thomas since he was in training that he was going to be an agent for the MDPD. Bronze replied, "Yes, they call me out for certain missions, with an emphasis in Middle East and other international relations." Thomas replied, "What position do you hold, do you work undercover?" Bronze replied, "Yes, I work as an undercover detective. However, I only do it on weekends and during the week only if it is absolutely necessary, because I am an ophthalmologist."

Thomas replied, "I see that is very interesting. I think it's fascinating how you lead a double life. It sounds sort of like a hero of a novel." Bronze replied and said, "Yes, many of my confidants think about it that way. But it isn't always fun and games though." Bronze then said, "Why are you asking me this though? Is everything ok?" Thomas smiled and started to explain.

Thomas said, "Yes, but a flag has been raised regarding one of my clients within the last week or so. This client is actually an American, so it is within your jurisdiction. His name is Andy Walker, and he is a wealthy banker. I don't know too much of the details, because he gave very little information to one of my banks when he opened an offshore account here. I do however, have a picture of him here." Thomas handed Bronze a small headshot of Walker. Bronze told Thomas that he looked familiar but couldn't make a match. Thomas then continued, "It seems that Mr. Walker has been depositing exorbitant amounts of money into the account without specifying where the money is coming from. Normally, I wouldn't bring up this sort of case to you, but the amounts that Walker is depositing are the highest amounts I have seen in all my years of working." Bronze thought for a moment, looked at the picture of Walker, and said, "Let me guess. You think that he is illegitimately earning this money somehow and depositing it in one of your offshore banks." Thomas replied saying, "You haven't lost your sting

Charles. That's exactly right. Do you think you can investigate?" Bronze replied saying, "I'll try and talk to my boss and get back to you. Normally, he is the one that assigns me missions, but I'll correspond with him and get back to you." Thomas replied saying, "Thanks a lot Charles. I really appreciate this favor you are doing for me." Bronze smiled and said, "Now let's eat this exquisite food, shall we?"

Bronze returned to his hotel room and thought long and hard about what Thomas told him. It was now the day before his departure back to Miami. Bronze went around the island one more time, and his eyes started to get watery because it truly was such a long time since he was last in Barbados. For the first time, Bronze didn't want to leave.

As Bronze was getting his luggage in Miami International, he turned on his black Motorola and dialed Lt. Baker. It was around 2pm in the afternoon, so Baker would be in the office. Baker answered and said in his husky voice, "Good afternoon Detective. How was your holiday?" Bronze replied, "It was excellent sir. Do you mind if I come of the office for a few minutes? I have to talk to you about something very sensitive." Baker sounded a bit surprised (he was always the one to call Bronze) and replied, "OK, not a problem. Come on in around 4pm." Bronze replied in the affirmative, picked up his luggage, went home to change, and drove in his Lexus LS to the MDPD station.

He entered the station, being greeted by the receptionist. She said, "Good afternoon Detective Bronze. You are looking rather well tanned today. Were you at the beach?" He told her, "Thanks, and no I was in Barbados on vacation." She smiled and said, "Lt. Baker is waiting for you." Bronze thanked her and proceeded to his office.

It was Sunday and Bronze was thinking about the swarm of patients he would have to return to tomorrow. However, his focus right now was informing Baker of the information he found out from his friend Lawrence Thomas. Bronze entered the office and Lt. Baker shook his hand firmly. "Welcome back," Baker said. He then asked, "How was your vacation? I see you got quite brown." Bronze laughed and said, "What can I say Lt. Baker? It's the tropical sunshine." Bronze became very serious and said, "You are probably wondering why the hell I am here especially because in all my years working for the police department, you are the one to call me, not the other way around." Baker smiled and said, "You are spot on, but I have come to trust your judgment. So go ahead."

Bronze said, "One of my most confidential and well respected contacts in Barbados who is the managing director of all of Barbados' offshore banking operations told me that there is a man by the name of Andy Walker who is depositing exorbitant amounts of money in an offshore account. My contact is getting worried, and he thinks that the money is illegitimate. He told me that the man is American, and he wants me to investigate." Baker was shocked and said, "Detective Bronze, I am disappointed. I understand that this man is a friend of yours, but you can't just trounce on into my office and want me to investigate. Need I remind you that I am the Lieutenant and you are the detective." Bronze replied firmly, saying, "I understand that sir, which is why I haven't come to you just with my contact's hunch. I did some research on this Andy Walker gentlemen and it seems that all the Andy Walker's in the U.S. don't make more than $100,000 a year. If my contact is suspicious of this money, then I have firm belief that we should investigate." Baker thought for a while and replied, "Alright, we'll see what we can do. However, I have many things to do for this week but I'll do a little investigative work and see what I can find. Consider it a favor for your loyalty." Bronze thanked him and left the station.

It was the following Thursday since Bronze's meeting with Baker, and he had a really hectic week at work. There were many patients who had to reschedule since Bronze was on vacation, and a lot of paperwork to be done. Claire Scarlet was so happy to see him again; very analogous to when Bronze went on vacation in Mexico. Anna prepared dinner for Bronze one night, and they had a romantic dinner over lit candles. That evening, the black Motorola rang. It was Baker, and he told Bronze to come quickly to the police station, for he had a lead. Bronze sped in his Lexus LS to the station.

Baker then said, "Well I've done some investigative work through my contacts in the FBI and CIA and it seems that you have very trustworthy friends in high places Detective. It seems that Andy Walker doesn't exist. It is a pseudonym for the CEO of Bank of America, David Johnson. Mr. Johnson has very close ties with the Central Banking System for the entire United States, and receives money from the government bailout that is going on now. He has become so trustworthy in the U.S. government that the government doesn't even monitor what Johnson does with the money. Johnson is supposed to be helping the housing crises here in America and delegate the money to small businesses. However, he is using between half and three quarters of the bailout money to fund illegitimate Presidents and Prime Minister's in South America and selected parts of Africa. My friends in the CIA have told me that all the illegitimate profits made from these dealings goes into that offshore account he has in Barbados. The CIA has been investigating for quite some time, but hasn't had a lead. Johnson is a stealthy thief, and hasn't been at work for the past few weeks probably because he got the tip off that the CIA is after him. The question though Bronze is why would he use Barbados instead of Switzerland or Bermuda for his banking?"

Bronze replied, "I think I can answer that one. Barbados is known for its confidentiality, and Johnson didn't want to use the normal Swiss banking because even though it is very confidential, it seems too typical. Barbados is a hidden gem when it comes to offshore banking. Since Johnson is dealing with very large amounts of money, he wanted to fool everyone. What is Johnson doing with the profits that he is storing in the offshore account?" Baker replied, "A mystery I'm afraid. That's what you have to find out Detective Bronze."

David Johnson went to his underground office where his board meeting was being held. He found out from his old comrade that the CIA found out about his dealings, so he decided that he had to lie low. Within the past two years, an elderly gentlemen probably in his 60s, was appointed to the board. He was referred to Johnson from an old contact as a thriving organic chemist who has been involved in projects that yield millions of dollars. Johnson met privately with this gentleman when he was first appointed to the board. Johnson recalled the conversation as if it were yesterday. At this point in his career, both legitimate and illegitimate, he reflected back to the conversation.

They met at a café because the old gentleman insisted on meeting somewhere low key.

He introduced himself as "L" and said that no one ever calls him by his real name. When Johnson asked him why, L's face went a little red but said calmly, "Don't worry about it." It was at that point when L gave Johnson the idea of where to delegate funds received by the U.S. government for the bailout, and how this money would be a great benefit to him and his family when it was time to retire. Johnson was very impressed with L's attention to detail in order to ensure that the operation went successful. Most importantly, all L asked for in return was a small percentage of the profit, but asked for trust more than anything. Johnson was a bit concerned about the legality of the operation, but L told him don't worry about it because the U.S. government will never know. L had knowledge that Johnson was once involved with a crime syndicate, but Johnson used a contact in the government to wipe it off his record so the government would still bank with Johnson. It turns out that Johnson's government contact actually worked for L. Johnson of course, had no idea about this small yet important fact. After their conversation, L gave Johnson a white card with a red "L" on it, and told Johnson to keep it with him at all times. When Johnson inquired why, L told him not to worry for it was just a trust symbol.

Lt. Baker told Bronze, "I want you to travel to Barbados again this weekend. Take next week off from work and lie low in Barbados. Find out information from your well-established network there, including your offshore bank friend, and capture Johnson. I would prefer if you not kill him, but I'll leave it up to your discretion." Bronze replied, "Lieutenant, it will be very difficult to tell Dr. Henry Smith, my boss, that I'm going to have to leave for another week after just coming from vacation." Baker replied, "You just worry about catching Johnson, and I'll take care of Dr. Smith."

Bronze left the police station and headed back to his Miami Beach penthouse. As he was parking his Lexus LS, his Blackberry rang. It was Dr. Smith. Smith said, "Good evening Dr. Bronze. Someone from the government called me, telling me that you have to go on an assignment all of next week. Don't worry about it; I will take over for your patients next week. Good luck and I hope to see you bright and early tomorrow morning." Bronze was surprised how quickly the government had contacted Smith and told him, "Thank you Dr. Smith for understanding. I'll see you tomorrow sir." Bronze hung up, smiled, and went to the elevator to go to his penthouse.

Bronze entered his penthouse, and put on some John Coltrane jazz music. He called Anna, asking her how her week was going and they had a long conversation for about an hour about life. He told her that he is going to have to go back to Barbados next week on business and Anna chuckled and asked him if he needed any help. Bronze knew Anna, like himself, had a great aptitude in solving cases, but Bronze replied in the negative. Barbados was very familiar territory to him and he had enough contacts there to help him capture Johnson. Bronze fell asleep soon after speaking with Anna.

The next evening, he proceeded to the Learjet and headed to Barbados. He bid Claire Scarlet goodbye, who was a little worried when she found out that Bronze would be away again for the upcoming week. She felt very distant from him, but they had a lovely conversation over Friday lunch and Scarlet felt close to him again. She wished him the best of luck and kissed him on the cheek.

As Bronze was on the Learjet, he called Thomas relaying all the information that Baker told him. Thomas smiled and said, "I'm not surprised that this is the case. Once I started seeing a large amount of money, it raised a lot of suspicion. You are the professional Charles, so I'm leaving you to deal with this case. Thanks again for agreeing to it, I really appreciate it, and contact me if you need anything." Thomas hung up the phone. Bronze ordered a ginger ale and thought about his plan of action.

After getting a good night's rest in Barbados, Bronze decided to call his own security contact. The MDPD didn't even know about this contact, but if there were any person on the island who knew the most about Johnson, it would be his old friend Neil Allen. Allen was the head of security for the police force, and knew Bronze since his childhood. Technically speaking, Allen was a family friend, but the two always had a professional relationship. He called Allen and they agreed to meet at Champers, a restaurant directly on one of Barbados' south cost beaches.

Allen and Bronze embraced each other after not seeing each other for such a long time. They caught up for a while and Bronze got down to business. He asked Allen, "What do you know of a man named Andy Walker?" Bronze wanted to see if Allen knew fully about Johnson. Allen replied, "Hmm, Andy Walker. Ah yes! But of course. Andy Walker is David Johnson's alias name. Mr. Johnson is the CEO of Bank of America. He has been using money from the U.S. bailout in order to fund illegitimate Presidents and Prime Ministers in South America and some African countries. All of the profits from these illegitimate dealings are wired to an offshore account run by your friend Lawrence Thomas. I spoke to

Thomas a month ago, and he was starting to get suspicious about Johnson's dealings but I knew the American government would send someone, so I told Thomas not to worry about it. I just didn't expect it to be you, my old friend, of all people. It really is indeed a small world."

Bronze grinned and said, "Yes Neil, indeed it is. What else do you know about Johnson? Do you know any other leads that can help me capture this menace?" Allen replied, "Oh yeah. Two very important facts. Number one, Johnson always carries a white card with a red "L" on it. I don't know what it means but it is something he treasures so I believe it is something important." Before Allen continued, Bronze gasped and said, "Oh my God!" Allen asked, "What's the matter? It's just a card." Bronze told Allen, "No Neil, it isn't. The culprit behind this is someone who has been overseeing all of the criminals I have busted within the past year. This merely cannot be a coincidence. Anyways, continue on your trend of thought." Neil looked at him with intrigue and said, "Number two. I can tell you for sure that in three days, he is going to be withdrawing money from the main Royal Bank of Canada branch in Bridgetown. He sent an email to the director of the bank telling him he will be there with his banking information to withdraw some funds." Bronze then said, "Neil, I have a favor to ask. Can you have all warrants in place for Mr. Johnson's arrest and can you please have guards ready to take him?" Allen replied, "With pleasure Charles. That's why I'm here. I have a plan that I think you will like."

Johnson was about to hop on American Airlines from New York to Barbados when his phone rang. It was L. L told him that to go quickly to Barbados, withdraw the money, and get out. It was the time for Johnson to give L his fair share of profits. When L spoke to Johnson about it, he agreed without hesitation. After all, L had guided Johnson until now regarding the whole scheme while keeping his name clean from the government, so that they would never suspect it. L secretly took a private jet to Barbados, unknown to Johnson. He went to the famous Barbados Yacht Club for some rest and relaxation under his pseudonym, Danny Steed. L had to ensure that his investment was protected, and planned to somehow be present in the Royal Bank of Canada without letting Johnson know about it.

When Bronze reached his hotel suite, he became very depressed and annoyed. He couldn't believe that Johnson was also linked to this "L" person. Bronze became annoyed with the police department, for not being able to figure out who this person is. He was also depressed because he still couldn't figure out who L was and what organization he works for, or is running. He decided to call Anna for consolation. When she saw on her caller ID it was Barbados, she picked up the phone immediately, knowing it was Bronze. Anna said breathlessly, "How are you doing sweetheart?" Bronze replied in a melancholy fashion, "I'm doing ok honey." Anna said, "No Charles, you are far from ok. Why are you so sad?" Bronze replied, "The criminal that I'm here to capture works for that L character." Anna was shocked and said, "What? Are you serious? I can't believe that! Have you thought about why this L person would have recruited Johnson?" Bronze replied, "Not really. My vision is too fogged from the shock of the fact that Johnson works for L and also the fact that L keeps escaping my normal trend of thought and reasoning." Anna said, "Listen my love, you can solve this dilemma. You are one of the most brilliant men I have ever met and that is one of many reasons why I fell in love with you. Even though you think that L has the upper hand right now, I know for sure that you will figure this out. It won't be easy, but it is doable. Now let's think about this together. It seems that L has a trend; he likes people who are misogynistic, power hungry, and people who want to overthrow governments. For the time being, we are going to have to work with that knowledge and as time goes along and you solve more cases of this nature, you will find out enough knowledge about L. Right now, you have to focus on capturing your criminal, and as you have always told me, things will fall into place." Bronze was impressed and cheerfully said, "Thanks a lot Anna. I am very grateful. Take care and I'll see you when I get back. I love you darling." Anna replied, "I love you too hun," and she hung up the phone.

Bronze prepared some Caribbean food for dinner, ate heartily, and had a good night's rest. He woke up the morning of the capture fresh and alert. Detective Bronze was ready to make his catch in paradise. He went over the plan that him and Allen made, put on a Ralph Lauren suit, and hired a Mercedes taxi. He took it and arrived at the bank like an aristocrat. Johnson was distinguishably noticeable compared to the locals and the people working in the bank. He proceeded to the front desk, and asked to speak with the director. The director, wearing a suit as well, came out but ignored Johnson and walked straight past him. He proceeded to Bronze, who was carrying a briefcase full of cash. The director said, "Good morning Mr. Bronze. Please come into my office." Johnson, whose face was turning red said, "Excuse me Director. I was the one that contacted you, not this Bronze joker. May I see you for a moment?" The Director said, "Indeed you may Mr. Walker, after I take care of my good friend Mr. Bronze here." Johnson sat down and waited in shock.

When Bronze came out of the Director's office, Johnson took out a gun and pointed it at Bronze's head. Johnson exclaimed furiously, "Listen Mr. Bronze, or whatever the hell your name is, I have a very good rapport with the Director and you can't just come swaggering into this bank and deposit your money!" Bronze replied very calmly, "Actually Mr. Andy Walker, or should I say David Johnson, I can." Johnson gaped, sweating now with the gun in his hand, still pointing it at Bronze's forehead and said, "How do you know who I am?" Bronze replied, "C'mon Mr. Johnson, I think anyone who lives in America would know the CEO of Bank of America." Johnson replied, "Yeah, but my name is Andy Walker, and I have been told that I look like David Johnson." Bronze replied, "Please Mr. Johnson, spare me your lies. I know damn well that you have been depositing your profits from illegitimate dealings in this bank and have been fooling the director here the whole time." The director was scared and frozen. He was shocked beyond belief. Johnson then said, "Who are you? Some sort of policeman from America?" Bronze said, "Something like that. Here's the fact of the matter, I have a security officer waiting outside the front door so either you drop your weapon and walk towards the door with your hands above your head, or I'll have to kill you."

Johnson laughed and said, "I think you may have had too many drinks here Mr. Bronze. As you can clearly see, you are the one at gunpoint." Bronze whistled. With that, all of the bank tellers and staff who were dressed in professional clothing, all took out guns and pointed it towards Johnson. Johnson was about to escape, but the staff held Johnson and restrained him at gunpoint. Bronze reached into Johnson's inner jacket pocket, and took out a piece of paper with all of Johnson's banking information that Allen said would be there. He then asked one of the officers, who was dressed up as a bank employee, to call in Mr. Allen. Mr. Allen came in and arrested Johnson, ordering the officers to take him to the police station for questioning.

From the time Johnson had entered the bank before Bronze came in, L was stealthily positioned on the rooftop of the bank so that no one could see him. He saw the whole scenario of the director going to Bronze, talking to Bronze, Johnson having Bronze at gunpoint, and Bronze outsmarting Johnson with the help of Neil Allen. L was very impressed with Bronze's skill and ability. Once all the police had left and everything returned back to normal, L jumped off the roof quietly and went to the Yacht Club. He checked his iPhone, and all of the funds that were in Johnson's offshore account had been wire transferred to his alias name, Danny Steed's account in Switzerland.

Bronze was now on the Learjet back to Miami. After Johnson's capture, Neil Allen, Lawrence Thomas, and Charles Bronze had dinner at Sandy Lane Resort to celebrate the victory. They reminisced on the whole mission, and both Allen and Thomas commended Bronze on his strategic planning to capture Johnson. Allen told Thomas and Bronze that this was a fruitful capture for Bronze because it turns out that Johnson had a total of about $5 billion of embezzlement. Bronze bid them farewell, and promised both of them that he would be back in Barbados in the near future for social purposes rather than for work. Bronze called Anna while on the jet and told her that the mission was a success and thanked her for her consolation. He also told her that he has a good hunch that he will find out more information in due course about L.

After hanging up the phone with Anna, Bronze decided to ring Claire Scarlet, asking her how she was doing. Dr. Scarlet said that work was getting hectic, and she missed him a lot to help her cope with the situation. Bronze told her not to worry for he was on his way back to Miami and he would stop by her house. Claire Scarlet sounded ecstatic and had everything ready for his arrival. When Bronze arrived at her place, she nearly squeezed the life out of Bronze and kissed him on the cheek. They had lunch together, and he talked about his time in Barbados, not mentioning about the mission. All he told her is that his second trip to Barbados was for the government job. Claire Scarlet was still a little annoyed that Bronze was keeping this a secret, but she went with his little game. He kept her optimistic regarding work, and she was so happy that he was back to keep her in high spirits. It was time for Dr. Charles Bronze to leave her place to head back to his own penthouse. He bid her farewell, and drove off in his Lexus LS.

7

The Hidden Secret

The clock was ticking. He kept staring at his watch, waiting for the package to arrive. Finally, the doorbell rang. The deliveryman had a package. The gentleman signed for the package. He opened the package and saw an envelope with a red "L" on it. The man was sweating now, very nervous. He opened the envelope and saw where the rendezvous point would be. Gordon Robinson grabbed himself a glass of whiskey and gulped it down, for he was indeed going to need one of those tonight.

It was a Saturday morning and Charles Bronze was reading Ian Fleming's *Thunderball* while listening to some Sonny Rollins jazz music. The oven started beeping. Bronze put on oven mitts and took the macaroni pie he was baking out of the oven. The aroma of the food permeated throughout his penthouse. He laid the table, and had everything ready for when she arrived. Finally, the doorbell rang. Anna was right on time for lunch. Bronze opened the door and they lip locked. Anna said, "You really didn't have to go out of your way to cook lunch. We could have gone to our favorite restaurant." Bronze replied, "True, but remember Anna cooking helps me with my stress as a physician and a detective. Also, there really is nothing like home-cooked food." Anna smiled and replied, "Very true Charles." Anna and Charles talked for a while and were about to have dessert when the home telephone rang. The man calling was Charles Bronze's old friend, Musa Abdul-Aziz. Abdul-Aziz is the son of the King of Saudi Arabia. Abdul-

Aziz and Bronze were close friends during Bronze's undergraduate years at UM, where Abdul-Aziz was studying Biomedical Engineering, while Bronze was pursuing his degree in Chemistry. Abdul-Aziz and Bronze had all of their pre-medical classes together, and often used to study together as well. They maintained close contact after graduating, especially since Bronze had known Arabic. Even though Bronze's father was from the Turks and Caicos, his father's ancestry is Middle Eastern, so Bronze picked up Arabic very quickly and learned it when he was young. Abdul-Aziz didn't have a communication barrier since Bronze knew Arabic, and Bronze had a friend to practice speaking Arabic with.

Abdul-Aziz said in Arabic, "Good afternoon Charles. I'm sorry to disturb you, but do you have a moment to talk?" Charles replied in Arabic, "Hold on one second my friend." Bronze told Anna, "Darling, do you mind waiting in the living room while I talk to my friend? I'll bring out dessert in a couple of minutes." Anna replied nonchalantly, "Of course, not a problem." Bronze told Abdul-Aziz in Arabic, "Ok, the coast is clear. Is everything alright?" Abdul-Aziz replied, "Yes, but there is a great concern that I have that I want to share with you."

Abdul-Aziz said, "There is an English gentleman by the name of Gordon Robinson who is secretly channeling all of the world's oil from the big producers like Iran, Iraq, Kuwait, United Arab Emirates, Oman, Qatar and Syria to India and China for an exorbitant amount of money. I have a hunch there is someone behind the scenes who he is working for, but I am not sure." Bronze started to think deeply about what Abdul-Aziz was saying. He then started to think that maybe L had something to do with this. This is the sort of criminal that L likes to recruit. Bronze treaded with great caution as Abdul-Aziz was speaking. Abdul-Aziz continued, "I am calling you because Robinson wants to have a meeting with the King of Saudi Arabia in Paris. My contacts in Europe told me that Robinson is going to coerce the King into signing some sort of agreement at the Eiffel Tower. Is there any way you can help us get rid of this madman?" Bronze thought for a while and replied, "I'll talk to my boss at the Miami-Dade Police Department and see what I can do." Abdul-Aziz replied, "Thanks a lot Charles. Peace and Blessings."

Anna was sitting after Bronze and Abdul-Aziz's 20-minute conversation. He came out with some ice cream and apologized for the delay. Bronze said, "I'm really sorry Anna, but that call was from Saudi Arabia, and I couldn't just let the phone go." Anna smiled and said, "Don't worry about it Charles. I know you still have your vast network of people out there in the Middle East. Is everything ok?" Bronze replied, "Yes, but I feel that L has a man stealing oil from the Middle East." Anna's face dropped and said, "Babe, how can you be sure that it is L?" Bronze immediately responded, "Because I am using your wise judgment. My contact told me that it seems that this man who is stealing oil for profit is working for someone, and I am almost sure that the person is L. It cannot be merely a coincidence that after all my years working for the police department, only recently are all the people I am busting are associated with L." Anna replied, "You make a good point, but don't let it get to you. Don't go running on some sort of vendetta against L. From my case, which you closed and caused both of us to meet, I can tell you that he will make himself present when the time is right. All I can advise for you to do is to be prepared for it. I have no idea how he is going to pounce, but it will happen." Bronze replied, "Anna, how can you be so sure?" She replied, "Remember I was indirectly affiliated with him. He reminds me of those goons who used to think they could take advantage of my company because I was a woman. However, they all learned their lesson." Bronze chuckled. He said, "There are more details, but until the case is solved, I can't say any more." Anna replied, "O you and your rules honey. One day you will trust me to the fullest." Bronze pondered about Anna's latter statement. They talked for a little longer, savored the ice cream, and she left. As soon as she headed out the door, the black Motorola rang. It was Lt. Baker. He said in his husky voice, "Detective Bronze, we need you." Bronze replied, "Lt. Baker, you have perfect timing. I'm on my way."

Bronze drove his Lexus LS to the police station. He was greeted as always by the receptionist and entered Lt. Baker's office. Lt. Baker looked a little worried. Bronze saw a printout that Baker was reading with Arabic writing on the letterhead. Bronze figured out swiftly that it was to do with Robinson. Before Lt. Baker could say anything, Bronze held up his hand and said, "Let me guess. A man by the name of Gordon Robinson is pumping oil from the largest Middle Eastern oil producers in the world to India and China for a large profit." Lt. Baker was a little surprised and asked, "Detective, how did you know?" Bronze replied, "First of all, I noticed the Arabic writing on the letterhead of the letter you were just reading, so I knew it was regarding the Middle East. Second, I have a contact who is linked to the Saudi royal family and told me the issue." Baker replied, "Well it seems you know more than I do. I didn't even know Mr. Robinson's name." Bronze asked eagerly, "So Lt. Baker, what's the plan of action?" Baker studied Bronze's excitement carefully and responded, "Before I tell you, do you know anything else about Mr. Robinson?" Bronze replied, "I'm afraid not Lieutenant, only that Mr. Robinson is supposed to be meeting the King soon at the Eiffel Tower."

Baker replied, "I have some information that may help and will fill some gaps so you are well-informed for when you have to go to Paris. First of all, Mr. Robinson speaks French and various dialects of Arabic fluently; to the point where when he speaks French and Arabic, you cannot tell that he's a Brit. In fact he is so diplomatic and so good in Arabic that he disguised himself as a Muslim and went for the annual pilgrimage that the Muslims perform. Robinson knew that the Saudi government considers it a duty and honor to host so many Muslims a year, and he thought that it would be the best way to meet the King. Robinson met the King under an alias name during the pilgrimage, and used his diplomatic prowess to find out about the National Security and the flaws of the other oil producing countries. The King didn't volunteer the information, but Robinson made himself convincing enough that he was a representative sent by the British government. From then on, Robinson has formed a social web and has been channeling the oil. Robinson knows that China and India are hungry for Middle Eastern oil, and he charges billion dollar amounts to have the oil channeled from the Middle East to China and India."

Baker continued, "Your objective is to travel to London and lie low there. That way you will be close enough to Paris, without being in France. Our MI6 contact Mark Smithers will be able to give you more information. Because of security purposes, he couldn't tell me any more so you will have to physically go and see him. He has some valuable information regarding when and what the King and Robinson will be talking about at their meeting in the Eiffel Tower. I'm sorry to keep interfering in your work, but you are going to have to take next week off."

Bronze was eager to go to the Middle East, especially to help his old friend solve this case, but he was concerned about his work. Patients were starting to get a little concerned as to why Dr. Charles Bronze, one of the most gifted ophthalmologists they have ever met had to keep bumping back appointments. After talking with Lt. Baker regarding this issue for a while, Baker told Bronze, "Don't worry. I'll talk to Dr. Henry Smith and will promise that after this mission, you'll be back in the office unless it is an absolute emergency." Bronze reluctantly agreed, and told Anna and Claire Scarlet he was going to have to be traveling again on business. Dr. Scarlet got very worried and said, "Charles, you can't keep doing this. Your patients here need you." Bronze replied, "I know Claire, but the work I do for the government at this time is more important than ever. I promise I will tell you very soon about it."

Detective Bronze was drinking a cold ginger ale on the Learjet en route to England. He thought about how Smithers would recognize him. "Lt. Baker probably gave him a headshot of me," Bronze thought. Bronze also planned his modus operandi for communicating with Smithers and trying to find out as much information as possible. It wasn't always the most pleasurable experience to talk with contacts of Lt. Baker, especially because they only heard a few distinct yet salient qualities of Bronze. Also, Bronze was thinking in the back of his mind about L, and when the two would eventually meet face to face.

Gordon Robinson drove his black Mercedes to the anointed meeting place. He drank another glass of whiskey. Robinson had heard of L through some gangsters he had worked with on another project and heard of L's ruthlessness. Robinson considered it an honor to be summoned by L, but still didn't know what to expect. However, Robinson had a mind of his own. He had a feeling that L would exploit his desire to cause corruption to the Middle East. Robinson had a sour relationship with the King of Dubai, and vowed revenge against all of the Middle East. A black limo finally showed up at the meeting place. An elderly gentlemen between two armed men approached Robinson. Robinson said shakily, "You must be L." L replied in a slow, creepy fashion, "Yes indeed. Utter one more syllable and I'll have your throat slit right here, right now. Never ask me what my name is, and we'll be best friends." L extended his frail hand to shake Robinson's. Robinson's hand was sweating, and L said, "Now now, no need to be nervous. After all, I am here for your benefit."

Bronze landed in a hanger for private jets in Heathrow. All of his immigration information had been taken care of. A tall gentleman, only an inch shorter than Bronze, approached him and said, "Good morning Detective Bronze. My name is Mark Smithers, and I'm your MI6 contact here. Please come with me." Smithers escorted Bronze to a brand new Rolls-Royce Phantom, and the two sat in the back seat. Smithers said, "I assume Lt. Baker told you why you are here." Bronze replied, "Yes indeed Mr. Smithers, but there is still more to be explained." Smithers looked at the driver and said, "For the interest of the government, let's wait until we reach headquarters." Bronze looked at the driver as well, smiled and replied in the affirmative.

L started to explain to Robinson an exact plan of how Robinson is going to channel the oil from the Middle Eastern countries and make a large profit. L said that in six months, Robinson would meet with the King of Saudi Arabia. L said, "Don't worry, by then you will have all control of the oil reserves in the Middle East, with the exception of Saudi Arabia. You will meet the King at the Eiffel Tower at exactly 12 noon. The King will find out when its too late and you will draft up a contract, forcing him to sign over all rights and privileges to oil all over the Middle East. It is more than likely that the King will come with his entourage but we will have a sniper outside the Eiffel Tower secretly hidden and as soon as the King's guards touch you, the sniper will kill the King. Then, you will become the Emperor of the world's richest and most easily accessible oil reserves and those foolish Americans will have to contact you if they want oil. Of course, it will be up to your discretion. Finally, you can shove it in Dubai's face for what they did to you." As L was saying all of this, Robinson grinned sinisterly and starting laughing. L laughed with him and said, "I have thought about any problems, and this plan is foolproof. There are only three things I ask for. First and foremost, I want your trust. Your trust is more valuable to me than any money. However, I have bills to pay. So second, I want 30% of all of your earnings. Lastly, in order for this operation to work, you will have to be wired whereby I can talk you through the negotiations with the King. The King is very smart and can outsmart you. However, with my Oxford and Harvard education, and your help, we will outsmart him. I will guide you as to what to say." L gave Robinson a piece of paper and a white card with a red "L" on it. L said, "Keep that card with you at all times. It is a sign of our trust. Also, here are the highlights of the plan." L then said malevolently, "We'll be in touch my friend." Robinson looked at the paper, and looked back to thank L, but L was gone.

Smithers and Bronze finally arrived at MI6 headquarters and entered the two large front doors. Bronze looked around in amazement. Bronze was always impressed with cultural architecture, but this was beyond words. Bronze had not been to MI6 since his very first mission over ten years ago, and it had changed a lot. Smithers took Bronze to his office. Smithers said, "Don't worry Detective, no one can hear us. The MI6 are well aware of my confidentiality, and out of respect for that, they granted me an office with soundproof walls." Smithers said, "Alright, here are my updates. I have an associate who shadows the Saudi security and was able to give me more details than everything you guys have. Tomorrow at 12 noon, Gordon Robinson and the King of Saudi Arabia will be meeting in the Eiffel Tower. Robinson is going to force the King to sign an agreement whereby the King will transfer over all right and privileges to oil all over the Middle East. I did some extra research with the help of my associate and he told me that Robinson is doing this out of revenge for a disagreement with the King of Dubai, and not to mention that Robinson is an oil tycoon. The King will have his entourage, but I have reason to believe that Robinson will attempt to assassinate the King then and there. Therefore, you have to use your Arabic skills. I will be in contact with you. Here." Smithers handed Bronze an earphone. Bronze looked at it and said, "And you will be communicating with me as to how I can speak to the King himself before the meeting with Robinson." Smithers replied, "Exactly."

Bronze's face was pruned. Smithers noticed and asked, "What's wrong, don't you like the plan?" Bronze said, "Yes, but did you think of any ramifications? Suppose Robinson is bluffing, what if Robinson has a man somewhere pointing a gun at the King in a distant place, and how do you expect me to talk to the King himself? That's a bit bold, don't you think?" Smithers smiled and replied; "I don't think Robinson is bluffing because he has done enough damage to the Middle East already. As for the man pointing a gun, yes, it is a possibility that Robinson would do something like that. I'll have our men do a full parameter sweep of the Eiffel Tower around that time and tell them to note anything suspicious. With regard to talking to the King, I think you are perfectly capable of doing that Detective Bronze. You do know his son after all, and from what Lt. Baker has told me, you are very diplomatic which is why you are assigned so many international missions." Bronze replied, "Thank you for the compliment, but it's all in a day's work. Is there any more information you can tell me about Robinson?" Smithers replied, "There is one more thing which may be of some help." Smithers continued, "Robinson carries a white card with a red "L" on it." It seems that Bronze's assumption was correct. He smiled and exclaimed, "I knew it!" Bronze then asked Smithers, "Do you know anything about this L character?" Smithers nodded and when Bronze heard what he had to say, Bronze gaped.

Robinson was going over the highlighted plan L gave him six months prior. He was ready to attack. L corresponded with Robinson frequently and called him last night. L said, "Alright Gordon, tomorrow is the big day. I don't want you screwing this up, otherwise you will never become the Emperor of Oil that you've always dreamed of. Most importantly, you won't have revenge on Dubai. Put the earphone in your ear, and call at 11:00 a.m. I will answer and we'll do a test run." It was now 11 a.m., and Robinson called L. L answered, "Good job Gordon, you called on time. I want to show you something. Open the email I sent you with the picture attachment. Tell me what you see." Robinson replied, "Good God. That's the house where my parents live, the house I grew up in." L said, "Exactly. I have planted a bomb in the basement and if you don't follow my orders exactly as I tell you, I will detonate it and say goodbye to your parents. Most importantly, I will tell them of the stealing and blackmail you are doing before I kill them." Robinson's voice went high pitch to the point where he was about to shriek and exclaimed, "L, that wasn't part of our arrangement!" L replied, "Well, it is now. Get your ass to that Eiffel Tower."

Bronze was still in amazement with what Smithers told him. Apparently, Smithers noticed a trend in all of the cases that Bronze had solved within the past year, and how the majority of them were somehow related to L. He contacted his most confidential associates, and was able to find out a little information. Smithers couldn't get a real name; all he got was that L was a thriving organic chemist. As soon as Bronze heard this he told Smithers, "He must be some sort of drug lord." Smithers said, "You know, I was thinking along the same lines but someone who has multi-billion dollar operations and uses manipulative powers to control some of the most power and money hungry people couldn't just simply be a drug lord." Bronze was still very grateful for at least a little information for him to gnaw on throughout this mission.

It was now 11 a.m. and Detective Charles Bronze was around the Eiffel Tower area. Smithers was communicating with him through the earpiece. Smithers said, "Alright Bronze, we've done a field sweep of the Eiffel Tower and we don't see anyone here." Bronze was still very suspicious and told Smithers, "Do one more field sweep. I see the King's Rolls Royce is approaching. I'll take care of this Smithers." The King of Saudi Arabia got out of the Rolls Royce with four armed men clad in his long white robe and white Arab headdress. Bronze, dressed in an Alfani suit, came up to the armed men and asked in fluent Arabic if he could speak to the King. The men said no, and the King was right behind them. Bronze said, "Please tell him my name is Charles Bronze, an old friend." Upon hearing this, the King came forward told the armed men not to worry. Bronze and the King shook hands and the King said in Arabic, "Good morning Mr. Bronze. My son Musa told me you would be here today." Bronze replied in Arabic, "Yes, it is an honor and pleasure to finally meet you." The King smiled from ear to ear. Bronze said, "As you are aware, you are going to be meeting a certain Gordon Robinson. He will be offering you a document." The King replied, "Yes, that is what he called me for, but I have no idea what it is about. However, from his diplomatic skills and his outstanding resume, I trust his judgment." Bronze replied, "While that may be true, he is actually deceiving you. That's why he asked you all those questions regarding the flaws of the other Middle Eastern oil producers. He has gained control of all of them, and the contract he will be presenting to you may seem fluffy and have a lot of perks, but in the end, he will force you to give up all of Saudi Arabia's oil and your privileges to oil access in the Middle

East." The King was shocked and said, "What do we do?" Bronze replied, "Do not worry, I am working with the British government on this assignment and we will take care of it. All you have to do is stall Robinson, and we will take over from there." The King agreed and Bronze disappeared.

Gordon Robinson entered the Eiffel Tower and took the elevator to Le Jules Verne, the agreed restaurant where the King and Robinson were meeting. Robinson entered the restaurant and went to the meeting place. Robinson said, "L, can you hear me?" L responded, "Yes, from the sound of things, you have entered the restaurant." Robinson replied, "Yes, I have. I am going to the agreed spot. Is the sniper ready?" L said, "No, not yet. There are some usual Eiffel Tower guards snooping around, but don't worry my sniper is trained to sneak past them." Robinson was getting a little nervous and started breathing heavily. L said, "For God's sake, stop being so nervous!" Robinson replied, "I'm sorry sir, it's not everyday that you get to talk to the King of Saudi Arabia." L replied, "If you really want to be as powerful as you say, then it wouldn't matter whether he's the King or a servant because you are more powerful than him." Robinson calmed down and waited patiently for the King.

L's sniper was dressed in all black. A helicopter dropped him off at the tip of the tower, and he crept his way down carefully. He had on his iPhone a blueprint of the tower and where exactly the King would be seated among his guards. The sniper got into the proper position. He looked around to make sure he wasn't noticed. "No one in sight", the sniper said to himself. He positioned himself accordingly where he could escape easily just in case, but was inconspicuous. The sniper assembled his sniper rifle and waited like a fox waiting for its prey.

Bronze was on his way to the restaurant after leaving from his correspondence with the King. He checked his gun holster and his Smith and Wesson .40 handgun was lying there patiently, waiting to be used. Bronze grinned and went to the main entrance of Le Jules Verne. He told the person at the front that his name was Charles Bronze, and he was meeting someone for lunch. The person said, "Of course, you're table is ready. Is it still for two only?" Bronze replied, "Yes sir." The man said, "This way Mr. Bronze."

Smithers called in when Bronze had entered and told him the updates. Bronze listened carefully. "Still no sign of anyone on the exterior of the restaurant?" Bronze asked. Smithers replied in the negative, and Bronze said, "See if your French partners can do a heat scan of the whole Eiffel Tower and look for anyone located outside the restaurant where they have the windowpanes and rooftops." Smithers said, "Bronze, I think you're getting a bit obsessive about this. I already told you that no one is there. We've checked the place three times." Bronze replied, "Listen to me Smithers, I have experience of dealing with L's associates. If I know L, he has someone on that damn roof. If the heat scan doesn't pick up anything, then I'll believe you." Smithers said, "Ok Bronze, we'll do the heat scan. Wait a few minutes."

The King had entered the restaurant with his entourage and approached Robinson. They shook hands whereby the King said, "It's nice to finally meet you. Before we begin, please remove any concealed weapons. Although these guards are here, I don't like negotiating with weapons around. I give you my word that my guards will not shoot you." L told Robinson, "Do as he says, but be very careful. I'll take the King's word but again, be on your p's and q's." L continued, "Now open the briefcase, take out the agreement, and explain it thoroughly to the King just as we discussed." Robinson did as told. He told the King, "Here is the fact of the matter. I have control of all of the oil in the Middle East and it is too late for you and your regime to retaliate. This agreement says that when you sign it, you will transfer all rights and privileges of the Saudi oil to me." The King laughed and said, "My English may not be as good as yours, but who do you think I am? Do you think that you can just use your power and tramp over me? Do you know whom you are talking to? You need to show some respect." Robinson said, "I knew you would say that. Hence, we have an offering. We will pay you one billion dollars for you to sign this agreement." The King thought for a while and continued to stall.

A few minutes later, Bronze heard through his earpiece, "Detective Bronze are you there? Are you there?" Bronze replied, "Talk to me Smithers." Smithers replied, "You were right Bronze. There is a sniper positioned exactly in shooting distance of the King. How are we going to capture him? If we send a helicopter, he will hear it and shoot the King. What do we do?" Bronze thought for a moment. Smithers heard silence. Smithers got worried and said, "Bronze, Bronze, are you still there damnit?!" Bronze replied, "Yes Smithers, don't get worried. I'm thinking for a moment." Bronze then said, "Fly your best man in the helicopter, but don't fly the helicopter right next to the sniper. Fly the helicopter 200 feet above the top of the Eiffel Tower, and let your man parachute down. Then, instruct your man to parachute right above the sniper, and shoot the sniper from above with a silenced gun. L probably is wired to the sniper like how you Smithers are wired to me, and I don't want him hearing that the sniper got shot. Make sure that when your man silently kills the sniper, he covers the sniper's mouth so the sniper doesn't utter a peep." Smithers replied, "Ok Bronze will do."

The King said, "Sorry my friend, but unless you have a better pay off, I can't agree to anything." L was becoming furious and started telling Robinson through the earpiece, "You fool, why did you give the King your weapon? We are going to give the King five minutes to agree or my sniper will shoot him. Tell the King that a sniper is in firing range within him and he has five minutes to decide." Robinson did as told, and when the King heard about this, the King was in shock.

Smithers activated the earpiece. "Bronze, Bronze do you copy?" Smithers said. Bronze replied, "Yes Smithers, I copy. Did he kill the sniper?" Smithers said, "See for yourself." Bronze saw a man approaching the sniper from above. The man had a Smith and Wesson .40 handgun with a silencer. "What a fine choice, I couldn't think of a better gun myself," Bronze said to himself. He saw the man descend on the sniper shoulders, covered his mouth, turned him over so the sniper was facing the man, and shot him in the heart. The sniper died quietly. The man then cut the wire that was connected to the headset. Bronze told Smithers, "Excellent work. Now get up here in the restaurant."

The King was starting to get worried. However, he saw Bronze a few feet behind Robinson as Bronze was putting on the silencer on his Smith and Wesson. The King smiled and told Robinson, "It's over my friend." With those very words, Robinson felt a cold muzzle at the back of his head. Bronze took out the earpiece from Robinson's ear and flung it a distance. L said to Robinson, "Hello Robinson. The sniper is going to kill him now." L didn't realize that the earpiece had been disconnected. L said, "To hell with Robinson." He switched to talk to the sniper and said, "Hello my friend. Kill the King now." However, L heard static and then a disconnection. L exclaimed, "No!" and switched back to Robinson. He called for Robinson, but Robinson didn't answer. With that, he ordered his men to detonate the bomb, killing Robinson's parents. L realized that Robinson got caught, but L didn't care. He wanted Robinson to feel the pain of loss in jail, just like how L felt that pain since he lost Robinson to justice.

Bronze said, "Do not utter a word Gordon Robinson." Robinson was nervous, and all of the King's armed men pointed their guns at him. Mark Smithers had arrived and called his French police friends, and they arrested Robinson. During his arrest, the police informed Robinson that his parents died. Robinson sobbed as he was handcuffed. The King shook hands with Bronze saying in Arabic, "Peace and Blessings my friend. Thank you very much. My men will take it over from here and make sure that the oil pumps to China and India are stopped." Bronze replied, "It is our pleasure to serve the King himself. Please give my regards to Musa." The King smiled and left with his entourage.

Since Bronze and Smithers were at Le Jules Verne, they decided to have lunch and savor the victory. "That was a close one," Smithers said. Bronze replied, "Yes indeed. However, sometimes you just have to go with your gut feeling." Bronze's Motorola rang. Lt. Baker said, "Excellent work Bronze. This was a tough one, but I knew you would make it though. Please congratulate Smithers as well." Bronze thanked Baker. Baker replied, "I just got word that a bomb placed by an unknown person killed Robinson's parents. The article just came out on the BBC. It says that both his parents have a red "L" branded on their foreheads. Do you think this has to do with L?" Bronze was shocked and said, "Yes it does, Lieutenant. That is one of his trademarks. We'll talk more when I return." Baker said, "Ok Detective. I look forward to seeing you soon." Baker hung up, and Bronze told Smithers everything Baker said. Smithers was surprised, and said, "Bronze, you are the one tracking down his associates, so you are the only one that can stop him." Those words echoed in Bronze's head as he headed back the U.S.

When Bronze returned to Miami, he told Lt. Baker everything that Smithers told him. Baker listened very intently and said, "It's going to be hard trying to search for a professor of organic chemistry with the letter "L" in his name in all universities." Bronze said, "Maybe so, but perhaps you could inquire about crimes linked to organic chemistry. Perhaps we can get a lead there." Baker replied, "I'll do what I can, but we're still working on limited information. There is only so much I can do. For now, there's no trace."

Bronze drove his Lexus LS back to his Miami Beach penthouse. He called Claire Scarlet and told her that he had a great time in London and he had supper in the Eiffel Tower. Claire started to get jealous and say, "Charles, you have to take me with you on these government assignments. I look forward to hearing about this government job exactly soon. Take care darling and I'll see you on Monday." She hung up, and Bronze was a little worried. Even though he promised her that he would tell her, it would still be a while before he did. The time wasn't right yet. He was about to go to sleep, and opened his side drawer in his dresser near the bed. He took out the white card with the red "L" on it he got from one of his previous cases, stared at it for a while, and went to sleep.

8

The Black Widow

Charles Bronze was gripping at the edge of his seat and his palms were sweating. He was sitting on a chair at gunpoint. Mr. Chang was an associate of the mastermind known as "L", an organic chemist who has been the kingpin of various recent operations that Bronze has been overthrowing. Mr. Chang grinned sinisterly at Bronze and asked, "Any last words?" Bronze heard the police cars arriving at the front of the building. However, Bronze couldn't take the risk of getting shot so he dove for Chang's abdominal region, and grabbed his right wrist, pointing the gun away. Mr. Chang held onto the gun tightly, and he wouldn't let go of the gun despite the pressure. Bronze kicked Chang in the nose, and it started bleeding. The police broke into the building and swarmed around Chang. Bronze got off of Chang and took Chang's gun from his right hand.

Lt. Baker arrived at the scene, and gazed around. The building had gone through a massive shootout, as Bronze had to avoid and shoot some of Chang's goons before proceeding to the main hall of the building. The police helped in the clean up process, while the other policemen who had Chang at gunpoint started escorting him out of the building. Baker preceded to Bronze and said, "Excellent work Bronze. Mr. Chang is one of L's close associates, and we are gathering more evidence about L every day. With your help, we will capture him eventually. We're going to sweat him so he can tell us everything he knows." Bronze smiled.

As the police were escorting Chang to the front door, Bronze saw a laser pointer aiming at Chang's head. Baker was talking to Bronze about another case when Bronze laid flat on the ground and pulled Baker to the floor. In a split second, Chang was shot in the back of the head by a sniper that was positioned on the roof. The police started shooting the roof wildly, while Baker and Bronze ran outside, trying to see if the sniper had escaped. They saw a man dressed in all black running towards a nearby hanger. Lt. Baker ordered the police to chase after him. However, the sniper was too fast. He ran to a one-person jet and flew away. Bronze asked, "Is there any way we can track him?" Baker's face was red now and said, "I'm afraid not, Detective. Damnit! Chang had to be killed! He was the only lead we had to finding out more about L!" Bronze calmed Baker down and said, "Clearly, the sniper was working for L." Lt. Baker coolly replied, "Indeed. L must have sent the sniper as a method of last resort. L has been studying you, Bronze. He's been studying your movements and the way you intelligently capture his investments. You have to tread great caution from here on out. Don't worry though, the government will keep you well protected."

Bronze was a little shocked and asked Baker, "But Lieutenant, how can you be so sure?" Baker replied, "We've had large kingpins like this before, but never to this extent. L has been operating globally and conducts some very large deals, as you have seen from your previous assignments." Bronze replied, "True, but if that's the case, then why does it just so happen that all of L's associates are assigned to me?" Baker replied, "I honestly have no idea. It seems as if L wants you to capture his associates so he can learn more about you. Go and get some rest and don't worry about it too much. Since you are the one who is capturing all his people, you are going to be the one to confront him when the time is right." Bronze thanked Baker for his insight, but said sternly, "Yes Lieutenant, I agree, but let's hope that it's very soon, especially since my safety is at risk."

Bronze drove from the location where Chang was captured back to his Miami Beach penthouse. As he enjoyed the comfort of his Lexus LS, he was trying to soak in what Baker was telling him and how L is after him. Bronze started to get a little paranoid. He started thinking, "If L is really following my movements as Baker says, he probably knows about my romantic relationship with Anna, and my friendly relationship with Claire." Maintaining his composure, Bronze parked his car.

Bronze called Anna, asking her to come to the penthouse at once. Anna detected anxiety in Dr. Charles Bronze's voice and asked if everything was all right. Bronze replied in the affirmative but still urged her to come immediately. As Bronze was preparing dinner, he heard the doorbell ringing. Anna was wearing a long fitted blue dress. Her blue eyes stared at Bronze like the ocean and she had her long blond hair untied. She kissed Bronze hard on the lips. She went to sit at the table and Bronze finished up cooking dinner. He then poured some Martinelli's and Bronze started to give Anna limited details.

Bronze said, "Now Anna, I don't want you to get worried, but L has been studying me carefully. He probably knows of you through your friend that worked for L, but I'm afraid he may use you to get to me." Anna's face started to become serious and said, "Charles, I think you make an excellent point especially since you have been arresting his people, but paranoia is really quite unnecessary. It will block your judgment both as a detective and as a physician." Bronze eyes opened wide as he was listening carefully to Anna's insight. He now realized why he fell in love with her, for she put everything into its proper perspective.

Bronze was clearing the table when Anna approached him. She hugged him, squeezing him so tightly he nearly suffocated, reassuring him not to worry about being tracked by L. She whispered in his ear, "You've been working for the government for a long time, so don't fret for they will have your back. Also, I will be on guard." As she finished making this statement, Frank Sinatra's "The Way You Look Tonight" started playing on Bronze's sound system whereby Anna and Charles Bronze started slow dancing. After the dance, Bronze pecked Anna on the cheek, thanking her for a wonderful evening.

Bronze went to work the following morning, jolly and bright thanks to Anna's words of encouragement. His week consisted of various retinal surgeries and a variety of post-ops. Claire Scarlet continued her normal routine at work; always admiring how respectful Bronze was, especially to his female patients. They talked about various patient cases for Scarlet and Bronze often sought each other's advice about the best course of action. If they disagreed, they did so in a friendly manner and consulted Dr. Smith and the medical journals as to the best solution.

Friday approached much more quickly than Bronze expected. He was sitting in his office, still wearing his white coat, and pensively looked through his patient files for the week. Bronze came across a variety of cases. The clock struck 5:00pm, and it was time to leave. Bronze gave his regards to both Dr. Smith and Dr. Scarlet. Claire Scarlet talked with

Bronze for a few minutes and brushed her lips on his cheek. She congratulated him on a job well done for the week. Bronze smiled and walked out to his car.

Five years ago, Bayani Sanga was looking outside his office window 45 stories high. He looked out at the city skyline of Makati, Philippines and thought pensively about his time in office. He had been the President of the Philippines for the past 30 years, and a lot of new rules and regulations were implemented during his tenure. Out of all the improvements that took place, he enjoyed education reform the most. However, compared to the West's standards, it was still a second-class education system. His wife entered the room. "Hello love", Sanga said. His wife replied, "Good evening. How was your day? Are you leaving again soon?" A frequent traveler for corporate reasons, Bayani Sanga often left his wife alone. Sanga replied to his wife, "My day was very good my dear. Normal Presidential things that you really don't need to know about. As for my traveling, yes, I will be leaving in two days." Sanga's wife smiled and said, "Alright darling, so you're leaving me again huh?" Sanga replied, "Yes, you know the nature of my work, it always involves traveling." Sanga's wife said okay and kissed him, wishing him the best of luck. She left the office abruptly.

Sanga was overthrown three years ago by his former Cabinet, consisting of 13 men and women from various countries in the world. Sanga deceived his cabinet, telling them that he traveled on business in order to fundraise to improve the Filipino economy. However, the cabinet was shocked and disappointed to find out that Sanga used the billions of dollars raised embezzling the money to purchase large properties and assets in global cosmopolitan countries. The cities included but are not limited to: Dubai, Tokyo, Sydney, New York City, Los Angeles, Cairo and Singapore. Because of this scandal, Sanga's wife was appointed to take over the Presidency.

Sanga's wife was born in the Philippines in a poor village, but raised in California. When her parents moved there, they salvaged pennies off the street and collected food stamps. She grew up with food and water, but at the sacrifice of her mother. Her mother was often impoverished and her father worked in a clothes factory to make ends meet. Sanga's in-laws eventually were able to rent an apartment. They sent Sanga's wife back to the Philippines in order to find a suitable husband. While she was back home, both of her parents died, leaving her traumatized. She was a very caring person and humble, understanding where she came from. Sanga's wife met Sanga at a charity event. Sanga immediately fell in love, especially because she was the perfect height for him, with golden brown skin and well endowed. Her buttocks were lifted and tight, and her voice was a breath of fresh air. Sanga and his future wife to be started dating and eventually got married. Sanga was appointed President of the Philippines after their marriage and became very wealthy. At that point, Sanga's wife became very greedy. She forgot her past and acted in front of Sanga's cronies as if she were born into a rich family. She became arrogant and flaunted her money often.

Ten years after Sanga was overthrown, the same thirteen membered cabinet decided to reinstate Sanga back into power. Eight members of the Cabinet agreed, while five disagreed, making it a tough decision. After Sanga was arrested for embezzlement, he served his time accordingly.

However, during those ten years, the status quo of the Philippines deteriorated, and they agreed that since Sanga was tried, his greed would be subsidized. Because of the status quo of the Philippines, he was still the best choice, even though Sanga would have a lot more baggage coming into power for the second time. The five who disagreed argued that there was still a missing link. However, the eight who agreed were convincing enough whereby Sanga restored his power.

Sanga had to agree to stringent terms in order to return to power. The only way he would be regranted his power were if he paid back all of the embezzled money. Onye Galang, one of only two Fillipino Cabinet members, started to suspect Sanga's wife for the embezzlement and downfall of Sanga. She was the only person associated with Sanga's global contacts, which were for diplomatic and embezzlement purposes, and Sanga's cabinet. Galang commenced discussions with the other cabinet members and after presenting some convincing evidence, they all became suspicious. Thus, in order to confirm their suspicions about Sanga's wife, whom they called the Black Widow, they reappointed Sanga.

The Black Widow wore only black fashionable clothes, making her name suitable. The Cabinet member responsible for the nomenclature was a British English linguistic scholar. Even though the word "widow" was normally in reference to a wife with a dead husband, it also means a wife whose husband travels often. The British cabinet member liked the ring of Black Widow, so they stuck with it.

Sanga agreed to the terms and was reinstated. However, because of his fraudulent scheme, people started to distrust him. Nonetheless, they did consent that Sanga was trying to make an honest comeback, so the people still accepted him. However, his cabinet members started putting severe pressure on Sanga because they wanted to investigate the Black Widow. Sanga was becoming old, as it was 45 years since he first became President of the Philippines. Since he was aging, he started coaching his wife, and the Black Widow began presiding over the majority of presidential decisions Sanga had to make. The Black Widow became even more arrogant, and started using an iron fist to help her husband rule by permanently eliminating any upstarts who seemed to be a threat. A few months later, Sanga died.

As Bronze entered his Lexus LS and was about to start the car, the black Motorola rang. It was Baker's raspy voice saying, "Detective Bronze, we need you at once." Bronze replied nonchalantly, "But of course Lieutenant. Actually, you have perfect timing, for I'm in the car heading over as we speak." Lt. Baker replied, "Great. See you soon." Baker hung up the phone and Bronze drove to the Miami-Dade Police Station.

Bronze entered the station and paced towards Baker's office. Lt. Baker said, "Good afternoon Detective. Have a seat please." Bronze sat down and listened carefully to what Baker had to say. Lt. Baker gave him a file. Baker said, "I was asked by the CIA to give this file especially to you. I do not know what is inside, for it has a seal, but I was given instructions on how to brief you for this case." Bronze took the file from Baker. It said, "Detective Charles Bronze." Bronze broke the seal and opened the file, while Baker read an email from his computer.

Lieutenant Baker began the briefing, "As you can tell Bronze, this is a very confidential case. I am aware that Anna has been using her business-oriented problem solving skills to help you, but she is not privy to this information." Bronze replied seriously, "I understand sir." Baker said, "Good, now let's continue." Baker started reading his email, saying, "The woman you are looking at is the wife of former President Bayani Sanga of the Philippines. She took over the Presidency after Sanga died from a heart attack, but we don't know exactly why because the members of Sanga's cabinet disliked her immodest ways. There are thirteen members of Sanga's cabinet, one of which is a mole working for us. His name is Onye Galang. He contacted Interpol and the CIA and has sworn to secrecy. However, you use your reasoning Bronze, for I know very well that you don't trust anyone, and rightfully so. The woman is known as the Black Widow. She doesn't talk to the media at all, for she detests the media and rules the Philippines with an "iron fist" as Galang phrased it. Mr. Sanga was involved in an embezzlement scheme that caused him ten years in prison." Bronze replied, "An interesting case indeed. I do know of Mr. Sanga through my Asian contacts. However, I didn't realize that the Widow was so involved, but I'm not surprised."

Baker continued, "There are many objectives for this mission Detective Bronze so please pay keen attention. We have reason to believe that the Widow was the real motivation behind the embezzlement of the money that caused Sanga's prison sentence in the first place. Your objective is to find out the location of the embezzled money through your Asian contacts and make a plan with our mole, Galang, in order to extract the Widow. You are eventually going to have to confront the Widow, but when you do, it is very important that you have all the trust deeds, financial documents, and property agreements retrieved and in the possession of the government so that everything will be recovered after the Widow's execution." Bronze replied, "I understand sir. You know the amount of respect I have for women, but a sinister female like the Widow doesn't deserve my respect. In addition, I see that you all want a clean kill of the Widow. I will do my best. I do have one question though. Does the Widow work for L?"

Baker replied, "I am not sure. However, since the CIA requested that you handle this case, I won't be surprised if she does. As you can see Detective Bronze, this is an international affair so do the best as you can. I know you'll make the MDPD proud." Bronze laughed and said, "Thank you very much sir. I am humbled by the compliment." Bronze was about to leave when Lt. Baker asked, "Hold on a minute Bronze. How are you going to approach this case?" Bronze was a bit surprised. Normally, Baker gave Bronze some time to think about his approach; never once was Bronze asked right away. However, Dr. Charles Bronze thought extemporaneously and said, "I'm going to travel to Japan this weekend and meet my old friend, Mr. Watanabe. He will be able to give me some more detailed information about the Widow so I'll be more well-informed when its time to work with Galang to enforce a plan of action. Plus, I haven't been to Tokyo in a long time." Baker smiled and said, "Very well then. Do what you need to do."

After Sanga's unexpected death, the Cabinet was faced with a tough decision as to who should be his replacement. However, because they wanted to know exactly what deteriorated Sanga's health so quickly plus their suspicions of the Black Widow, they decided to appoint her to be the President. She already took over most of Sanga's decisions since he became feeble in his final years, so although they were reluctant, she was the most experienced for the job.

A few months after the Widow took over, the associates were surprised by the transformation of the widow's behavior. She was being suspiciously kind to them, and reached a point where the Widow was being seductive to the male members of the cabinet. She granted the male members, and female members to a lesser degree, any wish they wanted as a bribery tool to remain in power. In addition, the cabinet noticed that the revenues increased drastically. It didn't take long for the cabinet to realize that the last time the revenue increased by such a large amount was when Sanga started embezzling during his first Presidency. However, they decided to keep it quiet and gather more evidence before making a move.

The Widow was sitting in what used to be Sanga's presidential office doing work when she received a phone call. A dark, alienated voice said, "Hello Black Widow. Congratulations on becoming the President of the Philippines. I want to assure you that you are being watched. We will come after you." The Widow responded calmly, "I don't know who the hell you are, but if you think you can attain my power, you are sadly mistaken. I've been running this country since Sanga took over, it was just a matter of time before his flesh and bones were going to wither away." The mysterious voice said, "I'm afraid you misunderstood me. I will come after you because I have some useful information that will help you run the country. You'll be hearing from me soon." The phone line went dead and the Widow hung up the phone. She resumed her work as if nothing had happened.

Bronze was flying to Tokyo on the Learjet. He called Mr. Watanabe and said, "Kon'nichiwa Mr. Watanabe. How are you?" Watanabe recognized the voice immediately and said, "Charles! How have you been my friend? It's been a long time." Bronze replied, "Yes indeed! I'm actually coming to Tokyo on business, and I want to see you." Watanabe replied, "Of course! I am retired now just taking it easy you know. Time for the younger generation to work, I work hard enough in my life. I will send my chauffeur to pick you up at the airport. His name is Kenji." Bronze said, "Excellent. I'll see you for some tea then." Mr. Watanabe said, "Absolutely. I also have some of the finest soba noodles. I look forward to seeing you soon my old friend." Bronze hung up and smiled to himself. He always loved Watanabe. He was like an old uncle, short and lean yet strong. He had a long drawn face, with the signs of aging and white hair.

The Learjet arrived at the airport. He saw the white Rolls-Royce Phantom that Watanabe described to him. Also, Bronze checked the number plate that Watanabe gave him to ensure it was the right car. The young driver introduced himself as Kenji, and drove Bronze to Watanabe's palace. Bronze asked Kenji, "So how long have you worked for Mr. Watanabe." Kenji replied, "Well, Mr. Bronze, I'm actually Mr. Watanabe's son." Bronze looked a bit surprised and said, "That's strange, I didn't know Watanabe had any sons." Kenji smiled and replied, "Although we aren't blood related, we are all his sons, and we become his family." Bronze smiled as the car headed towards Watanabe's palace.

Bronze went through a half acre of beautifully crafted Japanese botanical gardens before reaching the main door. He knocked. Watanabe answered the door smiling and hugging Bronze. Watanabe smiled and said, "Charles, it's so good to see you my old friend. How have you been? Come this way." Bronze removed his shoes as he entered the palace and Watanabe took Bronze to a smaller room where the tea and soba noodles were being served. Bronze looked at the tea and immediately said, "Mr. Watanabe, you know me to a tee." Watanabe smiled and said, "Of course Detective, I haven't forgotten that gyokoru green tea is your favorite."

Watanabe asked Bronze a few questions. He asked, "Still working for the MDPD?" Bronze smiled and replied, "Yes indeed. Also, I'm still working as an ophthalmologist." Watanabe replied, "How do you manage Charles? So much to do in so little time. I hope you have found yourself a good woman." Bronze laughed and said, "Yes Mr. Watanabe, I'm actually seeing a girl now." Mr. Watanabe smiled and asked, "Well, whoever she is, she is with a great man. Treat her with respect and honor young one. But then again, I know you don't have that problem." Mr. Watanabe's face went serious and said, "Now Charles. Enough chitchat. Why are you really here?"

Bronze admired the shift in personality of Mr. Watanabe. It further validated why he was one of Bronze's greatest contacts. Bronze asked, "What do you know of the Black Widow?" Watanabe replied, "Oh yes, that woman. She's one that you definitely don't tango with. As you are probably aware, she took over after Sanga's death. However, she has become very seductive towards the male members of her cabinet since taking office. Very power hungry and will do anything to stay as President. I don't know how the cabinet can be so foolish in appointing her President. She has caused the cabinet to deteriorate, the same cabinet that saved Sanga's skin when he was caught for embezzlement. Bronze, do you know why the country is doing so well now? I found out from one of her cabinet members who is an old friend of mine that some criminal mastermind has given her the keys to all of Sanga's old embezzlement contacts. Thus, she is embezzling money just as her husband did. However, she is being more discreet about it by threatening to kill the cabinet members who say anything about it."

Bronze listened intently and asked, "Mr. Watanabe, do you know anything about a man named L?" Watanabe replied, "I'm afraid not. The only thing I know is he has come up a few times, but a man of mystery I fear. He does not leave a trail or clues." Bronze then asked, "One more question. Do you know who the Widow's contacts are that she is giving this embezzled money to?" Watanabe replied, "All I know is there are two kingpins in Sudan who are secretly holding some of the money. However, the majority of it is in Switzerland and an offshore bank in Bermuda. Give me a few minutes." Watanabe left the room, made a call, and returned within five minutes. Here is the current location of the two Sudanese kingpins. Luckily for you, they are in adjacent rooms in the Al Salam Rotana hotel in Khartoum. Also, here are the account names which the Black Widow is using in both Bermuda and Switzerland." Bronze replied, "Thank you Mr. Watanabe. How were you able to find out the information so quickly?" Watanabe grinned and replied, "I have another contact who works for the London Financial Times and monitors banks all over the world."

It was time for Bronze to leave. He needed to head back to Miami in order to get to work on time on Monday and of course to relay the information to Lt. Baker. Watanabe asked, "Are you sure you don't want some gyokoru and soba to go?" Bronze said, "No thank you Mr. Watanabe. Thank you very much for your hospitality and the information." Mr. Watanabe replied, "No problem Detective Charles. I know the information will be put to good use. Good luck."

Bronze was a little disappointed that Watanabe didn't know about L, but still his trip felt worthwhile because he found out some important information that the government agencies have yet to discover. He was traveling on the Learjet back to Miami from Tokyo when he called Lt. Baker. He told Baker everything Watanabe told him, and Baker complimented him on his efficiency. Baker relayed the information to Walter Helms, the CIA director who transferred the information to Interpol. Baker then told Bronze, "Alright Bronze, we will take care of Bermuda and Switzerland, so you just need to travel to Khartoum next weekend and negotiate with the kingpins. You are going to have to sweeten the deal by offering them double of what the Widow is paying them to side with us and sign over the embezzled money." Bronze replied in the affirmative.

The following week, Bronze traveled to Khartoum. Anna was becoming worried and phoned Bronze while he was on the Learjet en route to Sudan. She said, "Charles, what have you been up to? Why is the MDPD sending you all over the place?" Bronze replied, "I'm sorry my love, but I am not privy to give any information right now. This is a very sensitive case and I cannot even tell you. I hope you've been doing well." Anna replied, a little disappointed and said, "Okay, I understand. If you have to keep it confidential, I honor the fact that you are keeping it a secret, even from me. Take care and good luck."

Bronze met an associate he rendezvoused with the last time he was in Sudan a month ago. The contact told him exactly what room the two kingpins were in. The associate had a good rapport with the manager of Al Salam Rotuna and arranged for the two to be together in a conference room for a presentation. Bronze wore an Armani suit and presented his case accordingly. He said, "Good morning gentlemen. I am a personal representative of the government in the West. We are aware of the fact that you are holding embezzled money from a woman known as the Black Widow. We want you to sign the money over to us, and we will pay double the amount the Widow is paying you to keep it a secret." One of the kingpins replied, "How do we know you are who you say you are?" Bronze called in his associate. The kingpins recognized him immediately as the head of the Sudan police force. Bronze's associate reinsured Bronze's identity. Bronze said, "So do we agree? All you guys want is money, so we will double whatever the Widow is giving you." Bronze's associate took out a document from his briefcase. He asked the kingpins to sign on the line, agreeing to relinquish all the embezzled money to Interpol. The kingpins then gave the account numbers to Bronze and Bronze's associate. Then, the associate called the manager, and two briefcases full of money for each kingpin were given to them as ransom. The kingpins smiled, and light reflected on their golden teeth. They left the room quietly.

Bronze got a call from Baker saying to come back to Miami for the second part of the mission. Bronze agreed and headed towards Miami. On Sunday night in Baker's office, Lt. Baker informed Bronze that the CIA have transferred all the embezzled money from Switzerland and Bermuda to

Interpol. Also, Baker confirmed the agreement that the Sudanese kingpins signed was valid. Baker also confirmed that all the necessary trust deeds and property agreements are all recovered at the Interpol headquarters. Lt. Baker seemed pleased with the progress.

Baker then told Bronze, "Now you have to make the capture Detective. You are going to be a UN diplomat who is interested in improving the education system in the Philippines. Interpol and the CIA have been instructing their IT department to create articles about your award winning work in educational contributions to third world countries. When you first contact the Black Widow, she will do what any normal person would do and Google you to see who you are. The IT department will ensure that Google is flooded with articles of you as a hero and how you won a Nobel Peace Prize due to your educational contributions. The Black Widow also has her own IT department, but we will ensure that they do not see what's really going on. There will be enough evidence for the Black Widow to believe that you are legitimate. You will go as your normal name. You decide on your own how you are going to capture the Black Widow. However, please ensure that it is a clean kill. Her associates and guards will find out that she is dead, but use your techniques in Chemistry to eradicate any evidence that you were present. We want it to look like suicide. In order to do this, stop by our CSI wing before you leave to Makati. Our contact Galang is sending us a blueprint of the Black Widow's mansion so study it carefully." A few moments passed and Baker said, "Ah, I have just received the email of the blueprint. I'm printing it out now. You can study it on the flight. Good luck and be careful Detective." Bronze smiled and nodded, and left without saying a word.

The Black Widow was working in her office when she heard something strange. She went downstairs and said hello, but no answer. The Widow called her guards on the main walkie-talkie, but no answer. She knew something was wrong. The Widow crept around the house, going into a small private room on the side. The Widow thought she heard someone, but looked around and no one was there. As she looked out the window, a man put a cloth around her nose and mouth with a chemical that knocked her out.

She woke up in a dark room. The mysterious voice from a phone call she received a few days ago said, "Hello there. My name is L. Just L. If you utter one more syllable, I'll have your throat slit. That simple." The Black Widow replied, "Ok L. What do you want from me?" He replied, "I have something that will be of great use to you, as I said in our phone conversation. Here is a list of all of your husband's contacts that he embezzled from. You are going to continue what he started, but be more intelligent than him by not getting caught." The Black Widow laughed and said, "Well L, I don't know how you found out that I was looking for this private information, but I will definitely do it. I have been looking for that list for quite some time, and his cabinet is not uttering a word." L replied, "C'mon Widow, you are smarter than that. They only let you be President because they are suspicious that you want to embezzle the money. In fact, they probably rattled you to Interpol." The Widow's small eyes opened wide and said, "You are right L. Which is why my guards will have them at gunpoint very soon. What do you want in return?" L replied, "I don't desire money, I just want your trust. I will outline a plan for you that is foolproof. There is only one person who can stop you." The Widow asked, "And who is that?" L replied, "Charles Bronze. He works for the Miami-Dade Police Department, but is often sent on international missions. Here's a picture of him. He has been exposing all my recent recruits, so just outsmart him and make sure he doesn't catch you. If the government is foolish as it is, they will send him after you, it's just a matter of time." The Widow thanked L and said, "I will definitely keep an eye out." She was knocked out by L's henchmen and woke up in her bed the next morning.

Bronze studied the blueprint carefully, as Baker advised. He noticed there was a small room off to the side. In it, there was a large bookshelf, with a secret passageway to the roof. Bronze was going to compliment the Black Widow for her luxurious mansion and ask her for a tour. He said to himself, "Then, I will lure her into the room and escape through the passageway."

Bronze called The Black Widow's direct line. She answered, "Good morning, Madam President, how can I help you?" Bronze said, "Good morning I'm a representative from the United Nations and I have an interest in meeting with you in order to discuss the educational improvement of the Philippines." The Black Widow replied, "Alright well I have some free time a little later today, so why don't you come over for tea and we'll discuss your plan." Bronze replied, "Very well then. What time will suit you?" She replied, "Come around 4pm. By the way, what was your name again?" Bronze replied, "Oh, I'm terribly sorry I forgot to tell you. My name is Charles Bronze."

The Black Widow laughed to herself and said, "If L is correct, then Bronze is going to trap me, but I'm going to outsmart his skin. Let's see if what he is saying is true." She opened a new window on her computer and went to Google. The Widow googled, "Charles Bronze UN". A whole bunch of results came, many of them saying, "Charles Bronze of the United Nations wins a Nobel Peace Prize for his contributing work to the expansion of education in Third World and African countries." The Black Widow kept looking at article upon article and realized that Bronze may actually be legitimate. She contacted her computer people who hack the government networks. The Black Widow said, "Check all of the files you have for a man named Charles Bronze." The head IT man replied, "Yes madam. Charles Bronze. I'm afraid he doesn't work with any government agencies except the United Nations." The Black Widow was shocked. She looked at the file L gave her on Bronze and said, "Check the Miami-Dade Police Department's database." The IT man replied, "Ok, checking the MDPD database...I'm sorry ma'am but no results." The Black Widow was very perplexed. She thanked the IT man and hung up.

Before Bronze left the Learjet, he got a call from the IT department at Interpol. They said, "Detective Bronze, The Black Widow's hackers have tried to hack into our databases. Don't worry we've caught them red handed. As far as we are concerned, you don't exist as a MDPD detective." Bronze and the IT department laughed together and Bronze said, "Excellent work guys. Thanks for all your help."

Bronze cleaned and loaded his .40 caliber Smith and Wesson handgun and put it in his shoulder holster. He slipped on his jacket and was chauffeured in a Rolls Royce to the mansion. It was now 3:55pm as Bronze was waiting anxiously. He was ready to kill his target, but he had to be discreet about it. Bronze then asked himself if he would be frisked. However, he decided that he wouldn't since he is a UN diplomat and as far as the Widow is concerned, he doesn't even work for the MDPD.

Bronze had a full reconnaissance go around the mansion and was informed that there were only two guards guarding the front door. Greeting them, Bronze told the guards that The Black Widow was expecting him. One of the guards called the Widow on the walkie-talkie and she said, "Okay thanks. I'm expecting Mr. Bronze and I'll be down in a minute."

She opened the door, and looked a little surprised at how tall Bronze was. Bronze then said, "How do you do?" and she replied with the same phrase. Bronze then knew that she was well trained in the old way of greeting people. The Widow said, "Welcome Mr. Bronze. It is such an honor to have a man of your stature at my mansion." Bronze replied, "Yes indeed. That piece of art on the right wall is from the European Renaissance, from 1531 I believe." The Widow smiled and said, "I'm impressed Mr. Bronze. Yes indeed, it is a piece of art from 1533 actually. Still, very good guess. Would you like to see the rest of my mansion?" Bronze smiled, realizing that the Black Widow fell right into his trap and said, "Of course, that would be lovely." The Black Widow gave Bronze a grand tour of the mansion, explaining the significance of each room while Bronze listened intently. They then drank some tea and talked about world politics. Afterwards, the Black Widow escorted Bronze to a large conference room. Bronze lied and said, "I actually have claustrophilia, for I'm afraid of large spaces. Can we move to that small room off to the side?" The Widow replied, "But of course."

They went into the small room. Bronze opened his briefcase and explained the education plan. He explained, "Your husband contributed greatly to improving the education system here in the Philippines. However, it is still second class compared to the West." Bronze then spent 20 minutes highlighting the pitfalls and holes of the reformed education system and explained a clear systematic solution of how to make the literacy rate 100% and retain a stellar high school and college graduation rate. The Black Widow was very impressed with Bronze's explanation, and if it weren't for L's warning, she would have taken Bronze hook line and sinker.

The Black Widow listened carefully and said, "Well Mr. Bronze, this is an excellent plan. However, I know who you really are. You work for the Miami-Dade Police Department." Bronze kept a poker face and said, "I'm sorry Widow, but I don't know what you're talking about." She replied, "Oh I think you do. My superior L told me about you." Bronze's face dropped. The Black Widow kicked him off the chair and tried punching and kicking Bronze in a disciplined manner. Bronze realized that she was well trained in martial arts. He resisted some of her kicks and punches and kicked her back. She defended accordingly and tossed Bronze onto the ground.

Bronze was laying on the ground, bruised and could barely move. He then realized that he had his gun lying in the holster. She attacked him again. He ran behind the desk, tilted it on its side to use as a shield. The Black Widow tried to do a running kick over the desk, but Bronze punched her straight in the face, causing her nose to bleed. He took out his gun and screwed on the silencer behind the desk. Bronze looked at the Widow and she was reaching for her ankle. Bronze planted two bullets in her skull with the silenced Smith and Wesson, whereby she fell to the ground. Bronze looked around. He went back to his briefcase, which had a hidden compartment with CSI materials. He cleaned the residue from his gun, put on gloves, and took her gun from her ankle holster (the one she was trying to reach) and put it in her right hand. Bronze dismantled his Smith and Wesson, took his briefcase and left through the bookshelf secret passageway.

As he was walking through the passageway heading for the roof, he phoned Baker immediately saying, "Target dead." Baker contacted the CIA and Interpol who then contacted the Philippines police, and they arrested her guards. Once they came, he jumped off the roof and talked with the police, explaining the situation. They complimented Bronze, and he then left in the Rolls to the airport, where he hopped on the Learjet back to Miami.

Bronze phoned Anna while on the Learjet. She was a little annoyed when she heard Bronze. However, he gracefully summarized the whole mission to her omitting some confidential parts, whereby she replied, "Wow, I now understand why you couldn't tell me. I guess I was wrong in being annoyed and I apologize honey." Bronze replied, "No problem baby. As long as you're happy." Bronze then fell asleep on the Learjet as it landed in Miami. He was so sleep-deprived that the pilot had to wake him up. Bronze then went through customs in the airport, and drove his Lexus back to the penthouse.

9

Revelation

Detective Charles Bronze was racing down the I-95 in hot pursuit of his target. The target was in a silver BMW 3-series coupe and moving in and out of traffic. Bronze tailed him accordingly in his black Audi R8, which was his personal vehicle only for special occasions. As they were driving south into Miami, the normal Miami traffic started from the northern border. The target braked heavily, forcing Bronze to do so as well. As Bronze and the target approached the Miami Gardens exit, the target started shoving his car over to the HOV lane to try and escape swiftly. Bronze decided to lie low, and let the target cause commotion. All the other drivers who were backed up in traffic started honking profusely, whereby the target turned down his window and started cursing everyone.

Bronze got trapped behind a huge concrete truck, and couldn't budge. He started honking at the truck and flickering the R8's headlights, to no avail. The truck wouldn't move. Bronze looked at the navigation of his R8, which was tracking the BMW. Bronze was so thankful that he threw that homing device on the silver BMW. According to the navigation, the target was stuck in traffic as well. The concrete truck that was in front of Bronze finally moved to a slower lane, and Bronze headed into the HOV. He drove carefully, even though there was a whole bunch of people honking behind him. Bronze disregarded the other drivers because he wanted to make sure he didn't lose sight of the BMW.

The target was still stuck to the lane adjacent to the HOV. Bronze pulled up next to him, turned his passenger window down, and asked him to pull aside. The target refused, and quickly nicked Bronze's front right fender, zooming in front of him and accelerating fast. Bronze pursued accordingly. He thought to himself, "Maybe I should just call in the police for backup." Then Bronze decided, "No, I'll chase him because it would take a while for the police to come anyway. Plus, I know for sure that one of the people in traffic will call the MDPD and they know who I am, so I shouldn't have a problem."

Bronze continued pursuing the target. They were now racing into downtown Miami, and the traffic buildup was noticeable. However, since they were in the HOV lane, they didn't have a problem. The target was now driving 130 mph and Bronze was directly behind him at 125 mph. Bronze thought to himself, "Ah, I have him now. The HOV lane is separated by plastic poles compared to the slower lanes, so it's now or never." However, the target slowed down abruptly to about 80 mph. Bronze mashed the brakes, causing him to lean forward sharply. The target bolted to the right, smashed through the plastic poles with no reservations, and continued whizzing down the lane to the right of the HOV lane. Bronze tried following him, but for some odd reason there was a truck in the HOV lane, even though it's not allowed. Bronze was trapped. He didn't want to break the plastic poles like his target, so he sharply changed to the pull over lane and swiftly yet skillfully drove past the truck. His target was still in the neighboring lane to the HOV, and Bronze followed him on his rear left.

Finally, they were heading to the South Beach exit where the HOV ends. Bronze thought to himself, "Now, I'll trap him." Bronze could faintly hear police sirens. Someone had called the police for backup, but they were still miles behind. Bronze got a call from Baker, answered his phone through the Bluetooth network in his car, speaking to Baker on speakerphone. Baker exclaimed, "Bronze, what the hell are you doing? I got your dropped call, and someone reported your tag number to the police!" Bronze replied, "I'm sorry sir, but I am currently in pursuit of the target." Baker exclaimed, "No doubt, but your life is at risk! Come in and debrief at once!" Bronze replied, "Sir, I almost have him, and don't worry about me, I'll be careful." Baker huffed and said, "Alright Detective, but you're doing this at your own risk." Bronze replied, "My car has already been damaged." Baker said, "Don't worry Bronze, you're doing a brave thing here. The department will take care of it. After all, you really don't need to go this far into the mission, but I see you really want to catch this guy just as badly as I do. Good luck." Baker hung up the phone and Bronze was now fully focused on the road again.

The target exited to go onto the Rickenbacker Causeway, which leads to Key Biscayne. He zipped in and out of traffic, and didn't even pay the toll to get onto the causeway. Bronze did the same exact thing, for Bronze could feel within that he was so close. They were both side by side now, driving about 130 mph. The target looked at Bronze's serious eyes, smiled, and stopped abruptly, coming to a near complete stop. The BMW screeched, and luckily, there were only one or two cars. Bronze mashed the brakes, turned the steering wheel and did an 180° turn, seeing the silver BMW parked on the side. Bronze then turned again, but not as sharp as before, and drove slowly, stopping about five feet behind the BMW. He saw the left arm of the target waving at him. Bronze loaded his .40 Smith and Wesson with a silencer, got out of the car and started walking towards the BMW. As Bronze approached the BMW carefully, he yelled, "Hands up and out of the car!" The target opened the door, put his foot out. However, he retrieved his foot back in and closed the door. The target yelled, "Good luck buddy!" With those few words, Bronze started hearing a beeping coming from the BMW. Bronze started running away from the BMW, pacing towards his R8 and all he remembered was a loud "Boom!" A huge explosion took place as he was running past his R8. The fire from the explosion had reached the R8, and narrowly escaped Bronze. Bronze felt a small burn, but it was very minor. In order to avoid any further injury, Bronze jumped over the side of the Causeway and into the water.

Bronze swam in the water, struggling because the water was very deep. He swam towards a pillar, and climbed himself back up onto the causeway. Bronze looked in the distance and saw that the police were on their way. He felt his face, and realized that he had a minor burn. His clothes and shoes were soaked as they were approaching. He looked at his well-roasted black Audi R8. Bronze wondered how this ever happened, and how he barely survived the explosion.

Bronze was sun tanning on South Beach with Anna. They were talking their personal and professional lives, and how they intertwined. Bronze always had endless calls to deal with being a thriving ophthalmologist in Miami Beach. As owner and CEO of Kris Cosmetics, Anna always dealt with phone calls from business partners. Anna was saying, "You know Charles, even though you work for the MDPD and are an ophthalmologist, I love you everyday for the fact that you are very humbled for your achievements and like to maintain a low profile. And of course, you still try to spend as much time with me as possible." Bronze smiled and said, "Well, Anna, not all women are as caring and accepting of my field of work as you are. So the candle burns at both ends." Anna giggled breathlessly and asked, "Do you want to go for a walk?" Bronze replied in the affirmative.

As Bronze felt the seawater gushing in and tickling his feet, he told Anna, "Tell me something, why do you like to come down here with the crowd, when we could get the same or better suntan from my patio?" Anna replied, "I like the crowd of people some times. Yes, I do like the privacy, especially when it's just the two of us, but its nice to come out in the public sometimes. Does it bother you?" Bronze replied, "No, not at all, I was just wondering." Bronze continued, "All my life, when I was a child, I always wanted to have my own place directly looking out to the ocean, far removed from civilization, if you will. That way, I could communicate with the ocean in a private and serene manner." Anna replied, "Relax darling. Although you make an excellent point, it is good to come out once in a while and remind yourself who you're among." Bronze admired her quick wit in the comment, laughed and said, "Yes indeed."

Charles Bronze and Annalina Kristensen were walking towards where they had set up their beach towels when the black Motorola rang. Baker said, "Bronze, we need you at once." Anna knew the ringtone of the Motorola as opposed to Bronze's Blackberry and said, "Do what you need to do honey." Bronze responded, "Thank you my love. If you want, you can stay out here for a while." Anna replied, "Yes, I think I'll do that. Then I will probably head home." Bronze said, "Ok dear. Enjoy the rest of your weekend." Anna lip locked Bronze hard and said, "Yes, you too. Be safe."

Bronze sprinted back to the penthouse, threw on a Tommy Bahama shirt and khakis, and drove the Lexus LS to the police station. He entered Lt. Baker's office, and Baker said, "Good God Bronze, are you always a beach bum on the weekend?" Bronze knew that Baker was referring to Bronze's smell of strong sunblock and said, "Well sir, with a dual job like mine, do you blame me?" Baker smiled and said, "No Detective, not at all. Now sit down and let's get to business."

Baker handed Bronze a manila folder and said, "Target: Exavier Mendoza. A Basque gentleman, and you will find a full physical description in his dossier. Our friends in Spain have been observing his behavior for a while, and he looks suspicious. What do you think Bronze?" Bronze studied Mendoza's face carefully, "Well, from the look of his chiseled features, I would say he looks like a Basque. His parents are also Basque, for he doesn't look like a person with mixed ancestry. Looks callous, but can change his emotions to negotiate successful business deals. It seems to me that he keeps a low profile." Baker replied, "Yes indeed, you are right Detective." Bronze analyzed his dossier carefully and asked, "What is the hard proof and motivation for the suspicion? And also, can't our contacts in Spain talk to him?" Baker replied, "I'm afraid not. Mendoza has been keeping a low profile in Argentina. Thus, Interpol delivered the message right to us. Mr. and Mrs. Fernandez, the current rulers of Argentina also keep a low profile, and Mendoza is a close friend with them. Mendoza also knows other powerful figures in

South America, one being the new President Mr. da Silva, who has been in power for a few months. However, according to our friends in Centro Nacional de Inteligencia, or CNI, Mr. da Silva has been showing communist tendencies." Bronze then asked, "Lieutenant, do you think it has to do with Mendoza's influence?" Baker replied, "No, at least not according to the CNI. Personally, I agree with the CNI. Even though da Silva is one of Mendoza's key contacts, because of da Silva's lean to communism, Mendoza does not trust him with any secrets. He has however, confided a few secrets, which even we don't know of, to Mr. and Mrs. Fernandez."

Baker continued, "A corn production factory in Brazil named Lewis Enterprises is holding a charity ball tomorrow afternoon at the Bahia Mar in Fort Lauderdale. All of the most successful and wealthiest businesspeople from South America will be there. The proceeds will go to the poor in Miami. Congratulations Bronze, you are on the guest list. You will attend, keeping an eye out for Mendoza. Keep in mind this time that we want him alive. I know that you don't kill people unless it is absolutely necessary, but please make sure that Mendoza stays alive. We need to question him. He is currently registered to a black Land Rover. Good luck."

Bronze left the office, thinking about how he was going to approach this case. "I'm going to have to make some sort of contact with Mendoza," Bronze thought. He looked in his closet for a suitable tuxedo. However, the ball wasn't until tomorrow, so Bronze had the whole night to work out a game plan.

It was Sunday afternoon, and it was time for Bronze to leave his penthouse to drive up north to the Bahia Mar. He put on his Calvin Klein tuxedo and thought it would be a good time to drive the black

Audi R8. Even though he had to keep a low profile for the sake of the mission, he thought the R8 would slate right in the middle, especially since many of the wealthy businesspeople would be chauffeured in Rolls-Royces and Bentleys.

Upon arriving at the Bahia Mar, Bronze sized up the place immediately, looking for escape routes. He went up to the bar, and ordered a ginger ale on the rocks. As he was drinking it, a golden brown woman with long black hair and green eyes approached him. She said with a somewhat thick, yet sexy Hispanic accent, "I've been watching you cutie." Bronze eyed her from head to toe. She was wearing a long white cocktail dress that was tight in all the right places. Bronze said, "Thank you darling. I'm honored. And what is your name?" She answered, "My name is Maria da Silva, and I'm the wife of the new Brazilian President." Dr. Charles Bronze replied, "It's an honor. My heartfelt congrats to your husband for becoming President. It must be a very dignified position for you as well, being the wife of the President." Maria answered, "Indeed it is. Do you want me to introduce you to him?" Bronze replied nonchalantly, "Sure."

Maria took Bronze's hand and headed towards Mr. da Silva. da Silva was talking to Mendoza, Bronze's target. Maria interrupted their conversation and said, "Honey, I want to introduce you to this wonderful gentlemen." Maria said, "This is," and Bronze said, "Charles Bronze." da Silva looked at Bronze, shook his hand and said, "It's a pleasure Mr. Bronze." Bronze replied, "Please Mr. President, the pleasure is all mine. Congrats on your victory. Brazil is in a terrible situation, but from what I have read, you have been doing a great deal in stabilizing the economy." da Silva replied, "You are well-informed Mr. Bronze. Let me introduce you to a friend of mine, Mr. Exavier Mendoza. We are talking about Lewis Enterprises, a corn producing factory." Mendoza and Bronze shook hands. da Silva continued, "Before I took over the Presidency, Lewis Enterprises had been there for quite some time. We are looking into expanding it, and its opportunities." Bronze said, "I see. I think that expanding it is a proactive move on your part, especially since Lewis Enterprises is funding this ball. Congrats to you Mr. Mendoza. You must be very proud." Mendoza stared at Bronze with his cold eyes and said in a thick Basque accent, "Thank you sir." Bronze then said, "Well, if you'll excuse me, I have to mingle with some other officials." da Silva smiled at the fact that Bronze was talking to two powerful people, yet Bronze knew his place as a guest. da Silva replied, "Absolutely. It was a pleasure meeting you Mr. Bronze."

Bronze continued walking around, mingling with other wealthy businesspeople. He reflected for a moment on his meeting with Mendoza and how cold those eyes were. Bronze then thought about Mendoza's operation in Brazil, gasped, and put his hand over his open mouth.

Bronze started making educated assumptions in his head. He thought that from the Mendoza's body language and the way his cold eyes gazed upon him, it was almost as if Mendoza was afraid of Bronze. "But why?" Bronze thought. Bronze couldn't stop thinking about it, but he needed more information. He walked around the main room, searching discreetly for Mendoza. Bronze saw his face, and his face was starting to go red and sweating.

Mendoza got a call on his cell phone, but had a Bluetooth headset. He started talking. Mendoza said, "Hello." A cold, creepy voice said, "Hello Mendoza. Have you made contact with Bronze?" Mendoza replied, "Yes L." L said, "Mendoza, why the hell do I detect nervousness in your voice? I thought you were prepared to deal with Bronze." Mendoza replied, "Yes sir, but from Bronze's cool demeanor, it's so hard to believe that he is responsible for the seizure of so many of your operations." L replied, "Yes, I have noticed that as well from my observation. You need to calm down. Bronze is going to notice that you are getting nervous. He's onto you. Bronze is already tracking your Land Rover; so don't go back to it. I have a silver BMW 3-series that will be valeted to the front entrance in exactly ten minutes. Get your ass in there and drive off. Don't race, just drive." L hung up and Mendoza went to the bar and ordered a drink.

Bronze realized that from the operation that Mendoza was running, he was working for L. He also recognized that L stands for Lewis. Since Bronze knows that L is a professor of organic chemistry, his surname must be Lewis. Bronze said to himself, "Damn, Lewis is such a common name. I have to let Baker know about this." Bronze kept an eye on Mendoza and went into a corner to call Baker. However, in a swift moment, as the phone was dialing, Mendoza headed for the front entrance whereby Bronze had no choice but to hang up the phone and follow him.

Bronze paced behind Mendoza. Mendoza ran to the valet, picked up the keys, and was entering the car quickly. Bronze threw a homing device that stuck onto the trunk of the car as the BMW drove off rapidly. Bronze ran to his black Audi R8 and raced off behind Mendoza.

At present, the police arrived. Bronze was

now soaked in his Calvin Klein tuxedo. The policeman said, "Good evening Detective Bronze." Bronze replied, "Good evening sheriff. May I use your phone?" The sheriff said, "Sure." Bronze said, "Detective Charles Bronze for Lieutenant Baker please." The person who picked up said, "Ok, Detective Bronze, one moment please." Baker picked up and said, "Bronze, what's going on? Is everything ok?" Bronze replied, "Yes sir, but I'm afraid our target Mendoza committed suicide. There was a timed bomb on the silver BMW. Mendoza apparently knew that the bomb was present, so he used his cell phone to detonate it." Baker then said, "Did you get injured? You took on a dangerous race Bronze, despite my warning." Bronze replied, "Yes, but nothing serious. When the car exploded, I got a minor first-degree burn on my left cheek. But don't worry about me, the fire rescue will take care of it." Baker said, "Ok. I need you to come in and debrief afterward." Bronze said, "Yes sir."

The fire rescued had arrived. They took care of Bronze, and taped gauze to his left cheek, so now his speech was somewhat muffled. The paramedic told him, "You can take it off in two days." Bronze asked the sheriff to take him back to the police station. Baker was standing outside, frantic.

Baker said, "Bronze! Thank God you're ok. Bloody hell, what happened to your face? And where is your Audi?" Bronze replied in a somewhat muffled manner, "I'm ok sir. The paramedic said the burn was only minor and I can take off the gauze in two days. My car was bombed I'm afraid. That R8 was my prized possession." Baker got angry and said, "You see Bronze, I told you not to follow him. What the hell is your problem? I gave you specific orders to let the police take care of this situation. Now we have to buy you a new R8, not to mention the city costs we have to pay for the damage you did!" Bronze raised his voice slightly above the normal and said seriously, "Lt. Baker, I'm aware of my blunder. And yes, I should have listened to you. However, you know damn well that I would not have chased Mendoza if I didn't have good reason. He was definitely not a nobody. I found out from him that L, our old friend that we've been tracking, and once again the mastermind behind this operation, stands for Lewis. His name is Professor Lewis, and he is a professor of organic chemistry." Baker calmed down and said, "No wonder why you called me for a change, not to mention extemporaneously. Damnit, and Mendoza had to go and commit suicide!" Bronze said, "Yes, unfortunately, no doubt L trains his associates with committing suicide as a last resort because this has happened to us before if you recall." Baker replied, "Yes I do. Now get yourself to bed and take care of that burn. I'll see you next weekend. I will do some investigating this week about Lewis Enterprises. I'll have a nice long chat with my friends in Brazil and see what they have. Meet me in my office this upcoming Friday at 5:00pm as soon as you get off of work." Bronze replied, "Yes, Lt. Baker. Have a good week."

Bronze returned back to work the following morning, adhering to his normal morning routine. He woke up, went for his beach run, came back, took a hot shower, and got ready for work. He drove his Lexus LS to work. The gauze was still on his face from the burn, but it wasn't paining as much as the preceding day. When Claire Scarlet saw him, she nearly shrieked at the huge white gauze protruding out of Bronze's cheek. "Charles!" she exclaimed, running from her desk towards him to look at it in more detail, "Are you ok? What happened?" Bronze replied, "I'm ok Claire, just got a little bruise that's all." Claire inspected his cheek carefully and said, "Sorry honey, but don't lie to me. This is a burn, what happened?" Dr. Charles Bronze was now thinking very quickly as to how to respond. Claire Scarlet still didn't know that Bronze was working for the MDPD after all these years, so he lied and said, "I had an accident in the kitchen, that's all. I can take it off tomorrow evening, so I'll only be in this condition until tomorrow. I have to ask the lady at the front desk to reschedule all my surgeries until Wednesday, because I can't operate with this gauze jutting out of my face." Claire replied, "Indeed, I thought it was from the kitchen. C'mon Charles, I'm a doctor too you know, and I know a burn when I see one." Bronze laughed and then proceeded towards his office.

Wednesday came around very quickly, and the gauze was finally removed from Bronze's face. There wasn't any more pain, and Bronze didn't have to talk in a muffled fashion anymore. However, there was still a mark, but the doctor told him that it would disappear in a few days. During Scarlet and Bronze's lunch hour, Bronze decided to stay in his office for a change. He had to think about an important event that had to happen soon, and the ramifications.

After eleven years of working in for the Miami-Dade Police Department, Bronze agreed that it was time to reveal to his dear friend Dr. Claire Scarlet, the nature of his work. Charles Bronze was starting to sweat, and became very nervous at the thought of telling her this secret he kept from her for such a long time. Scarlet and Bronze always had an open relationship, from the time they met many years ago at Johns Hopkins Medical School, and this was the first time that Bronze was borderline frightened.

He was not scared at the way he would have to present this revelation because Bronze was an excellent orator, but he had trouble predicting what her reaction would be.

Claire Scarlet walked in his office abruptly while these thoughts were zipping through Bronze's head. She said, "Charles, is everything ok? You weren't in the lunch room today as you normally are." Bronze responded calmly, "Yes, everything's fine, something crossed my mind that's all." Before Claire could respond, Bronze asked, "What are you doing for dinner tonight?" Claire Scarlet smiled and said, "As of now, I don't have any plans." Bronze replied, "Let's go to the Ritz Carlton for dinner tonight. My treat." Scarlet giggled quietly and said, "Of course, it has been a long time since we had one of our interesting conversations. However, would Anna be ok with this?" Bronze answered, "But of course. Strictly professional." Claire smiled again and left his office.

The Ritz Carlton was located north of the office, and since both Scarlet and Bronze lived south of the office, Bronze drove Scarlet in his Lexus to the Ritz Carlton. He ordered the smoked salmon, staying true to his pescetarian diet, and she ordered the Mediterranean salad. They talked for a while about world politics, and for a brief time about work. Dr. Charles Bronze then said, "I have something important to tell you." Claire's face went serious. Bronze started sweating, and his palms were getting greasy. He had butterflies in his stomach, and the hair on his skin started to rise. He never felt so nervous in a long time, probably since the first time he performed eye surgery as a resident. Claire noticed this, and held his hand. She said, "Hey Charles, if there is something that you want to tell me, then by all means. You know very well that I'm a good listener." She was right. Dr. Claire Scarlet always had innate acute listening skills. Bronze took note of this when they met at Hopkins, and the art of listening was a skill that Bronze had to learn, while for Claire it seemed so natural.

Bronze still couldn't determine how Claire was going to react. This was one situation that Bronze felt was totally unpredictable. "To hell with it," Bronze said to himself. He then said, "Ok Claire, its about my government job." Claire's face wanted to crack a smile, but refused to. She tried to maintain her composure and seriousness, but Bronze knew that she wanted to run around screaming in joy. Claire Scarlet was finally going to find out the one thing that Bronze kept hidden from her. Before Bronze said anything, Claire told herself, "Wow I never thought this day would come."

Bronze said, "As you are aware, I have been working my government job on the side for the past eleven years. Well, I am an undercover detective for the Miami Dade Police Department. My specialty is in international relations, and because I speak Arabic, I am sent frequently to the Middle Eastern region. However, my missions have spanned the seven continents." Claire didn't know what to say, but the first question she asked was, "I don't understand. How can you travel to so many places over weekends? Doesn't it take like 27 hours to fly to Australia?" Bronze replied, "Yes, but I ride in a special jet that travels five times faster than the fastest airplane. Therefore, I arrive in Australia much quicker."

Bronze detected sorrow and worry in Claire's voice when she asked, "Why did you choose to tell me this now? Why didn't you ever tell me this before?" Bronze replied, "The time wasn't right." Claire became slightly angry and said, "Charles, you're going to have to give me a better excuse than that. I've known you longer than I have known anyone except my family and we have always confided in each other. Did you wait to tell me now because of the burn that you received? Was it from a case?" Bronze replied, "Yes, the burn was from a mission. And I'm sorry I lied to you." Claire looked frustrated and asked, "Charles, you answered one of my questions but not the other. Why did you wait so long?" Bronze was trying to keep his composure, but his feelings were too strong for Claire. Bronze never had any siblings, and Claire was the closest thing he had to a sister. He wanted to weep, but held his emotions and said sternly, "I didn't tell you before because I didn't want your life to be at risk. If the opposing parties, those whom I have been sent by the MDPD to capture, found out how close we were, your life could be at risk. Believe me Claire, I wanted to tell you a long time ago, and every time you ask me or allude to the government job, it created a bigger wound on my heart for not telling you, but I couldn't risk it."

As Bronze was talking, Claire's eyes started to water and fill with tears. It was at that point when Claire Scarlet realized that Dr. Charles Bronze would be more masculine than any male she ever met. She took the napkin off her lap, stood up, walked over to Bronze, sat on his lap, embraced him closely, and kissed him on the cheek. Claire then whispered breathlessly, "Its ok love. I appreciated your concern and I honor who you are, and why you waited so long to tell me. We have always trusted each other, and I applaud you for being able to keep the nature of your government work from me for such a long time." She kept holding on to him tightly, and the waiter arrived. The waiter saw her sitting on his lap and the waiter said, "Oh dear," and left. Bronze laughed and said, "Alright darling, shall we have dessert?" Claire smiled and went back to her seat, "Absolutely Detective Bronze."

As Claire Scarlet and Charles Bronze were savoring the rich dessert they ordered, the black Motorola rang. Bronze said to himself, "I thought I wasn't going to hear from Baker until Friday. What's going on?" Bronze asked Claire, "Will you excuse me for a moment?" Claire smiled and nodded. Bronze left the table abruptly, and answered, "Yes." Baker said, "Sorry Detective. I know its Wednesday and I said I wasn't going to call you until Friday, but we have some important information." Bronze replied, "I'm really sorry Lieutenant, but I'm eating dinner with a business partner. I'm afraid I can't come now." Baker replied calmly, "I understand. Call me in an hour." Bronze replied, "Will do." Bronze hung up the Motorola and went back to the table. He paid the bill as promised, took Claire back to the office so she could pick up her car, bade her goodnight, and went back to his Miami Beach penthouse.

It was almost an hour after Baker's call, so Bronze called Baker on the Motorola. Baker said, "Alright Detective, here's the scoop. I've been working with our friends in South America. Apparently, the core of the suspicion with Lewis Enterprises is the fact that even though it's a corn production plant, it has a lab in it. We don't know what kind of lab, but with your lead that Lewis Enterprises belongs to L, and your knowledge in Chemistry, you are the best person to investigate." Bronze thought for a moment and replied, "No problem Lieutenant. I can't do anything until Friday because I have a lot of surgeries scheduled over the next two days. I'll come to the station after work on Friday, and if you need to fill me in on anything you can do so on Friday." Baker replied, "Ok Bronze. Sounds like a plan. See you on Friday."

It was Friday afternoon. Bronze felt a large weight lifted off his shoulders since revealing his job with the MDPD to Claire. Also, it was easy because Claire and Bronze had his detective work disguised as "the government job." Bronze didn't have to keep that secret anymore, which he was perfectly fine with.

Bronze however, did keep some things from her. Claire Scarlet was a woman of sophistication, so she didn't ask any questions that seemed too nosy. For example, Bronze didn't tell her of the people whom he had to kill, even though he would have left them alive if it was his choice. Also, he didn't want to scare her with L, but now Bronze had the worry in the back of his mind that L would find out about Claire. It didn't matter anyway, because Bronze knew where he stood. "As smart as L is," Bronze thought, "L has been monitoring me, but in the job. The government will keep all my personal information secret, so no worries there."

Bronze drove to the station, and was briefed by Baker. Baker said, "Ok Bronze, we haven't found out anything else. However, we did get a picture of the factory. It's pretty salient, especially since it's located in the outskirts of Sao Paulo, away from the main city." Bronze studied the picture carefully. Baker continued, "It's pretty run down. I'd be interested to see what kind of lab is located in there." Bronze said, "Yes indeed." Baker then said, "We aren't looking for anyone in particular Bronze, we just need you to gather information about the factory and come back. I don't want you running on some wild goose chase like what you did with Mendoza. I understand you wanted to take care of it yourself, but your desires can cloud your judgment. Go to the factory, analyze the lab carefully using your skills in Chemistry and come back. No one needs to know that you were ever there." Bronze smiled and replied, "Yes sir, I understand. I'll report back on Sunday with a detailed report." Baker grinned and said, "Excellent Bronze. Off you go then."

Bronze ordered a ginger ale with a lime wedge as he was flying in the Learjet destined for Sao Paulo. This was actually Bronze's first visit to Brazil, so he got a map and researched on his laptop some of the popular destinations there. He called Anna and talked to her briefly, telling her that he was going to Sao Paulo and he would meet her Sunday evening. Anna replied, "Oh Charles, why couldn't you have taken me with you?" Charles laughed and replied, "Sorry darling, duty before pleasure." Anna laughed and said, "Exactly love. See you on Sunday then."

Bronze checked into the Emiliano resort and stayed for a few hours. He rented a small car, for he wanted to keep a low profile. He drove to the outskirts of Sao Paulo, beyond the hustle and bustle of the city. Then, he saw Lewis Enterprises straight ahead. He drove around in the parking lot, where many cars were present at the time. He parked in the back and put on a fake mustache and beard. Bronze couldn't risk being noticed, especially since it seems that L has been giving his associates a picture of him so they could identify Bronze. Bronze entered the factory, unarmed. He went to the bathroom, seeing that a factory suit was hanging inside. There was a gentleman washing his face. Detective Bronze knocked him out cold, and turned off the sink. He dragged his body into a toilet stall, locking the stall and jumping over so that no one would find him. Bronze took the suit and started taking a self-tour of the factory.

Bronze looked around and saw that there was nothing suspicious. He saw machinery that any corn production plant would have. Bronze observed the workers for a while. They noticed him, but didn't care. He continued walking around, trying to find a lab. Bronze went to the elevator, and saw a keyed button with a red "L" on it, the same trademark that Lewis has been using. He took out a pin, and picked the keyhole in the elevator, pressing the button with the red "L" on it. It took him underground.

The elevator doors swooshed open. Bronze approached carefully, trying not to make a sound. He turned on the lights and saw what the government agency was talking about. It was a whole chemistry lab, full of equipment. Bronze was shocked to find all the equipment up to date. He tried looking for a storage locker. He thought, "If I were hiding chemicals, I would have a big locker to put everything in." Bronze walked around for a while. "Wow," he thought, "this is some very sophisticated equipment." It reminded him of his days at the University of Miami, and the equipment he observed was very advanced, equipment he couldn't use until he reached high-level advanced chemistry. Bronze said to himself, "No doubt our friend Professor Lewis is an astute organic chemist."

Bronze finally found the locker. He smiled to himself, opening it. There were a large amount of organic chemicals, and Bronze recognized that the chemicals were the main components of illegal drugs. Bronze realized that L was using this factory to synthesize illegal drugs. "But which ones?" Bronze thought. He took out a notepad and started to jot down the names of the chemicals. Charles Bronze said to himself, "Let me write down these chemicals now, and I can make the association later when I have time to think." However, as Bronze was writing, he heard the elevator creaking. It was going up. Someone was coming down to the lab.

Bronze started to get a little panicky, looking for a place to hide. The lab was so wide and open spaced, it would be difficult to find somewhere. There was no way out, except through the elevator. Bronze was so intrigued by the up-to-date lab equipment, that when he was investigating the place, he forgot to look for an escape route. Bronze was stuck. He couldn't move. He did his best and hid behind the large cabinet, squeezing himself behind.

Bronze heard a man with a thick Portuguese accent saying, "Tell L that the drugs are ready to be shipped. With the addition of this compound, the law enforcement will never detect it. Also, tell him that this drug operation won't last long. He will have to relocate the lab somewhere else, or open a new more recent lab." The assistant said, "Yes sir. I will inform L of what you said. I am impressed that even though you work for L sir, you have done a good job of keeping this lab under your control." The man said, "Thank you young one. Now let's go. Everything must proceed according to plan."

The two gentlemen went back into the elevator that went to the main factory area. Bronze was breathing heavily, realizing that he barely escaped. He couldn't believe that he was so foolish in judgment, but he didn't dwell on it. Instead, he kept cool as a cucumber, and opened the cabinet doors again. Bronze jotted down a few more chemicals and left. However, as he was going up the elevator, the elevator jammed on him. Bronze got a little scared and observed that he may get caught, even though he is wearing the factory uniform. The elevator was old and rusty, explaining its flawed mechanics, but it started working again and took him up safely.

Bronze exited the factory and drove his car back to the resort. He studied the chemical compounds carefully, and the conversation he had overheard between the two gentlemen in the lab. He continued looking at the compound names. "There must be some sort of relationship," Bronze said to himself. He continued, "Let's see, what illegal drug has all the components?" Bronze made a list, scratching off the ones that didn't apply. He said aloud, "Cocaine, no, heroin, no, meth, no, marijuana, definitely not. LSD?" Bronze told himself, "Well, these chemical compounds do make up the foundation of LSD with the exception of this one added randomly. Unless…maybe this random compound is the one that causes the LSD to be undetected." Bronze did some research from his online sources he used as an undergraduate to write research papers. His hunch was correct.

After flying back to Miami, he immediately went to see Baker. Bronze said, "Ok, Lieutenant, I have a lot of information." Baker replied coldly, "Good, that's what the government paid you to do." Bronze ignored his brashness and said, "Now, these are the chemical components that I found in the lab." Baker was not amused and said, "In English please." Bronze said, "Based on the ingredients I found in the main cabinet, and the equipment in the lab, L has a whole underground operation going on. He is using organic compounds in order to synthesize LSD. However, he adds a certain component to them, which I won't bother giving you the Chemistry jargon and is quite unnecessary for the purposes of this conversation. The component allows the LSD to be detected as a regular pharmaceutical. Thus, it passes through U.S. Customs with ease. In addition, there are some other minor extra components that alters the psychological effects of LSD, more than usual." Baker looked a little surprised and said, "It's a good thing we sent you out there Bronze. The lab is a bigger operation than I anticipated. Don't worry, we'll contact our friends in the DEA and they will take care of it. However, we are not ready to pounce just yet. I need to report all the information you told me to Interpol and our friends in South America. Is the lab noticeable?" Bronze replied, "No, in typical L fashion, it is hidden. The only way to reach it is to take the elevator via keyed access down to the lab. The lab is underground and with good reason. That way, when the factory has to undergo the normal inspection by the government, they will never discover it." Baker nodded at Bronze's witty explanation and said, "Ok Bronze, we have enough information for now. Go home and get some rest. Good work. We'll keep you updated." Bronze replied in the affirmative and left.

Bronze drove back to his penthouse, calling Anna on the way. He told her to meet him at the house, whereby Anna agreed. Bronze didn't have enough time to cook, so Anna took him out to dinner for a change. They talked their usual conversation, and Bronze gave as little information as possible regarding his South American investigatory trip. Bronze tried to switch the conversation to more lighthearted things, such as comedy and music. Anna was telling Bronze about the profitability of Kris Cosmetics and how it was booming. As she was talking, Bronze didn't seem to care. He noticed that even though she was well dressed and looked gorgeous as usual, his mind drifted off to the dinner he had with Claire the other night whereby the revelation took place.

Showdown

Dr. Charles Bronze entered the room and was very nervous. He scrubbed in, prepping for surgery. It was a while since he performed glaucoma surgery. He was a little melancholy whenever he had to perform this type of surgery because Bronze has a family history of diabetes. Nevertheless, Bronze contended with these emotions before entering the operating room. Once he was inside, it was strictly business, and Bronze kept his usual professional profile.

Bronze had arrived at the office at 6:00am to do the pre-op right before the surgery. The surgery was scheduled to begin at 7:00am. However, it actually worked in Bronze's favor because he needed to leave early from work. Bronze received a call from Baker that he would never forget.

Baker informed Bronze that the DEA busted one of L's biggest operations, Lewis Industries. He also thanked Bronze for making a valuable contribution towards the capture. If Bronze had not infiltrated the facility a few weeks ago, L would still be getting away with his clandestine synthesizing of LSD. Bronze told Baker that it wasn't a problem, and told Baker, "This is the big one." Baker replied, "Yes indeed, Bronze. L is going to be very disappointed." Baker gave a laugh of satisfaction and hung up the phone.

Bronze was in his penthouse on his laptop when he read a significant BBC News article. The title said, "Largest Illegal Drug Factory in South

America Busted." Bronze smiled, but was a bit surprised. This was the first time in all the years Bronze worked for the MDPD that one of the missions that he contributed to actually make international news headlines. Most of his white-collar crime busts were well known people, but inconspicuously made local news, not international. It seemed to Bronze that Lewis Industries was a bigger operation that he suspected, especially after investigating the lab.

Bronze's house phone rang. Anna said, "Charles, did you read the headlines in the BBC?" Bronze replied, "Yes, I'm reading it now honey." Anna said, sounding a little apprehensive, "May I come over?" Bronze replied, "Absolutely, is everything ok?" Anna replied, "Yes, but I have something important to tell you."

As Anna was on her way to Bronze's penthouse, Detective Charles Bronze sat on his couch pondering what Anna needed to tell him. Due to the seizure of Lewis Industries, Bronze was possibly going to get a little more free time. Bronze knew this meant that he could finally spend more quality time with the woman he loved, rather than have an interruption arise from Baker whenever he was with Anna. He thought to himself, "As brilliant as L is, which I'm not going to deny, with Lewis Industries gone, he will probably go hiding like a caterpillar becoming a cocoon and look for more contacts." Bronze smiled to himself, and directly afterwards, the doorbell rang.

Anna laughed and nearly tackled Bronze with a strong embrace. She kissed him hard on the lips and said, "It's so great to see you Charles." Bronze replied, "Anna, I only saw you a few days ago. Does it really feel that long?" Anna replied, "Yes my darling because I feel like we've been dating so long that you have become a mate to me." Bronze was a little perplexed with Anna's behavior, but went with it. He took Anna by the hand and said, "Listen Anna. We haven't been dating for even a year. What's going on with you?"

Anna responded, "Nothing, just a little worried that's all." Bronze said, "Yes, I know from your phone call. I detected a great anxiety in your voice, and looking at your body language and shaken dialogue, no doubt you are. What's the matter?" Anna responded, "You don't realize it, do you?" Bronze replied, "Anna, do you want some tea or something? You need to be more specific." Anna replied, "Charles, isn't it obvious? Since Lewis Industries made international headlines, this means that L is hiding God knows where and he is seeing it as well. All of his operations, or at least the ones you have told me about, have avoided international attention, but with this bust, no doubt he's going to come after you and the entire MDPD. Your life is at risk." Bronze listened intently as she continued.

When Anna finished rambling, Bronze held her face between his hands. "Look in my eyes," Bronze said. Anna stared at him with her big blue eyes, and Bronze saw them clearly, looking like aquamarine gems. He said, "For about eleven to twelve years, I've been working for the Miami Dade Police Department. My job is definitely a risky one. It just so happens that my missions recently have been connected to L. However, I am always prepared for anything, it is part of my training. L is tracking me down, not you. Therefore, you don't need to worry. Let me handle this. Don't worry, I'll keep you safe." Anna kissed Bronze again and smiled. Bronze could see the anxiety being lifted off her shoulders.

Anna and Bronze continued talking for an hour or so. Anna then left, winking at Bronze. She said, "No matter how at risk you may be, just know that I love you so very much." Bronze's face went red and said, "And I love you too my dear." As she shut the door, Bronze thought for a moment, chuckled, and went to his study room. He opened his patient file for the following morning, and saw he had to perform a retinal surgery together with his dear friend, Claire Scarlet.

The next morning, Bronze went through his normal morning routine and again had to go early to the private practice. Bronze and Scarlet needed to discuss their plan of action for the surgery and what roles they would play before seeing the patient. The surgery was a bit more complicated than usual, but Bronze and Scarlet have done surgeries together numerous times over the past fifteen years so it seemed very natural for them. Dr. Henry Smith, the owner of the practice, and Bronze and Scarlet's mentor, also showed up, much to the surprise of Bronze and Scarlet. Smith said, "Don't worry Charles and Claire, I am only going to observe the surgery. We haven't had a retinal procedure like this in a while, plus I want to see how you all will work together as a team." Bronze and Scarlet looked at each other, smiling. They knew what the other was thinking. Dr. Henry Smith was in for a treat, because when Scarlet and Bronze worked together, they were unbeatable.

Dr. Charles Bronze and Dr. Claire Scarlet scrubbed in. Bronze noticed Scarlet was a little more nervous than usual and said, "Don't worry Claire. I'm sure you'll do fantastic. Let's do this. Don't fret over Dr. Smith, just stay concentrated on the patient." Scarlet smiled and said, "Thanks Charles. I needed that."

It turns out that the surgery was a great success. Bronze and Scarlet finished earlier than expected. Smith checked the inner working of each step from the area where he was standing and was very satisfied. Smith congratulated them both on a job well done and they proceeded with their other patients for the day.

Lunch came around pretty quickly, especially since both Scarlet and Bronze only saw two patients, since their team surgery took a long time. Claire asked Bronze, "Charles, I know we always have lunch here, but can we go outside for a minute? I want to talk to you privately, without any distraction." They advanced outside and she said, "Thanks for your help when we were scrubbing Charles." Bronze replied, "Not a problem. You didn't bring me out here to compliment me, did you?" Scarlet looked down and said, "No." Bronze said, "Claire, what's wrong honey?" Claire responded, "Charles, I read the international news regarding the bust of Lewis Industries. I understand that the production plant was in the same region you traveled to a few weeks ago. Did you have to do with it? Did the MDPD send you there to investigate?" Bronze replied, "Claire, I told you about my job right before I went on that mission. Let's not talk about this now. Let's grab dinner tonight and we can talk." Claire said firmly, "No Charles. I need to know this info now." Bronze looked at her and said, "Why is it so important to you?"

Scarlet responded, "Charles, I'm worried about you. No doubt that whoever is behind the industry will find out that you are the person who initiated such a large-scale investigation. It was because of your mission that led a series of events, which therefore led to the arrest of the factory and its inhabitants. He or she will track you down. Doesn't that bother you?" Charles Bronze was intrigued at how the two most important women in his life were worrying about the same thing, when he was the one L was tracking, not them. Nevertheless, Bronze understood where they were coming from, and he also figured out that there is a slight possibility that L will find out about them.

Bronze put his left hand on Scarlet's right shoulder, and lifted her face by the chin with his right hand. She stared at Bronze eye to eye, looking up at him. Bronze said softly, "Listen to me Claire. I know that with the nature of my work there will be criminals tracking me down. However, I can assure you that everything will be ok. I wouldn't be good at my job as a detective or even more as a doctor if I worried about that fact all the time. I don't want you getting worried about me. You know that I will always love you as a sister and a dear companion." Scarlet looked in his eyes and hugged him.

Bronze felt her warmth yet again. After they embraced, they went together back to the lunchroom. Dr. Henry Smith was sitting down eating lunch. He said, "Ah, there you two are! I've been looking all over for you. Please sit down." Bronze and Scarlet sat side by side, across from Smith. Smith said, "Listen Charles and Claire, I'm getting old. My health is somewhat going down, and my doctor told me that I need to start taking it easy. As you know, all of us as doctors make terrible patients because we think we can cure ourselves. However, I began really thinking about what my doctor said and realized that he's right. In one year, I will fully retire. As for who will take over the ownership of the practice, I have decided to equally split it 50/50 between the both of you. I am strongly against joint ownership of a practice, for I think that this place ran a lot better when I alone headed the whole operation. However, after witnessing the respect and honor that you two have for each other all these years, I've decided that this is the best choice. The joint surgery you both performed this morning was the cherry on top of the cake. I will be training you two bit by bit. There really isn't a big difference, just a larger responsibility and a few administrative things to do. Are you two ok with this?"

Charles Bronze and Claire Scarlet looked at each other, somewhat surprised. Neither of them saw this coming. They smiled at each other, and again, they both were thinking the same thing. Bronze told Scarlet, "Why don't you tell Dr. Smith, Claire." Claire Scarlet said, "It would be our honor Dr. Smith. I do agree that both of us together as a team would be able to manage and lead this practice better than either of us individually because Charles has his government job and I have other obligations. However, splitting the responsibility is a perfect idea. It will be difficult filling in your shoes Dr. Smith." Dr. Smith replied, "Excellent! Thank you Claire for the compliment. I'm glad you all agree with my reasoning. We'll have a congratulatory party for everyone in the office in the next few weeks."

Lieutenant Baker was sitting in his office going through some old case files. He decided that with the freeze on Lewis Industries, it was appropriate to put all cases pertaining to Dr. Lewis, or L, in one drawer so he could do some more research on him. As he was putting what seemed to be like pieces of a puzzle together, his private corporate cell phone rang. The cell phone was given to him by the Chief of the MDPD and was only used in communication with NYPD, LAPD, Interpol, CIA,

DEA, and other prominent international police organizations. Since it was such a confidential phone line, the IT department at the MDPD was always monitoring the line to make sure that it couldn't be tapped or infiltrated. A cold voice said, "Good evening Lt. Baker." Baker didn't recognize the voice and said, "Who is this?" The voice said, "C'mon Baker, you've been doing so much research on me and you don't even know what my voice sounds like? What kind of officer are you?" Baker's mouth opened wide and asked, "Is this L?" The voice replied, "Very good Baker. If you utter one more syllable, I'll have you hunted down and chopped to pieces." Baker was starting to sweat and quasi-confidently replied, "We know your last name L." L replied, "Yes, I am aware of that, but you must not say my name." Baker's shirt was started to get wet. There were so many things he wanted to find out, one of which was why did the IT department not catch onto this.

L told Baker eerily, "Listen Baker, I don't have time to talk crap so I'm going to get straight to it. I know your friends at the DEA busted my operation in South America. After all, it made international news. I know about your detective, Charles Bronze. I've been tracking him for a while now. I notice that you always have a plainclothes guard watching over and protecting him 24/7, even though Bronze doesn't realize it. It is obvious that Bronze is holding secrets for you. He has been assigned to you for quite some time now, so you obviously trust him. He is a high valued asset to you. I called you this evening because I want you to know that I swear I will do whatever it takes to get Bronze. He has caused too much harm to my operations, and busting my goldmine, Lewis Industries was the last straw." Baker got really scared now. For all he knew, L could have a sniper waiting to kill the plainclothes policeman watching over Bronze tonight and then shoot Bronze cleanly and quietly. Baker then thought for a moment and asked, "Tell me something L, why would you contact me instead of Bronze himself?" However, it was too late. L had already hung up the phone.

L entered his mansion, hot and sweaty from his training. He was dressed in uniform, arriving home from the dojo. L smiled to himself. He said, "Alas, my training is almost complete." L met his karate master, Master Morimoto in Japan when he was there on business. Since then, Morimoto has become a mentor to L to channel his thoughts and learn the way of the Japanese. This had not only a profound effect on L's mental abilities, but it definitely took a toll on his physique. For a man in his mid 60s, if one had seen him on the street, one would think that he was in his 40s. He was ripped, but not in a bulky bodybuilder fashion. L was lean and strong, ready to eviscerate anyone or anything in his path.

L turned on his sauna in the master bathroom and went in for about half an hour. As he could feel the extreme heat relaxing his muscles, he thought about his training. He thought how Master Morimoto took him as a flabby man in his late 50s, and trained him to push his body beyond the limits of a man in his 60s. L was fascinated with the sword wielding skills of those in the Far East. Morimoto taught him precise technique, analogous to the way of the samurai. After cleaning himself up, L went to his living room. He poured a glass of scotch and felt the burning sensation down his throat. Then, L put the glass to an adjacent coffee table. He turned on the TV to the BBC, and saw that Lewis Industries had been busted. L's blood started to boil, and he drank another glass of scotch. He became frustrated with himself for allowing the opposition to come so close. L told himself, "All these years I've been running criminal operations, and this bloody Charles Bronze comes in the picture and starts crumbling my empire." The news report however, didn't mention anything of Bronze. L thought, "Of course they wouldn't. If Bronze is as smart as my dossier on him says, then he was probably there a few weeks ago snooping around and found my LSD production lab. Then he got the DEA to do his dirty work." L had his scotch glass in his left hand, and struck his right fist hard on the coffee table, causing it to shatter.

L went to Master Morimoto's dojo to see if he was still there. Morimoto was arranging everything back in its place, cleaning up for the night. L came in and said, "Master Morimoto, I need to talk to you." Morimoto said, "What is it L?" L replied, "The DEA busted one of my big operations in South America." Morimoto replied, "I'm sorry." L said, "Don't worry about it. However, this is the last straw. My goal is clear, to hunt down and kill Charles Bronze." Morimoto said, "Yes, revenge is an interesting feeling. However, you are too high ranked in our criminal world. Do you want me to call my friend who heads the Yakuza in Miami? He will be a great asset to you." L replied, "No, no, I need to take care of Bronze myself. First thing tomorrow morning, I need to complete my training." Morimoto replied, "Of course sir. I'm working on a little gift for you to celebrate the completion of your training." L asked what it was, but Morimoto refused. L left with a feeling of rage burning inside him, ready to complete his training. The first utilization of the training will be to extinguish Charles Bronze once and for all.

Lt. Baker was frightened for Bronze's safety. He called Dr. Charles Bronze. Bronze was reviewing some patient files when the black Motorola rang. He answered, "What is it Lieutenant? You do realize it's a weekday right?" Baker replied nervously, "Yes Detective, but you need to come in at once. It's an emergency." Bronze noticed that Baker was nervous, which was very abnormal of him. He told Smith and Scarlet that he would be away for a few hours and then return. Bronze raced in the Lexus LS to the MDPD.

Bronze entered Baker's office. Baker was pacing back and forth. When Bronze entered he said, "Thank goodness Bronze you're here. Sit down." Bronze sat down and asked, "Lt. Baker, what's going on? Why are you so nervous?" Baker replied, "Today I got a call on my private corporate cell phone. Not even you are permitted to contact me on this line. It is so private and secure that the IT department here analyzes all incoming and outgoing phone calls. If an incoming call looks suspicious, then the call will not come through and I would never hear it ring." Bronze looked confused and asked, "Why are you telling me about this now Lieutenant?" Baker replied, "I got a call from him. From L. I don't know how the hell he was able to pass by the IT department, but he did. He saw the news story, as everyone did in the world, that the DEA busted Lewis Industries. Apparently, it was one of his biggest operations. He's been watching your every move Bronze. He told me that he's been observing how you handle the cases pertaining to him. However, he sounded really annoyed. Lewis Industries was really close to him, and metaphorically speaking, it is as if the capture of the industry caused a bullet to go through him without killing him." Baker paused for a moment, but didn't give Bronze enough time to reply. Baker looked down and said shaking, "Bronze, he's threatening to kill you. He told me that he would use whatever means necessary to hunt you down." Bronze was flabbergasted.

Bronze said, "A few things. First of all, do a lie detection test and thoroughly check all of your workers in IT. One of them could be a mole for L because as you said, the line is secure. Second, why would he contact you instead of me personally? If he is as well connected as he says he is, he probably has my phone number to reach me on the black Motorola, so why go though you to deliver the message?" Baker replied, "I don't know." Baker continued pacing and said worryingly, "Who the hell is this man Bronze? How is it possible for him to be in every circle, and yet we barely know anything about him?" Bronze looked at Baker in a melancholy fashion. Baker reached for a drawer and took out a crate that was one quarter full. He said, "This is everything we have on L Detective. I fear for your safety. I'm going to have plainclothes men posted close to Anna and Claire's houses." Bronze got annoyed, stood up, and said, "Now listen Lieutenant, that really isn't necessary." Baker was about to flare and said, "Bronze sit your ass down. It is obvious from all the evidence thus far that L is hunting you down. He is going to try and get to them in order to make a move on you. I've seen cases like this happen before, you know, use a relative as hostage to lure someone out. They need to be well-guarded." Bronze noticed Baker's face was getting red. Bronze calmed himself down and said, "Ok. I need to get back to the office, but I'm going to drop my patient files home and then I'll come right back here and we'll go through everything we have on L together." Baker smiled and said, "My sentiments exactly. I fear my own safety as well, and the safety of my family. Therefore, I suggest that we spend the night here at the station. It's guarded 24/7 and there is a room with cots, analogous to the on-call room in the hospital you work in." Bronze replied in the affirmative and left.

It was the following morning, and L went to Master Morimoto's dojo. In order for L to complete his training, he had to sword dual with Master Morimoto. Morimoto told him, "You must defeat me in order to pass your training. Whoever receives three marks of blood first loses." L said, "Yes sir." They bowed to each other and began. Morimoto moved around quickly, hopping all over the place like a bunny, moving swiftly. L tried to strike, but Morimoto counter attacked with a slice on L's arm. Morimoto said, "That counts as one." L and Morimoto continued they're fighting, and Morimoto struck again. L became furious and Morimoto said, "Now L, channel your thoughts. Visualize your sword strikes before you actually strike." L did as told and after five minutes, struck Morimoto twice. Morimoto said, "Excellent. Now we're even. Who receives the next strike loses. Don't think however that I'm going to let you get away that easily." Morimoto attempted to strike L, but L ducked quickly. He tripped Morimoto over and struck him on his leg. L exclaimed, "I win Master Morimoto." L helped Morimoto up. Morimoto smiled, hugging him. He said, "Congratulations L. You have completed your training. Come now and I will show you your gift."

Master Morimoto led L to a special room in the dojo, a room L had never seen before all the years he trained there. There was a large cupboard with double doors. Morimoto opened it gently, and as the doors creaked open, L saw a single sword in the middle. Morimoto took the sword out of the case and said, "This is for you L. It has your pseudonym Danny

Steed in Japanese. Use it wisely." L received the sword in his hands, bowing. He knelt on one knee and said, "Thank you Sensei for all of your training." Morimoto replied, "It's been my pleasure. Good luck."

Bronze returned to the police station after dropping off the patient files home. Before he went home, he stopped by Claire's office and said, "Claire honey, don't worry about me. You'll be fine. Be safe and stay strong." Claire smiled and said, "OK." Bronze also called Anna. She sounded a lot better and Bronze said, "Anna, you are the love of my life. I can tell that you're not as worried. Stay that way and be on your p's and q's." Anna replied, "Thanks Charles, and yes, I will."

When Bronze entered Baker's office, Bronze asked, "Did you position the plainclothes guards strategically?" Baker replied, "Yes, no one goes in or comes out of both Claire and Anna's abodes this evening." Bronze smiled and said, "Excellent." Bronze and Baker were up in the wee hours of the morning rummaging through all the closed cases pertaining to L. However, neither Bronze nor Baker could find any tendencies. Baker said, "It just goes to show you how malicious and intelligent this man is. In all my years on the force, I have never seen someone with such a wide span network." Bronze looked at Baker sternly and Baker said, "When I was about your age, we had a drug lord to bust. He had a vast network very similar to L. However, he didn't cover all parts of the globe like L does. I was sitting alone in my old office wondering how I was going to catch him. I tried and tried, thought until my head felt like it was going to explode. Then, I realized something. Maybe I should stop looking and start waiting. I waited patiently for a few days, and got a lead on where he was hiding. It turns out that I captured him single handedly. That very case is what promoted me to Lieutenant of the MDPD." Bronze looked at Baker now instead of the files. Baker stared him in the eye and said, "Bronze, listen to me. I think we should do the same thing. Let's both get some rest. I have a gut feeling something will turn up in the morning."

L returned to the mansion from the dojo. He laughed sinisterly with his sword in his hand. L told his sword, "My friend, the first person you will slaughter is Charles Bronze." L called the head of the Yakuza, a contact provided to him by his dear Master Morimoto and said, "Sir, I need your men to come to my mansion at once." The chief of the Yakuza, Jai, said, "Yes sir. I've heard about you through Master Morimoto. We are indebted to you. My men will be there within the hour."

An hour later, the men arrived. L told them, "Good evening gentlemen. I have the coordinates here for two ladies, one of them named Claire Scarlet, and the other named Annalina Kristensen. I need you all to infiltrate their homes. They are being heavily guarded. Wipe out all the guards, quietly. Then kidnap the two women softly, not leaving any trace." L went to Jai and gave him a piece of paper. L said, "You will take Kristensen and Scarlet to these respective addresses and wait for my order. Do you understand?" Jai replied, "Yes sir." L said, "Very well then." Jai and his Yakuza left, and L chuckled. He told himself, "The best way to lure out a warrior like myself is not to pounce on them physically, but attack his heart. Bronze will be dead soon, and the first victim to my sword."

Bronze and Baker overslept a few hours in the room full of cots. An officer came in and woke them up. The officer said, "Lieutenant Baker, I'm afraid we have some bad news. We found all the plainclothes guards that were guarding Ms. Kristensen and Ms. Scarlet dead this morning." Bronze felt his heart sank. He said to himself, "Don't tell me that L captured the two most important women in my life." Baker asked, "Where are Anna and Claire now?" The officer replied, "We don't know yet sir. We have a search out for them, but we haven't seen them." Baker then asked, "Do you think they've been kidnapped?" The officer said, "We're not sure yet. CSI is there right now trying to figure it out. As soon as we get a lead, I'll call you." Bronze and Baker were getting out of the cots when the officer said, "One more thing Lieutenant. We received a package this morning addressed to you. It's at the front desk." Baker and Bronze looked at each other, and Bronze thought, "This could perhaps be the clue that Baker was talking about."

Baker and Bronze went together all freshened up to the front desk. The receptionist said, "Good morning Lt. Baker. This packaged was received this morning." Baker said, "Thank you," and Bronze and Baker went to Baker's office. Bronze analyzed it carefully and said, "Well Lieutenant, go ahead." Lt. Baker swallowed his apprehensiveness and opened the package. There was a lot of bubble wrap, but when Baker fully unwrapped his parcel, he found an audio CD. He inserted it into the computer. Bronze and Baker couldn't believe what they heard.

A cold voice, the one Baker recognized as L's said, "Good morning Lt. Baker and Dr. Charles Bronze. My name is L, and you probably know me by now. Bronze, you have caused a great deal of pain to me. I currently have your lovely girlfriend, Anna Kristensen at a specific location, and your old friend Claire Scarlet at another specific location. In case you don't believe me, here they are. The audio background changed and Anna said, "Charles, please help. They have a bomb attached to me and its ticking!" Afterwards, the audio background changed again and Claire said, "Charles! Help me! They have a bomb here!" The audio background changed back to L's voice. He said, "You will meet me tonight at 7:00pm on the rooftop of the Bank of America tower, now known as the Miami Tower, in Downtown Miami. The bomb is ticking only to scare them. However, my cell phone detonates it. If I do not see you here by 7:00pm sharp, then both of them will die." L laughed sinisterly over the recording and it went blank.

Tears started to fill in Bronze's eyes. His felt many emotions at the same time. One was sadness and remorse since L had his two ladies hostage. Another was revenge and anger because of L's doings. Lastly, Bronze felt a large amount of guilt because he put the two women he loved the most in serious danger. Baker noticed this, went to Bronze and tapped him on the shoulders. Bronze shook a little at Baker's motion, but Baker said softly, "Listen Detective, this isn't your fault." Bronze said weeping, "Yes it is Baker. And I'm going to fix it. You have no idea right now how I feel. If my eyes meet with L's, one of us will die before we break eyesight. I want to just plant a bullet through his forehead right now. However, that will be foolish. We need to make a plan." Baker smiled and called Bronze by his first name for the first time ever, "Charles, I'm proud of you. I thought you were going to do a one-man job, but clearly, you are the most intelligent detective I've ever had since I've been Lieutenant."

Baker said, "Alright Bronze, you are too emotionally shook up to talk, so just listen. Here's what we're going to do. L probably has a whole bunch of armed men to stop you or anyone from reaching the rooftop. You will enter the building first calmly as you always do. Dress in one of your designer suits, because you are going to need to look professional. As you enter, L's men will most likely start shooting. Directly behind you will be our officers ready to take them down. When the shoot off starts, run to the elevator and hit the penthouse button and take the stairs to the rooftop. You will have to confront L face to face in order to settle your business with him. Before you go to the Miami Tower, you will stop here at 6:30 tonight first. We will give you under armor to wear underneath your suit. Also, we'll equip you with guns and grenades. L is in his mid 60s according to our files, so he's probably just a weak old man with a brilliant mind. This is why he would want you dead before you reach the rooftop. Confront him, take his cell phone and make sure before you kill him that you find out where the girls are." Bronze's tears dried up and he blew his nose as Baker was talking. He was back to normal and said, "Sounds like a plan sir. See you soon."

L was getting ready for the final showdown. He told himself, "Finally, I'll be rid of Bronze once and for all so my international operations can continue for hundreds of years." L went to his closet, and wore a shirt, tie, and suit pants. He put on a black trench coat and a black fedora. L took his sword with him, and put his cell phone in his pocket. The Yakuza escorted him to the Miami Tower rooftop just in case Bronze came early. He told them, "Gentlemen, guard every corner of the Tower. I don't want Bronze coming up here. If you see him, kill him. Each of you have a walkie talkie so let me know when he is dead and then I'll detonate the bombs on his girlfriends."

The Yakuza nodded. L called Jai and said, "Jai, I want you to be ready to kill either one of the girls when I give you the order. Is that clear?" Jai replied in the affirmative.

L's plan went into action. The Yakuza shot dead all of the civilians in the Tower at the time. They escorted L to the rooftop as planned. Jai was in close proximity to Anna, and he had his second in command in close proximity to Claire, ready when the call came to kill them both. Even though L could detonate the bomb, in the end, L wanted both of them to die of gunshot wounds so he could brand his red "L" on their foreheads. L waited patiently on the rooftop alone, sword at the draw, in case Bronze showed up.

Bronze was at his penthouse, sweating and slightly nervous as he was putting on his Calvin Klein suit. He washed his face, and felt the cool water permeate his hot, sticky skin. It felt refreshing and helped Bronze calm down. Bronze knew that even though there was a risk to get into a car chase, the Audi R8 was the appropriate car for this mission. As he was driving to the police station, he started thinking how this was the most emotional mission yet. It blocked his judgment for he could no longer see things clearly. The only way the cloudiness could be lifted was if he knew that the two girls were safe. Bronze arrived at the police station. He went inside.

Baker was waiting in his office for Bronze. He looked at his watch and said, "6:30. Right on time Detective. Here is your bulletproof under armor." Bronze took off his jacket and shirt and put on the under armor. It covered his chest and back. It felt tight, but Bronze knew that's how it had to feel. Bronze put back on his shirt and jacket. He asked, "What about the guns and grenades?" Baker took out a box and opened it. He gave Bronze three grenades and said, "Use them wisely." Then he gave Bronze ammo for his .40 Smith and Wesson. Baker said, "I would give you a machine gun, but since the police will be right behind you, I don't think its necessary." Bronze told Baker, "Lieutenant, I don't know what is going to happen out there. In case I don't come back alive…" Baker interrupted Bronze and said, "Listen Bronze, if you talk like that then you're not going to win. You can do this. L is just an old geezer. He's a wimp. Now get in there and whoop his skin." Bronze laughed. Bronze's face went serious, and he said sternly, "Now your turn to listen Lt. Baker. I need you to be on call at any moment. As soon as I get the word from L where the girls are, I'll go after Anna, and you go after Claire. Agreed?" Baker smiled and said, "Yes Detective. Good luck."

Bronze drove his Audi R8 to the Miami Tower, but parked away from the normal parking lot. He didn't want to be conspicuous. The police arrived without their sirens, but still had their lights on. The Yakuza were strategically positioned in the tower. They talked to Jai via walkie and Jai told L, "Just like what you said L. The police are here all in uniform, but no sign of Bronze." Bronze decided to pull a last minute trick. He let the police enter first, and then he went in afterwards, surrounded by police.

It turns out that Bronze's idea worked. The Yakuza purposely turned off all the lights in the Miami Tower, but Bronze and the police had night-vision goggles. The Yakuza shot wildly, and the whole inside of the tower started shattering. It sounded like a gun range. The policeman yelled at Bronze over the gunfire, "Detective, there's the elevator!" Bronze threw a grenade at some Yakuza who were guarding the elevator, killing them, but the grenade didn't harm the mechanics of the elevator. Bronze entered the lighted elevator swiftly. Some Yakuza tried shooting at the elevator, but the elevator doors closed. Bronze hit the penthouse button and waited patiently.

While waiting in the elevator, Bronze tossed off his night-vision goggles and put a silencer on his Smith and Wesson. He had his gun in his right hand, and a grenade in his left. As the elevator was going up gradually, Bronze felt a lump in his throat. He swallowed the lump. He went to the side of the elevator so that when the doors opened, anyone looking directly inward wouldn't see anyone. The elevator dinged as it reached the penthouse floor. From this point onward, Bronze was alone.

L waited and waited, but didn't hear from Jai. He looked at his watch, which read 6:50pm. He said to himself, "Ten more minutes before those two women die." He called Jai and asked, "Jai, what the hell is going on? Is Bronze dead yet?" Jai heard the transmission and was scared out of his mind. He replied trembling, "L, I'm sorry but it seems that Bronze got away on the elevator. He's proceeded to the penthouse floor as we speak." L exclaimed, "Damnit! Can't you all do anything right?!" Jai apologized, but L didn't listen. L stood up and waited for Bronze's arrival.

The elevator doors opened. There were four Yakuzas blocking the stairwell. They looked at each other confused, because the elevator doors opened but no one was there. Then, all of a sudden, a grenade flung out. They tried to run, but as soon as the grenade hit the ground, it exploded, killing three of them and leaving one alive, but injured. The alive Yakuza was bleeding and on the ground. Bronze shot him twice coldly with his silenced Smith and Wesson. He went to the stairwell. There was no one there. He opened the door, climbed up the stairs, and saw rooftop on the next door. Bronze pointed his Smith and Wesson to the door and flung it open.

There was selective lighting on the rooftop. L was standing facing Bronze a good 100 feet away, and Bronze had his Smith and Wesson pointed at him. Bronze scaled him from head to toe, looking around swiftly to see if anyone else was on the rooftop. L said in his cold voice, "Don't worry Detective Bronze. No one else is here. I wanted to make sure that this fight to the end was just between you and me." Bronze smiled and said, "I'm glad you extended that courtesy, and I feel the same way." L said, "Good job, Bronze. You're right on time. I anticipated your arrival, even though my Yakuza are all over the Tower."

As L spoke, Bronze was watching L from head to toe. He was an average height man, and from the little Bronze could see since L was wearing a trench coat, L's posture was well poised. Bronze knew that he was a very fit man, contrary to what Baker thought. L said, "I must say Bronze, you've caused me a great deal of pain." Bronze replied, "Yes I know. But then again L, you have caused me the more pain by kidnapping Anna and Claire. Baker was right." L laughed and said, "The Lieutenant? I thought that wack job would have left a long time ago considering his record." Bronze asked, "And what do you have to do with Baker might I ask?" L replied, "Nothing at all. I have never seen him with my own eyes. However, I have a file on him, just like I have my file on you." Bronze asked, "And where do you get your information L?" L said, "C'mon Bronze, what do you think? You are obviously a man of great reasoning since you have been able to successfully capture many of my associates around the globe."

Bronze said, "Well from your quips about knowing so much about the MDPD, it would be fair game to assume that you have a mole within the MDPD, specifically within IT." L grinned and said, "Very good Bronze. But my man isn't in IT." Bronze looked confused and asked, "Then how were you able to get passed Baker's secure line?" L replied, "Simple. I made an invention, which allows me to bypass government phone tapping. How do you think I have been able to contact all my people around the world without letting the government know about it?" Bronze smiled and said, "Touché L, touché."

Bronze was still pointing the gun at L, while L had his right hand ready to withdraw his sword. Bronze asked, "I don't understand L. You have a PhD from Harvard, according to our file, yet you spend most of your time making money through illegal means? Why?" L replied, "Detective and Dr. Charles Bronze, you will never understand a criminal mind. Trust is my main priority, more than money and power. I give my associates what they want, which is money and/or power, and they pledge their allegiance to me. It's a very simple act and is not unconstitutional." Bronze replies, "True, but when it's for illegal means, that's not constitutional my friend." L said loudly, "Enough chit-chat Bronze. You really expect to question me all night, and answer every single gap that I've purposely created in your head about me and the people I work with? I know the rage you feel against me, and my rage is greater and even more. Let's end this the old fashioned way." Bronze replied, "As you wish."

Bronze shot at L, but L was too fast and dodged the bullet. L attacked Bronze with his sword, striking the Smith and Wesson out of Bronze's right hand. Luckily for Bronze, he has a black belt in Tae

Kwon Do and is still well trained. Bronze dodged L's strikes swiftly. Bronze noticed that L moved very spritely. He had the speed of a 30 year old. Bronze told himself, "No doubt L has been trained very well in martial arts." L struck Bronze with the sword, slicing through his shirt and causing a cut through his armor. Bronze grabbed L's right wrist, trying to force him to let go of the sword, but L head-butted Bronze causing Bronze to fall to the ground. Bronze got up quickly and dodged another slash by L. Bronze was looking for his gun.

L charged towards him, but Bronze moved to the side, causing L to nearly fall over. Bronze charged a right fist towards L's back hard, causing L to fall to the ground. Bronze pressed L's right wrist to the ground, forcing him to release his sword. Bronze took hold of his sword, but L flipped and punched Bronze in his face, causing Bronze's nose to bleed. L kicked Bronze's wrist, causing him to fling the sword. Bronze kept a guarding stance, and spat out blood telling L, "You've been well trained my friend." L said, "Thank you Bronze, and I see you still remember your skills from when you obtained your black belt in Tae Kwon Do ten years ago." Bronze was shocked at how L knew exactly when Bronze got his black belt. Bronze let down his stance for a moment, and as a result, L struck him. Bronze got back up, ducked down as L was going to hit him again in the face, and Bronze swept his leg, tripping L. L fell straight to the ground, shrieking in pain. Bronze choked him from behind and asked him, "Where are the girls?" L replied muffled, "Forget about it."

Bronze bashed L's head into the ground and looked for his phone while L was unconscious. He found his cell phone and Bronze threw it over the rooftop. Bronze told himself, "At least he can't detonate the bombs now, but I need to find out where they are." Before L regained consciousness, Bronze ran to his gun. He picked it up and ran back to L, pointing the gun to his head. L woke up, and Bronze asked cocking the gun, "Where are the girls?" L's head felt fuzzy, but he said, "Ok, ok don't shoot! I'll tell you!" L said, "Anna is at 7122 Biscayne Boulevard and Claire is at 9178 Flagler Street in Hollywood." Bronze said, "Thanks L. Now you're going to die my friend." L said, "Go to hell Bronze." L kicked Bronze in the chest, causing Bronze to release his gun. L ran towards his sword. Bronze tackled L before he could reach his sword. L turned around and choked Bronze. Bronze choked L back.

They were both choking each other with their left hands, Bronze trying to reach his gun with the other hand and L trying to reach his sword. They were both about to faint by each other's choking, but L grabbed his sword and Bronze got a hold of his gun. Both L and Bronze released their left hands on each other, and L pointed his sword at Bronze's left shoulder, while Bronze pointed his gun at L's left shoulder. It was a stalemate. L said, "It seems we can't kill each other. I thought my completed training would be able to kill you immediately, but you are full of surprises." Bronze smiled and said, "You may have a file on me L, but nothing beats the flesh. And I feel the same way, I thought you were going to be a feeble old man." L and Bronze smiled at each other. At exactly the same moment, a fraction of a second, Bronze shot L in the left shoulder with his gun, flinging him back, while L stabbed Bronze in the left shoulder with his sword in and out. L still had the sword and Bronze was trying to aim for him, but it was too late. L struck Bronze hard on the neck, knocking him out.

L quickly went to one corner of the rooftop and opened a briefcase that was lying there. It had a parachute inside. L could hardly move, but he told himself that he had to. He realized that Bronze was a bigger threat than he anticipated and had to flee quickly before Bronze regained consciousness. Bronze threw L's cellphone, so L couldn't detonate the bombs. L couldn't feel his left shoulder, and his left arm was weak as a result. L had blood spots and wounds all over him. However, he channeled his mind like Master Morimoto taught him to not think of the pain right now. He called Jai on the walkie. Jai said, "Yes sir?" L said, "Listen we've been compromised. When I reach safety, I'll phone you. Then, kill Annalina Kristensen. Also, tell your second in command to be ready to kill Claire Scarlet. Do not act until I call you." Jai said, "Yes sir." L put on the parachute. As Bronze was regaining consciousness, L jumped off the rooftop.

Bronze's head felt like a boulder that had been smashed, but he started regaining consciousness. He saw a blurry figure jumping off the rooftop. He yelled, "No!" Bronze came back to his senses fully, and went to the side where L jumped off. He saw L release his parachute and fly away. Bronze's left shoulder was gushing with blood from his wound. He took off his jacket, and looked at himself. His white shirt was stained with blood from his injuries. Bronze took off the tie he was wearing, and wrapped his shoulder with it to control the bleeding. He dialed Baker on the black Motorola. Baker answered immediately. Bronze yelled, "Baker! We don't have much time! Claire is located at 9178 Flagler Street in Hollywood! Go and get her ASAP!" Baker responded, "Bronze! What's going on? What happened?" Bronze said, "Listen Baker I don't have time to explain now. Get Claire now! I'll go after Anna. She's located at 7122 Biscayne Boulevard. Call some backup to meet me there."

Bronze ran down the stairwell as fast as he could and ran out the Miami Tower through all the gunfire. The policemen saw he was leaving and two of them followed him. Bronze told them, "Listen guys. I need you to follow me to 7122 Biscayne Boulevard. That's where L has Anna! Meet me in two minutes, exactly two." The two men agreed. They went to their police car and waited. Bronze drove out of nowhere in his black Audi R8. Bronze turned down the window and yelled, "Follow me!"

There was still gunfire going on in the tower, but Bronze didn't care. Bronze knew all of Miami like the back of his hand, and he knew that 7122 Biscayne Boulevard was a warehouse where he would find Anna. Baker, on the other hand, took the helicopter option. He flew a helicopter to where Claire was being held at 9178 Flagler Street.

Bronze raced as fast as he could. Baker called, whereby Bronze answered via the Bluetooth connection of his R8. Bronze said, "Baker, where are you?" Baker replied, "Easy Bronze, easy. Relax. We'll get them in time. I took a helicopter since it's quicker. We'll be there in five minutes." Bronze said, "Yeah, me too. I really need Anna now."

L had reached safety. He called Jai and said, "Jai, kill Anna now." Jai said, "But of course sir." Jai called his associate, but heard no answer. Jai said, "Hello, hello." Jai called back L and said, "L, we have a problem. My second in command isn't answering." L said, "Don't worry about him, I need at least one of them dead so Bronze can feel the pain. Kill Anna now!"

Bronze was in time. He entered where L told

him Anna would be. Bronze kicked the door opened. There was a man who had his gun pointed at Bronze's love, but he redirected the gun toward Bronze. Bronze shot the man coldly before the man could shoot back. When he turned on the light, he was shocked. It was Claire.

Bronze called Baker and said, "Lieutenant, lieutenant! Where are you?" However, Bronze heard no response. Claire was tied and Bronze asked Claire if she was ok. She replied in the affirmative and squeezed Bronze hard, kissing him on the cheek. "Thank you for saving my life Charles," Claire said flawlessly. Bronze said, "Anytime, but excuse me." Bronze tried Baker again but heard no response.

Lt. Baker left his phone in the helicopter, since it had successfully landed to where Claire was supposed to be at 9178 Flagler Street. Baker's had two policemen with him, and they headed towards the building. Before they reached the door, they heard two loud gunshots. The three men ran towards the door charging it down. Jai was running out through the back door. Baker exclaimed to the policemen, "Get him now!" Baker went where the lady was tied and said, "Claire, are you all right?" However, Baker saw that it wasn't Claire, but it was Anna. She had two bullets planted in her head, and was bleeding profusely. Baker listened carefully for breathing sounds and looked for a chest rise, but didn't see nor hear anything. Anna was dead.

Bronze was with Claire now and told her, "Claire, I'm so sorry for all of this. It is my fault that you got into this mess." Claire Scarlet replied, "Don't worry Charles. We'll talk about it later. What's going on?" Tears started to fill in Bronze's eyes and he said, "The bad guy, who goes by L is the one who had you hostage. He also had Anna hostage as well. I wish Baker would answer his damn walkie so I can know that she got out safely." Claire said, "Charles, look at me. I'm sure she's ok. Just relax." Bronze listened and calmed down. He finally got the call from Baker.

Bronze said, "Lieutenant Baker, where the hell were you? Is Anna ok? Did they hurt her? Is she alright?" Baker responded, "Bronze, I'm terribly sorry, but Anna's dead. L knew that we would come after them after you threw his detonator off the rooftop so he positioned two men to shoot Claire and Anna at his command. You were in time for Claire, but I'm afraid we weren't for Anna. I'm so sorry." Bronze hung up the black Motorola and threw it across the warehouse. His knees touched the ground, and he was sobbing. Claire hugged him and said, "I'm so sorry darling," and she started to weep quietly as well, consoling Charles Bronze.

It was the following morning and Bronze took the day off from work. It seems that Claire Scarlet was so shook up from last night as well, that she took the day off too. Bronze thought to himself, "It's a good thing that Dr. Henry Smith didn't give us the practice yet." Bronze drove his Lexus LS to the MDPD office because Baker wanted to see him. Bronze entered Baker's office in the normal fashion and said, "Detective Bronze, I want to apologize for my inefficiency. If I got there faster, we could have saved Anna. Anyways, I can't make it up to you, so I understand if you're going to be angry with me. However, we caught the man that killed her. His name was Stephen Jai, and he was the head of the Yakuza that are here in Miami. It seems L has some powerful people." Bronze was still a little shook up and depressed. He didn't say anything.

Baker said, "Bronze, you have you talk to me sooner or later. But for now, we'll stay quiet." After fifteen minutes of stalling, Bronze said, "Lt. Baker, I forgive you. It wasn't your fault that Anna died, it was because I let L get away." Baker said, "Bronze, in these situations, human tend to assign blame. Don't make it personal. Anna died, but she didn't die for nothing. I know you will need time to move on. Also, I don't want you going on a vendetta against L because of the death of your lover. The police department will not accept that." Bronze listened and said, "Any leads on L?" Baker replied, "Sorry, but none. He escaped somewhere to the Greek islands, but disappeared off the grid. The rat has buried himself under ground." Bronze replied, "Thank you Baker for your consolation. Revenge is for the weak minded. I loved Anna very dearly, and I'll miss her company, but I'm only in my mid 40s. I still have a whole life ahead of me and I don't want to carry around that guilt."

Baker was amazed at how quick Bronze was and replied, "Wow, Bronze I'm amazed. It's as if nothing ever happened." Bronze said, "Thank you sir. I've been through many trials in my life so I'm used to it. Also, Lt. Baker thank you for everything." Baker replied, "It's my pleasure." Bronze said, "Anna's funeral will be on Saturday. I would appreciate it if you came out." Baker replied, "Absolutely." Bronze replied, "Then it is with that sir, that after over a decade of service, I hereby resign from the MDPD." Baker was dumbfounded and speechless. Bronze handed Baker his badge and his Smith and Wesson. Bronze left Baker's office without uttering a word.

Saturday rolled by quickly, and over the course of the week Dr. Charles Bronze had to make funeral arrangements. The service went by relatively fast, and about ten people, who included Dr. Henry Smith, Dr. Claire Scarlet and Lt. Baker, attended Anna's funeral. Charles Bronze, even though her boyfriend when she died, gave a touching eulogy to Anna that caused Claire Scarlet to weep and even Baker was about to shed a few tears. He talked about how they were happy around each other no matter how stressed out they were. Bronze talked about their closeness and the intellectual conversations they had. Also, Bronze said that Anna was a person whom he truly loved, which was very rare for Bronze. He ended it by saying, "Goodbye Anna. Rest in peace, and you will be missed." Bronze's eyes went watery and his sinuses kicked up, but he didn't cry.

Baker met with Bronze as the entire funeral was being dismissed to offer his condolences. Baker asked Bronze, "Detective, why did you resign? We need you on the force. You are very observant and have observed my body language. You know very well that you were my best detective or officer for that matter." Bronze said, "Sorry Lieutenant, but the job is getting too much into my personal life." Baker asked glumly, "Is there anything I can do to get you back?" Bronze thought for a moment and said, "At the moment no." Baker said, "Well, it has been a pleasure Bronze." Bronze replied, "Indeed." Bronze continued, "I only resigned because I need some time off. However, we'll see after that." Baker smiled. Bronze smiled back. Baker hit Bronze playfully and Bronze laughed. Baker shook Bronze's hand firmly and said, "Keep in touch Dr. Bronze."

Claire Scarlet was the next in line and last to offer her condolences. She told Bronze, "Charles, I know you have known me for a long time and we never really talked about Anna very much. However, the way you gave her eulogy, I can tell that you really loved her." Bronze replied, "Thank you Claire. It's been tough, but I'll get over it soon." Claire Scarlet replied, "How are you so bulletproof?" Bronze replied, "Experience my darling, experience." They sat at the cemetery while everyone was leaving. Bronze talked for a good hour about Anna to Claire, and Claire listened intently as she always did. Everyone left by the time they finished talking. Bronze thanked Claire for always being a good listener. Claire smiled at Bronze and said, "Not a problem babe. Shall we?" Dr. Claire Scarlet took Dr. Charles Bronze's arm. Claire kissed him on the cheek and they walked arm in arm down the street.